SAINT UNDERGROUND

PUBLISHED BY DUNN BOOKS. FIRST PAPERBACK EDITION NOVEMBER 2015.
THIS TITLE IS ALSO AVAILABLE AS A DUNN BOOKS EBOOK,

AND AS AN AUDIBLE DIGITAL AUDIOBOOK.

LIBRARY OF CONGRESS CATALOGING-IN-PUBLICATION DATA
IS ON FILE WITH THE U.S. COPYRIGHT OFFICE .

ISBN: 978-0-9962082-8-4

DESIGNED BY ARCHIE FERGUSON.

MANUFACTURED IN THE UNITED STATES OF AMERICA.

EVIL

SAINT UNDERGROUND

A NOVEL

ADAM DUNN

db

DUNN BOOKS

GLOSSARY'S IN BACK

TO THE DOCTORS WHO HELPED ME GET THROUGH THE
LONG DARK TUNNEL THAT WAS WRITING THIS BOOK:

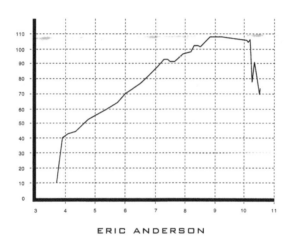

ERIC ANDERSON

ΕΣΤΙΝ Ο ΠΟΛΕΜΟΣ ΟΠΛΩΝ
ΤΟ ΠΛΕΟΝ ΑΛΛΑ ΔΑΠΗΣ

STEVE CALL

GRAEME DOWNES

It could probably be shown by facts and figures that there is no distinctly native American criminal class except Congress.

—**MARK TWAIN**, "Pudd'nhead Wilson's New Calendar"

Ordinary citizens have been wiped out time after time as governments come and go with exciting but often misguided new policies. As the years go by, they develop a deep personal distrust of "visible" domestic financial and real assets as a reliable store of value.

—**INGO WALTER**, *The Secret Money Market*

Eat quietly, play gently, and take secretly.

—Catchphrase among Chinese officials in response to government-imposed austerity measures, from reporting by Ji Shaoting and Cheng Yunjie, Xinhua News Agency, January 23, 2013

Below the mine shaft holes
It will all unfold
There's a world
Going on
UNDERGROUND.

—**TOM WAITS**, "Underground"

AT POINTS UNKNOWN

"IT'S LOOKING BAD," the caller said tersely, wasting no time. "I need you back in New York."

There was only the slightest delay. Despite the satellite uplink, the encryption software, and the mammoth distance, the secure line worked very much like an ordinary one, a triumph of years of complaints by field agents and station chiefs the world over.

"The last time we talked, you said I should stay as far away as I could," replied the man on the other end of the line. Even through the software that secured the connection, the caller could hear the rust in the man's voice; it clearly wasn't used much.

The caller, whose name was Devius Rune, thought carefully before speaking; he badly needed the other man's compliance. "The last time we talked, you'd just turned the Bronx into Baghdad. The medical examiner still has open case files on the bodies. We let Justice and NYPD take the credit so I could get you out quietly."

There was no response. The man on the other end of the line, whose name was Everett More, could outwait erosion.

Rune bruxed his teeth and sighed through his nose. "Your 'partner' was promoted," he conceded. "He and his friends got the transfers they wanted. I saw to it personally."

Devius Rune was tall and rangy, with a creased face that had weathered hostile suns in covert ops on every continent. He was a senior officer in the CIA's Special Activities Division. Unlike many of his company peers now in their fifties, Rune preferred staying in the field, overseeing his operatives personally. This particular one demanded Rune's special attention; he was not an asset to be deployed lightly. Everett More had been working for Rune intermittently for years, since the end of his last tour in Afghanistan, before the drawdown began the previous decade. He had hunted and killed men all over South-Central Asia for years before that. And despite his occasional sideline projects for Rune, he was still, as they say, "attached," still formally part of the military. On the books, he was a Force Recon marine based in Camp Lejeune, North Carolina; in the shadow world of Special Operations, he had been one of the first men selected for MARSOC when the command was originally stood up in 2006.

The last time Rune had seen More in uniform, there'd been so many medals, ribbons, and citations on his chest that the cloth beneath was invisible. Judging from his service record, More should not have been alive; few who had fought alongside him still were. Then again, *none* of those who'd fought against More were. To those who had served with him, he was "Ever" More, and Rune regarded him as an unrelenting pain in the ass. After hearing the news about his partner's promotion, More finally gave Rune the result for which he'd fervently hoped: "So what do you need from me this time?"

Now for the hard part.

"It's Convention Week," Rune began carefully. "Both parties will be in Manhattan for basically the first half of August to make their choices for the presidential election and to raise funds. The Dems are backing the former secretary of state for president, and they want to lock it in. The GOP's a mess; they can't even agree to disagree over whom they'll nominate. But this year there's a hitch: An independent may declare a third-party ticket. First time in decades."

There was a moment of silence, then a glottal grunt. "Since when do you care about elections?"

"The newcomer's name is Alex Redhawk, maybe you've heard of him. Major-league financial player, came up on Wall Street, founded his own fund a decade ago, now he's got about a hundred billion dollars under management. He has a reputation as a maverick, and he's got some pretty hard-core ideas on tax reform that may not be in the nation's best interest. Which is where I come in."

"I'm not a babysitter," rasped the man on the other end of the line.

That, Rune reflected, had to be the understatement of all time.

More went on: "The black budget's safe no matter who sits in the Oval Office. What do you care who gets elected?"

Rune took a breath and continued, "Redhawk's been getting a lot of press lately. His attacks on both parties have been highly effective. When it comes to style, the pols have nothing on Redhawk—he runs circles around them at every debate. News polls are showing that he could pull a substantial number of voters away from either party if he throws his hat in the ring, depending on where he stands on the latest Dodd-Frank amendment, the new National IRA bonds." Rune included this last item to drive home his point. "On paper, the bonds are an investment to 'modernize' American infrastructure—that's the sales pitch, anyway. They're really a smokescreen to deflect voter attention away from how badly infrastructure has *deteriorated*.

"Worse that that—the whole National IRA thing's a time bomb. The GOP thinks it's a Trojan horse, more Democratic control creep over everything since health care. The Dems see it as their ticket to Four More Years of full control of Congress and the White House. Now, whether or not you agree, relations between the parties can't sink any lower. They hate each other like never before."

Rune paused to let his words sink in. He didn't want to cry wolf to More, who couldn't care less about politics. But he hoped he was getting the point across. The new bonds were the most crucial issue of the election. The amendment (an absurd piece of political theater commemorating the sixth anniversary of the bill's passing) was supposed to have been solely a tax-reform bill, one that did away with the charitable-contributions loophole. But at the last minute the house speaker, Caduta Massi, had tacked on the National IRA bond issue. It was a brazen, impulsive move, and it had brought the simmer between the two parties to a raging boil that threatened to overflow the pot.

Essentially another massive government bailout, the bonds were seen by some as control creep, a means to bring whole states, even regions, under federal management. By 2016 that was quasi-synonymous with the Democratic Party. The GOP was publicly, vehemently, rabidly opposed to the program. Republican congressmen denounced it regularly; more radical party members saturated the airwaves with cries of "killing America, one city at a time."

Now Rune cut to the chase. "One of Redhawk's ideas is to relax federal restrictions on foreign direct investment in the U.S. He thinks it's the fastest, easiest way for us to raise capital even before tax reforms are enacted, which he knows would be an uphill battle. He's even outlined a plan to roll back CFIUS." Rune referred to the interagency government body responsible for screening foreign money flows into the country.

"So they go through hedge funds instead," More said. "That was the impression I got from my last trip to New York. You remember."

Rune had to deliver good news and bad. He decided to start with the good news, to entice More. "I think Redhawk's plans for relaxing government oversight of foreign capital flows has less to do with him than with his new flame. Her name is Ing Kan, and she's a financial affairs attaché with Beijing's embassy in New York." He was holding the good part in reserve.

"I'm supposed to care about the guy's love life?" More growled.

Rune smiled into the phone. "She's PLA, one of the new hothouse plants. She and Redhawk met in Hong Kong about a year ago. At a party hosted by our friend there. You may remember him—the gent with the Chinese sub on call? Which you tried to blow up? Nearly starting World War III in the process?"

Again silence on the other end of the line, but it had a different feel. Rune knew he had More interested; now Rune just had to keep him that way.

"I think the reasons for Ing Kan's presence here are more professional than personal. I think PLA brass is finally feeling the heat from all the anti-corruption drives over there, and they're looking for ways to get their booty offshore. And while they're at it, gaining a real foothold in the top tier of American finance—not to mention a potential one in the White House—would be considered a nice bonus. Maybe even one that could stop the 'tiger hunts' there for a while," Rune added, using the jargon for Beijing's corruption investigations.

"Now, if you're looking at financial flows during an election year, you're bound to find funny money, both here and from overseas. Ing Kan is the latter. There are money games happening stateside, too, between the parties. Having both conventions in the same place at the same time is no accident, but it's a terrible idea. It concentrates the politicians and the donors in one tight spot on a tight schedule, under ridiculous pressure to grab as much of the loot as possible. With tensions this high between the parties, it wouldn't be hard for someone to pull off a stunt that would jeopardize the convention process, maybe even screw up the national elections. Do we really need that kind of instability right now?"

Rune could almost hear More frowning, though not out of impatience. More could wait in an ambush position for days, even weeks, for just the right moment to obliterate his target. Rune had seen the smoking aftermath more than once. He figured More knew what was coming.

"There's some weird stuff going on with the campaign money this year on both sides. You've heard what's happening with the banks—people are turning away from them in droves. That includes the politicos. I've got a source high up in the industry giving me detailed information. The money's going elsewhere, but no one knows just where. Now, you know that by law, I can't look into this stuff directly. But there are people who can. That chick from Treasury, for one."

More snorted derisively. Even after all this time, he couldn't stand Liza Marrone, a FINCEN agent from Treasury who'd crossed paths with both men several years earlier. Rune pressed ahead. "She's been getting information about financial irregularities related to Convention Week. She thinks it's coming from various banks and agencies, but it's coming from us, through back channels. I need help following the money, and I need a cutout. She's both. I know you don't like her, but you'll like this other part."

Rune paused before delivering the final payload. He could hear More out there, waiting. "We'll need NYPD liaison. A team for investigation and quick response that we could inter up with other agencies, like last time, if need be. Your former partner and his running buddies fit the bill. They can take the lead and take the credit—"

"—but you'll be guiding them the whole way, and I'll be your hand on the wheel," More finished for him. Rune knew he wouldn't hold More's attention much longer, but it was done now: More had put the pieces together, as Rune had known he would.

"I'll make all the arrangements, I'll give you whatever you need. But we've got to get this up and running right away. The first fund-raisers start in a few days. You'll have to move fast."

And damn him, More did, Rune thought, listening to the clicks and hisses of the broken connection. The bastard had hung up on him.

Which was just as well. More had let him off the hook.

Rune hadn't needed to disclose his deepest, most private suspicion.

If he was right, Convention Week was the fuse to a bomb the likes of which the United States had never seen.

One that could tear those states apart.

Permanently.

PART I

THE DESCENT

IN THE KINGDOM OF THE WICKED

"THE AMERICAN PEOPLE don't know what they want," the Speaker of the House, Caduta Massi was saying to her new aide, Corinne. "That's why they keep electing us."

The speaker's office was located in the southern wing of the U.S. Capitol, the gleaming gift of the pentangular commission of Thornton, Hallet, Hoban, Latrobe, and Bulfinch, who had bequeathed the core of a Francophilic monument to a new nation while France marched its own people to the guillotine by the thousands. The wing arose later, in the decade preceding the U.S. Civil War. Its architect, Thomas Walter, also designed the Capitol's distinctive "wedding cake" dome, with its oculus and statue of freedom, the construction carried out by slaves.

Pristine Virginia marble all round the wing was festooned with CCTV cameras, laser motion detectors, and snaking wires. The select few granted access to the House wing had to clear a triple-tiered security cordon (manual, chemical, and electronic), then whatever additional security measures each representative had added to his or her own office using whatever public funds they could divert. No prison in the country could top the United States Congress for surveillance and segregation. Each legislator hunkered in a fortified bunker, suspicious of everyone everywhere. Compromise and camaraderie were long dead on Capitol Hill, replaced with an air of paranoia and the stranglehold of slow coercion.

Caduta Massi's office was watched over by no fewer than three traversing CCTV cameras, a millimeter-wave body imager, a HI-SCAN X-ray system, a Centurion II HVAC air monitor, a seven-man Secret

LIP detail (segregated-channel radios, Glocks with extended magazines), and a dozy Rottweiler named Clarence, whose snores and farts carried throughout the marble halls.

Caduta Massi hailed from old Pacific Heights money, the daughter of a San Francisco flour magnate. Her marriage to the scion of a Central Valley agricultural tycoon had created a dynamo that had powered the California Democratic machine since the 1980s. With shrewd and adroit financial machinations, the couple parlayed their nouveau-riche family fortunes into true dynastic wealth. Their combined connections across the three-dimensional chessboard of local, state, and federal politics could not help but make them money. Land deals, stock trades made minutes after closed-door congressional committee meetings on pending legislation, blind trusts, offshore holdings: The money never stopped flowing. Money that accrued to them, of course. Caduta Massi diligently funded each move of her impressive career with public—i.e., taxpayers'—money, and if the corporate entity she and her husband created early in their marriage also reaped the benefits, so what? There was nothing illegal about profiting from advance knowledge gleaned on the job. It was all part of public service.

Even when the party ended with the passage of the STOCK Act in 2012, Caduta Massi—of narrow hips and broad vision—was in a unique position not only to weather the storm but to profit handsomely. And profit she had, becoming the richest congressional officeholder the Democrats had sent to Washington.

On the surface, her politics were textbook liberal Democrat ideology, Camelot and the Great Society refashioned for the digital age. No special interest was too small to go unnoticed, no electorate too insignificant to ignore, no fence-straddling vote not worth buying.

Caduta Massi was cunning, seasoned, with the flexibility to instantly flip-flop on sensitive issues that would earn her the envy of a teenage Olympic gymnast. One of the qualities most remarked upon by her opponents in the House and Senate was her tenacity, which was born of jealousy combined with a near-psychopathic competitive streak. The speaker was known to ruthlessly hound and claw any legislator who stood in her way. This included members of her own party; when the incumbent president threw her weight behind the bill that would later become the Reform Emergency and Administrative Medical Rights Law, those Democratic lawmakers who dared protest the bill's staggering cost and lack of spelled-out implementation found themselves hurled under the grinding undercarriage of the Democratic bus, a foaming Caduta Massi at the wheel.

She had been affectionately dubbed "Pile Driver" by the more conservative elements of the press. When she privately referred to these journalists, colloquialisms such as "shitheel" and "cocksucker" incongruously freckled the speaker's otherwise polished speech.

Corinne (freshly graduated from Brown, double major in IR/semiotics, with energy and piercings to spare) sensed that such a graphic lexical shift was in the cards that morning. Ostensibly, she had been called in to plot strategy for the party convention in New York City next week. She'd arrived early, pushing through the crowd of reporters, rushing through the security protocols, and ignoring the appraising stares of that jockish new senatorial aide to the Appropriations Committee chair.

Upon arrival, she found herself alone with the speaker, taking notes (later to be deleted) for an emergency tactical session on the Infrastructure Recovery Act, or National IRA bonds, as they were more commonly known.

Caduta Massi had long been on a "Vote for a National IRA" kick and had been infuriated by resistance from high-profile figures in high-profile cities—like New York. Passage of the National IRA bill would first require the isolation and neutralization of New York City's troublesome Mayor Baumgarten, who was being a pain in the ass about the party's latest attempt to issue yet another round of good-faith bonds to stave off yet another financial Armageddon in the Big Apple. The mayor (who had effectively inscribed his own name on Caduta Massi's personal shit list when he'd defected from the party in the previous election to run as an Independent and, gallingly, won) had shown himself to be an intractable opponent of the Democratic "spend now pay later" strategy.

Never mind that the biggest underwriters (like that cocksucker Julius Exmoor at Urbank) and hitherto staunch allies (like that shitheel Dicter Lanark at Electrum-Horn) were united in their obstruction to the bill. Flabbergasted, the speaker had gotten the president to schedule another bus tour in support of the bonds, on top of a special appearance during Convention Week, which would cause epic traffic jams from the security lockdown, making life miserable for millions of New Yorkers as long as she was in town.

The politics of this had become thorny of late, as the speaker put it, when that "asshole" (the mayor of New York City) and those "bloodsucking little pricks" (the bankers, most of whom worked for either Lanark or Exmoor) had begun to articulate to "those drooling, shit-eating maggots" (the press) their growing concern that the city would never be able to repay, let alone pay the interest on, the increasing mountain of debt brought on by the new bonds.

The aide had been on the job long enough to know that the speaker could not, *would* not, let such an affront go unanswered. What Corinne did not know was that Caduta Massi had an ulterior motive, a dark private dream that had festered for years. The mayor of New York City was weak, his city on its knees: the ideal time for making dreams (and political agendas) come true.

"Call Mario and confirm our meeting next week at the first one," the speaker instructed brusquely, referring to New York governor Mansoni and the first DNC fund-raiser, scheduled to be held in Manhattan the following week. "I want to talk to his man alone."

The aide dutifully tapped her orders into her tablet. "Should I call Mr. Fasciola as well? He'll definitely be there," she offered helpfully, alluding to the public advocate, the first municipal official in the chain of succession behind the mayor.

The speaker blinked in a slow, reptilian manner at her credulous aide. "Did I *ask* you to?" she said with an undertone of menace that made Corinne's jaw tremble.

"No," the aide replied hurriedly.

The moment passed. "We need to move fast on this bond-issue thing. I want all the local ward heads to start circulating attack ads. How many districts can we count on?"

The aide's fingers flew over her tablet. "Seventeen, with another five on the fence."

The speaker's lips pressed together in a thin blood-red line. "How much would we need for their votes?"

More tablet taps followed. "Two hundred thousand, give or take."

Caduta Massi thought silently, her eyes the color of schist. "Take it out of Take It Back," she ordered, meaning the super-PAC responsible for bundling millions of dollars in campaign contributions without overt links to specific candidates, thus neatly sidestepping federal restrictions.

The aide typed away rhythmically. "Distribution as usual?" she asked, referring to how the money would be divvied up and spread around the electoral districts.

Caduta Massi's eyes flashed gneiss. "No. *Now* you can call Fasciola. Tell him what we need to do, and let him tell you how to do it."

The aide hesitated. "But don't we have to—"

"No, we do NOT have to," Caduta Massi barked at her aide, her gaze now twin orbs of dark glinting mica. "Get it done and don't fucking question me again. The American people don't need four more years of waffling Independents with GOP puppet masters pulling their strings. This is for the party; it's *our* time. Now get out."

As the aide frantically scurried from the office, Caduta Massi picked up her secure cell phone, punching in a speed-dial number from a very private contact list. As she waited for the connection, she made a mental note to get herself an aide who could follow orders, keep quiet, and didn't have so many fucking piercings.

A low rumble began throbbing against her bulletproof office windows.

• • •

They were heard before they were seen, owing largely to the two DAP Black Hawk gunships flying cover overhead. Two GMVs and two M1078 "War Pig" trucks rode before and behind the armored black Sprinter Executive van, along with two Washington MPD prowl cars on either end. The convoy stretched a quarter mile and carried enough firepower to take out the entire Capitol complex; Beltway insiders who knew the man at the center of the procession whispered that might well be his intention.

The motorcade snaked around Southern Drive, approaching the Capitol from the House side—this was clearly intended. As the formation slowed, armored blackout shades slammed shut over Caduta Massi's office windows. The Black Hawks took up defensive hover positions overhead, their weapons fixed on the Capitol building, while the men in the vehicles trained their arms on windows, doorways, Hill journalists, and any civilians dumb enough to try for a closer look. The Capitol police were nowhere to be seen.

The Sprinter's door opened, the advance men of the LIP detail fanned out in a black-suited cocoon formation, and out he came.

Senator Mel Cordryceps. The Republican chairman of the Senate

Appropriations Committee and Caduta Massi's archnemesis.

Though he did not look the part. He was pink and soft, with graying blond hair brushed straight back from his smooth high forehead. Beneath this shone his well-publicized gaze, a level, wide-eyed stare that gave the glinting impression of irrepressible assurance. His eternal smile was wide and relaxing, his dentition not the slightest bit predatory, his speech always measured and steady. He gave off the comforting air of a good-natured parent (in fact, he had authored a bestselling children's Christmas book to offset his many polemics written for voting adults). His movements were smooth and practiced from years in front of the camera for his popular program, long the centerpiece of a conservative cable news network.

He was a hardy midwesterner, widely known to love his grandchildren and golf and good whiskey. His image had been carefully cultivated over decades to project a stately, unbroken facade without blemish, upon which he actively traded every waking moment of his life. Not even in private, to those in closest orbit of his inner circle, would he admit or even suggest that he was deftly manipulating the perceptions of a nation of brain-dead TV watchers; such cynicism simply did not occur to him.

With Mel Cordryceps safely inside the Capitol building, the military formation moved out. It could be summoned again at the senator's whim, in any configuration required and always Special Operations capable. Among the many protuberances dotting the membrane of his empire, Mel Cordryceps maintained a charity for wounded SOF veterans of the Afghan and Iraqi campaigns, which guaranteed him the votes of not only those in the U.S. Special Ops community but their families and friends as well—a most effective use of force multiplication. The senator was safely rushed through the corridors of Congress to his blast-proofed office, where an aide waited patiently, tablet in hand.

After the security detail had fired up the satellite, broadband, and RF countersurveillance array, Mel Cordryceps crossed one perfectly creased trouser leg over the other, steepled his fingers, and said over his manicured nails: "To business." His aide, a smiling blond jock fresh out of UMass who was decked out in Brooks Brothers, sat up even straighter, fingers laced over his tablet like the stitches of a football.

But the senator wasn't speaking to him; his gaze was focused on the man in the corner. This man was tall, broad-shouldered, and rangy, with hooded eyes that scanned, measured, and remembered all, and which had no difficulty meeting the senator's glassine stare. This man had grudgingly surrendered several weapons of unconventional make and manufacture before being granted his private audience with the senator. Mel Cordryceps had needed to pull rank on the head of his personal security detail to station outside the blast-proof doors.

"Mr. Hurt," Mel Cordryceps began amicably, "you have reviewed my proposal?"

The man in the corner nodded a fraction of an inch.

"And?"

"I have someone in mind," Hurt said, a touch of gravel in his voice.

"Just one?"

"He'll pick his own team. He'll be the liaison for all communications."

"Which will, of course, not be traceable to this office," Mel Cordryceps said dentally. His trademark grin was widening even as that of his aide vanished.

Hurt nodded fractionally again. "Do you accept his conditions for payment?"

The aide was starting to look uncomfortable, since all payments would fall upon him, in the form of a series of dead drops, locations shared only with the senator, who would dispatch his aide no more than one hour before each pickup. The aide was fervently hoping he would never meet or even see whoever collected the payment.

Mel Cordryceps casually waved one pink hand. "Of course. I see no reason to haggle with a professional who provides such a vital service to the nation. When do I get to meet him?"

Hurt said sandily, "You don't. You'll never see him or his team, and the direction of contact will be only from him to you, through me. You'll have no way of finding him."

The senator's smile shrank slowly, as though his feelings had been bruised. "Then how will I know it's really him?"

In a voice of thickening mud, Hurt replied, "By his code name."

Two fingers of Hurt's right hand curled upward—there was a paper matchbook held between them. Hurt waited three seconds, then flicked the matchbook across some of the most heavily monitored airspace in the U.S. He had already turned to leave by the time Mel Cordryceps opened the matchbook and silently read the name stenciled on the inside flap: ODIN.

With Hurt out of the room, there seemed to be a bit more air. The aide took a big gulp of it to steady his nerves and chanced a question: "Sir, how should I log this expense?"

Mel Cordryceps was firmly back in control. Pocketing the matchbook, making a mental note to dispose of it at home in his fireplace, he said grinningly: "Don't."

THE PONZIANI OPENING

THE HAND-CARVED PANELING in the ceiling and walls would cost the GDP of a small country to duplicate. The floors alone would pay for a new helicopter, and the rugs could equip it with premium surveillance gear. Taken together, the crystal chandeliers throughout the mansion would cover the cost of a small reconnaissance UAV. The paintings and sculptures—all original—displayed their provenance silently, having been covered countless times in auction-house catalogs, antiquarian publications, and design magazines for psychotic spenders. The furniture was a mix of period and modern that drew adjectives like *exquisite, neo-baroque,* and *deliciously decadent* from the gathered revelers.

These were a mix of local and state politicians and their attendant pilot fish, litigators both public and private (though equal in their slither), and of course, the top tier of what remained of New York City's business and financial elite. As well it should have been, for this was Convention Week, a time of promises and palm-greasing. It was when the Powers That Be convened and cajoled and tried to ease the considerable sum of their fears while deciding which scurvy figurehead coughed up by the parties would be the better horse to back.

The assemblage—drawn by the promise of money, the ultimate chum cloud—had congealed in what was once the Frick museum, bastion of Roman arch and lintel and neoclassical clutter. Now it was the private residence of none other than Julius Exmoor, the anuran CEO of Urbank.

How this had come about was the crux of this year's election morass—the unexpected, highly controversial, 2016 endgame to the Dodd-Frank Act of 2010. On paper, the recently passed law closed the loophole for all charitable contributions being tax-deductible. Permanently. In practice, it was a slow-motion train wreck.

Typically, the problematic item had been inserted into the bill's bulging paragraphs at the very last minute, with no debate, let alone any thought given to its future ramifications. No sooner had the legislators finished slapping each other's backs as the bill was signed than a nationwide ebb of capital support for educational and cultural institutions began to flow. Universities were gutted; museums were sold with or without their collections to private citizens who still had capital to deploy. Nearly every program for arts education or administration that had flourished for decades on steady donor contributions now withered to windblown flecks of bonemeal. Untold thousands of jobs vanished almost overnight, as did innumerable grants and scholarships. The hordes of unemployed casualties of Dodd-Frank got no help from the banks, which were being squeezed by the same law. Homeless colonies were springing up faster than the media could cover them.

Somehow this fiasco was viewed as a triumph in Congress, which marveled vociferously at its own achievements on the Sunday-morning talk shows, while the monster it had unleashed upon the country went about its work.

With Convention Week looming, both parties were at loggerheads over the ramifications of what they had brought into being. Anyone with a political career was doing his or her utmost to avoid the white-hot issue of the moment: the Repeal.

The Repeal was on the tip of every tongue, the lead-in of every broadcast. It was the trigger of a million interrupted conversations, violent arguments, and sundered friendships. Both parties were locked, from distance to azimuth to kill box, in a seemingly endless exchange of barrages over efficacy, rights made wrong, and wrongs gone on. No one knew who would wade into the toxic quicksand or if they would. Not since the crash had an election year shown such toothsome potential.

Amid the odious mountain of legislation Dodd-Frank had excreted into being, the associated costs (long promised to be negligible by the congressmen for whom the act was named) had spiraled up and out like a fire tornado, engulfing at first whole branches of government, then whole industries, then regions of the country, and finally, vast segments of the population.

Over its six-year metastasis, Dodd-Frank had lived up to its promise of preventing future economic catastrophe by strangling the financial industry with the methodical ruthlessness of an anaconda. As it grew, more staff had to be added to enforce the ever-growing list of regulations, and more departments created for the new regulatory bodies. Lawsuits followed hearings as the beast fed slowly on its quarry, occasionally pausing when thwarted (usually by congressional deadlocks over funding) before throwing another legislative loop around its prey. Allegations of market-rate manipulation, price-fixing collusion, high-risk trading, and mortgage fraud on an unprecedented scale were dropped on the heads of the largest banks from above, while from below, Dodd-Frank's tentacles worked tirelessly, slapping on higher reserve-capital ratio requirements, trading caps, and an endless and imaginative stream of new administrative fees.

All of which was being perpetrated in the name of ending "too big to fail" while actually enshrining it. That such blatant hypocrisy would be swallowed hook, line, and sinker by the public was a congressional snake-oil fire sale that would have done P. T. Barnum proud. The banks had been made the sacrificial lamb, the government the veiled priest, and regulation the death by a thousand cuts. This dynamic had been going on for six years now. It had traumatized millions and cost trillions but made for great television.

Such was the litany of woe now warbled by Dieter Lanark, the current chief executive of Electrum-Horn, the oldest, largest, and most powerful of the Wall Street investment banks. Its members went on to command multinational corporations, once venerable universities now offering little more than the shabby gentility of accreditation, and, of course, the highly influential K Street lobbying firms generating obscene profits from both sides of the bloody partisan rancor ravaging the nation's capital. *Vus nuch?*

Lanark and Exmoor were ensconced in a corner of the vast West Gallery, more to keep an eye on the crowd from a distance than to mingle. As usual, they were huddled over a claw-footed table of intricately carved marble, topped with an inlaid chess set of polished walnut and mahogany, the board bounded with a delicate filigree of braided gold. The exquisite piece was said to have belonged to Henry Clay Frick himself, and Exmoor was said to have demanded it as a condition for closing on the house. He'd phoned in his offer after the Frick Foundation's funding collapsed, exactly twenty-four hours after the Dodd-Frank caveat closing the loophole for tax-deductible charitable donations cleared the Senate floor.

As usual, Exmoor was brooding over a problem he had laid out on the board, this one being the Ponziani Opening, a complex maneuver involving multiple pieces and directions. It wasn't aimed at capturing enemy pieces. It was a veiled survival strategy. Smoke and mirrors.

Also as usual, Lanark was bitching. "Have you heard what those fuckers are proposing now?" His voice, while not quite to the point of honking, managed to register in Exmoor's ear as somewhere between a grunt and a whine. "It's like Basel Six. They're talking about doubling the reserve ratio requirements again. That'll put our Tier One up to nearly forty percent. And they want to put new caps on our trading ops. *And* they want us to lend more when nobody in the country, let alone the country itself, can pay bills. And *they* call *us* 'the engine of growth,' those hypocritical cocksuckers. How the fuck do they expect us to make any money?"

Exmoor said nothing, apparently pondering the problem on the board. But he was seeing much more than he gave away with the position of his head. Urbank was facing the same problems, and Exmoor had been brooding over them at much greater depth.

How, for instance, were both political parties paying for the obscenity of Convention Week? Neither one had touched its long-standing accounts or lines of credit with Exmoor's private bank, an arrangement that had stood for decades. Nor did he know why, as of that very night, the vaults and safe-deposit boxes at every Urbank branch that offered them carried only one third of their normal annual capacity. Nor did Exmoor have an answer for the steady hemorrhage of retail customers throughout the city—a critical erosion of Urbank's depositor base.

But Lanark was lost in his tirade. "We're going to have to raise processing and card fees again! That's the second time this *year!* You want to know how many customers we've lost this month alone? I've got the mother of all credit squeezes tightening around my balls, and those bastards in Washington want *more!*"

Lanark had a vain streak. While his status afforded him ample opportunity to indulge it, it had led to one particularly odd result. Like other wealthy men for whom image was all, he could stave off time's ravages to a certain extent. His hair and teeth were real and impeccably maintained. His body was well honed by personal trainers in private health clubs. But when confronted with the inevitable broadening of the bones that comes with age, he had taken the radical step of osteoabrasion, having layers of his cranial faceplate sanded down by CNC medical machinery, with the soft tissue of his face then pulled tight over the new landscape. The scale of his head was infinitesimally smaller than that of his body, giving him the look of a statue that had been decapitated and its head replaced.

While it had made Lanark's visage as youthful and handsome as that of one many years younger—if not altogether proportional—Exmoor thought the drastic procedure had also shaved off some of Lanark's brain.

Still, it wasn't like the man was spouting untruths. Dodd-Frank continued to wreak havoc on the financial industry in the name of saving it. But there was an insidious subtlety, which, though buried in reams of bureaucratic obfuspeak, had burned like a newborn star to Exmoor's discerning eye. The real danger of the act wasn't in the new governmental powers barely spelled out in the finished document; it was precisely their *unfinished* nature that had made Exmoor's blood run cold six years earlier when the bill was signed into law. It was the deliberate vaguery infecting the act's language that Exmoor knew would give the government nearly unlimited authority to penalize, tax, and otherwise shake down the financial industry for cash any time at all. With its parameters undefined, there were no effective restraints to the law. And since Dodd-Frank *was* now law, there was no recourse for the banks, brokerages, and funds.

It had started with the levies on lenders bogged down in the mortgage mess, then spread like wildfire to capital reserve ratios, proprietary trading limits, and new fees and regulations imposed at nearly every level of the transactive pyramid.

But Exmoor had known there was worse to come. He'd nearly had an apoplectic fit when the Commodity Futures Trading Commission filed a lawsuit against the hugely successful high-tech monolith, Kumquat, whose product pipeline set the standard for consumer electronics the world over. Everyone, *everyone*, had to have the latest Kumquat phone, computer, or content player, all interconnected, all user-friendly, all in annoyingly loud colors.

The government had filed suit alleging Kumquat's collusion with the country's largest remaining publishing companies over ebook pricing, *during* an election year, *after* Kumquat disclosed it had a ninety-billion-dollar cash hoard and was trying to decide whether to spend it on new acquisitions or return it to shareholders.

It made Exmoor shudder that such brazen extortion of private industry by a government agency had met with hysterical public approval. It was theft, pure and simple, cleverly done through a third party with no legal or historical precedent, engineered to provide a comfortable chasm of safe distance for its congressional wielders. Only Kumquat was big enough to withstand the years-long face-off in the courts that fighting the charge would bring. Nobody gave a shit if the government wrecked the nation's publishing industry in the process—hey, collateral damage. In what masqueraded as a war against industrial corruption. But which in fact was a smokescreen for the *real* source of the corruption, of government run amok and ravenous, stoking popular discontent to legitimize its own limitless appetite for other people's money.

A fact that was not lost on Julius Exmoor.

At first he'd been vocal in his protests, appearing more often in a month's worth of Senate hearings than many senators. He didn't stop when Dodd-Frank's teeth began to bite, forcing him to consolidate Urbank's trading operations and raise fees at its retail branches. He didn't stop when the multiple government lawsuits over interest-rate manipulation made him cough up hundreds of millions to settle the charges (some baseless, none proved) to keep his bank's name clear and vital signs normal. He didn't stop when some greedy shithead in the London office made a series of massive bets that ended up on the wrong side of the trade, costing Urbank over six billion dollars in losses and kicking off a new round of investigations, lawsuits, and popular uproar. He didn't even stop when forced to "settle" with the government over the mortgage mess that everyone wanted to forget, along with the cost of the government's own audit of the banks named in the case, which threatened to run into the billions.

What had stopped Julius Exmoor in his tracks was when the government started going after *foreign* banks. At first glance it just looked like a state thing, upstart New York AG grabbing the spotlight in a suit over sanction violations that didn't even hold much water. But Exmoor knew the AG, and he knew who pulled his strings in both Albany and Washington, and now found himself facing a world in which *every* financial institution, no matter how far away, was considered fair game for the U.S. government.

Exmoor knew the sanctions case was just the tip of the iceberg. Sure enough, the CFTC jumped in with both feet atop a host of other banks from England to France to Switzerland, and even though some of the prey successfully fought off the maraudings, the subsequent billions in settlements began to flow stateside.

Exmoor knew they wouldn't stop; there was too much money to be made. So he did.

He stopped fighting, stopped going to Washington, stopped going to Urbank's Park Avenue headquarters. He more or less stopped leaving his mansion, shuttering the windows to the howling mobs that encircled it daily. He augmented his personal security team, as well as upgrading the mansion's defenses. Within his modern motte-and-bailey, he hunkered down to wait out the storm, to plan and strategize, delegating much of the bank's daily operations to subordinates. He spent most of his time at the chess table—he'd begun studying the game as a college student—laying out problems, which, in his mind, corresponded to the times of decay and debilitation in which he lived.

However, a man of Exmoor's status could not simply isolate himself from the roiling waters of politics, nor the predators infesting them. Convention Week was a time of promises and palm-greasing. Fund-raising events were the conduits for campaign donations, the oil in the gears of the American political machine.

Exmoor could avoid going to see the other political and financial chieftains, but he could not avoid them coming to him, especially in an election year. The mansion's location meant proximity to the numerous private residences designated as fund-raising hubs for both parties. Its ample fortifications and security teams provided a well-protected comfort zone for a meeting between the heads of state and business, who no longer dared show their faces to an unruly and increasingly fierce populace. Those in Exmoor's professional orbit—men like Dieter Lanark—were precisely the sort of people sought out by politicians, lobbyists, and assorted other parasites seeking cash nutrition.

And in they came.

Just now, walking through the colonnaded connection to the North Hall, was Aniruddha Nayarit, last man standing after the feds raided GC Piso and Partners LLC two years earlier, who had bought his freedom by informing on his former colleagues. Despite being formally banned from participating in legitimate banks or hedge funds, Nayarit was now a silent partner in a dark pool that Exmoor knew oversaw a hundred billion in assets. A survivor.

Clustered in front of Rembrandt's 1658 self-portrait was a group whom Exmoor privately referred to as the Hatchet Men: Peter Fasciola, the city's public advocate; Anthony Ascaris, deputy state comptroller; and his courier, a pallid, damp wraith of a man whom Exmoor had heard referred to only as Necator.

A young female aide with commendable incurvation hovered briefly around the periphery of this group before flitting across the room to another, larger, and more heavily photographed one crammed on the divan in front of Turner's *Dieppe*. The aide, whose name, Tsetse Fly, always made Exmoor's mouth twitch, took her place standing beside her boss, City Council Speaker Isabella Trichinella, who was speaking sotto voce to New York state's governor, Mario Mansoni, who was packed in beside Senator Theodore Usanius Rickover Davidson III (D–New York). The couch's company comprised the very rungs of a ladder of power rising from City Hall to the statehouse in Albany to Washington. It was a couch, Exmoor knew, that signified slow death for himself and his professional peers.

For net worth, Lanark was the richest person in the room, with Exmoor a close second. The third richest person in the room had just walked in and was grabbing all the attention.

"Oh, great, it's bad enough we've got Caduta Massi's whole posse, but now fucking Redhawk's here," Lanark groused.

Alex Redhawk: billionaire asset manager and bon vivant, lone wolf of the money trade, with the chiseled physiognomy of a born liar and the easy gestures of one who didn't need to lie. His outspoken ideas on government spending and tax reform had earned him a reputation as a radical and an industry firebrand. There was a growing rumor, much louder than a murmur, that Redhawk was going to upset the whole Convention Week applecart by declaring himself a third-party presidential candidate, the first of the twenty-first century.

Exmoor liked Redhawk's go-it-alone spirit and respected his business skills but thought him a loudmouth who didn't consider the long-term implications of the reforms he advocated. Nor did Exmoor like the fact that Redhawk and his female companion angled their trajectory straight for the New York political power couch. No, Exmoor didn't like that one bit.

The woman on Redhawk's arm was sylphic and tractile, with the golden skin of the regions bordering the South China Sea. Her smile was opalescent, and her almond eyes glinted with something that might be mirth or cruelty. She wore a short dark tunic of semi-translucent silk festooned with thin strands of oxidized chain. The dress venerated every plane and curve of a figure that strained necks and loosened jaws throughout the gallery, male and female alike.

"Who *is* that?" Lanark gasped, twisting around in his chair.

Privately, Exmoor reflected that there was a certain symbiosis between politics and lust: The same passion roused by partisanship was now stoking Lanark's gonads. "Her name's Ing Kan," he grunted, returning his batrachian gaze to the chessboard. "She's an attaché from the Chinese embassy, foreign financial relations. Officially. Unofficially, she's Redhawk's new plaything." More likely vice versa, he thought. He had it on good authority just who and what the woman called Ing Kan was, from a decidedly well-informed source. But Exmoor wasn't telling Lanark that. After all, the man was his competitor.

"She's some piece of ass," Lanark drawled, taking a long pull on his Scotch and water.

"No, she's a cunt," Exmoor corrected him, "with friends in high places."

"Like Redhawk," Lanark sneered. "Look at 'em scurry. You'd think Redhawk was Christ returned."

"For some, he may be," Exmoor replied neutrally. Lanark wasn't wrong about the crowd. Besides the politicos fawning around Redhawk and his date—city councilors, state senators, the governor, oh my!—nearly every journalist in the room was jockeying for position. One of these was having better luck than most. This was a financial-news anchorwoman well known to Lanark and Exmoor, wearing a body-hugging dress over a figure second only to Ing Kan's. She was thrusting a microphone—and her décolletage—as close to Redhawk's face as possible. Ing Kan, for her part, seemed amused.

"Look at her. She's so desperate to be the one he's running to, she'd ball both of 'em right there on your rug," Lanark muttered disgustedly.

Neither man could hear the anchorwoman's question, but they caught Redhawk's baritone reply: "Taxes should be an economic incentive, not a political weapon. And I believe the same should apply to tax policy."

"*Fuck*, will you listen to this shit," Lanark nearly spat, twisting in his chair to face Exmoor, who was back to studying the chessboard. "Redhawk's building a groundswell on some bullshit platform about tax reform when nobody's talking about the *real* problem."

Here we go again, thought Exmoor with a mental sigh, leaning both hands on the custom-tooled cane he was never seen without.

"Dodd fucking Frank, the root of all evil," Lanark rambled on, gaining steam. "Six years ago Congress shat it into creation, and the government's been shaking us down ever since—us, Jules, guys like me and you, who run the banks that keep the world running—for a quarter trillion dollars. Now the tab's coming up on *half* a trillion. And American banks were just the beginning. You remember."

Exmoor sighed; Lanark was annoying, but he was right. It was time to head him off. "Dieter," he began gently, "do you ever wonder where all the money's gone?"

Lanark stopped and blinked. "The fuck are you talking about?"

"Convention Week," Exmoor explained, trying to keep his voice and body language calm in another attempt to bring Lanark off the boil. "Both parties have long-standing accounts with us. But they've been drawing down their balances for years. We haven't logged any campaign donations—*any* donations—this whole year. Don't you think that's a little strange? I mean, who's paying for all this?" Exmoor made a sweep of the room with his eyes, noting that Redhawk was speaking quietly with the governor, while Ing Kan was chatting up the TV anchor with the supermodel figure.

Exmoor continued: "What about your retail customers? Your volume's been dropping just like ours, hasn't it? As of this moment our deposits are down thirty percent, and over half our vault storage is empty. We're going to have to start closing branches soon. *Where have all the customers gone?*"

This only got Lanark revved up again, and Exmoor could see he was close to losing it. "Tell me about it! We're going to have to raise processing and card fees again! That's the second fucking time this year! You want to know how many customers we've lost this month alone?"

Lanark's fulminations were starting to draw attention. He was waving his arms, spilling his drink, threatening the pieces on the board. It was only when he felt the touch of Exmoor's cane in the middle of his chest that he finally got hold of himself. Lanark knew the custom cane housed a .45-caliber derringer. Exmoor was no fool, nor did he suffer them. In a very low voice audible only to Lanark, Exmoor growled: "Don't fuck with my chessboard."

Lanark slowly put his drink down and his palms up. Exmoor held his eyes for a few seconds, then lowered his cane to the floor.

The moment passed, and the revelry went on around them uninterrupted. Lanark shrank down in his chair, which made his head look a bit more in sync with the rest of him. "Sorry," he mumbled. "I'm just so fucking tired of this. I wish they'd all just go home."

"It's only show business," Exmoor murmured. "Smoke and mirrors." It was all so futile, he thought. Men like Lanark could only react to the political absurdities of their times without fully understanding them. And Redhawk, he only *thought* he could change things—if he cared enough, which was still to be seen. Despite the posturing and the obscene waves of money sloshing around Convention Week, it was all a sham. The office of the presidency had become a cipher, a smokescreen for the dominant party heads and the interests that paid them. True power rested behind the throne, not on it. Exmoor figured Ing Kan understood this quite well.

He returned his thoughts to the board. The thing about the Ponziani Opening, he recalled, was that it wasn't an attack or even a flanking maneuver. It was a doctrine of long-term offensive subterfuge for surviving a crowded, dangerous environment.

Most appropriate, Exmoor thought glumly. *Most appropriate indeed.*

THE LAST SUPPER

UZHKA IS CHOPPING CELERY ROOT with a machete over one of the garbage bins while I check the stocks simmering in their cauldrons on the stove; out of the ten people in the kitchen, we're the only ones working. Everyone else is coping with evening service by getting as high as they possibly can.

You could say there's good reason for it. Everybody knows the party's ending tonight. After weeks of angry calls from creditors, vendors refusing to ship unless we paid cash (our wine guy stopped shipping altogether), and the owner's increasing elusiveness, the general consensus is that tonight's dinner will be the last gasp of Le Tableau.

We never open before eight, to follow the nocturnal rhythm of the neighborhood's traffic. It's early enough in the evening that Nadia, the bartender, is taking a break. She's lying on the flour sacks by the pantry door, nuzzling her girlfriend over a joint that smells strongly of something besides weed. It was Nadia who found the gleaming new padlock and chain hidden behind a case of Verkhoyansk vodka when she came in this afternoon. No one has seen the owner, Ron, in over two weeks. As the fumes of cooking drugs vie with those of cooking food in the low-ceilinged basement kitchen, the conversation turns to Ron's possible whereabouts.

—'e's on a fuckin' plane to Brazil by now, dude, rasps Evan, our number one sauté man as he passes the smoldering glass pipe to Wendy, the pastry chef, an elfin figurine with a startling amount of body hair that threatens to ignite as she holds the lighter to the rocks simmering three inches from her nose.

—They'll love him down there, drones Kev laconically from the floor, where he sits staring intently at his shoelaces. Kev is my sous chef. Kev is also a heroin addict. I would've fired him my first day on the job had he not demonstrated his uncanny ability to perform all the myriad and dangerous tasks his position requires, while being stoned completely out of his gourd. His habit also prevents him from saying much, which is the other reason I've kept him on this long—he doesn't run his mouth and give me headaches.

Payne, our grill man, brings his nose off his wrist with a jagged snort and practically shouts: —Two-faced lying COCKSUCKER!

This draws a clenched giggle from Larry, the saucier, who's tapping out a line on his wrist from Payne's little brass coke cache.

John, our lead prep monkey, and Miguel (dishes) and Osvaldo (porter) are leaning on their elbows at the prep station. Their group silence means the acid they took about an hour ago is kicking in.

You could say there's good reason for this sort of behavior, but I wouldn't agree with you. I loathe irresponsibility, and everyone in this group knows it. But they also know why I don't care anymore. I've got something they don't: a way out.

And as though reading my mind, Caitlin, one of our waitresses, comes bounding downstairs and sings out: —So, Beth, do you, like, have to wear a uniform at your new private-chef gig?

—I don't know, I say, and it's the truth. They didn't cover that at the interview, and I didn't think to ask questions. I needed the job badly and didn't want to make waves. Also, I was pretty sure I was the only person in that room who didn't have a gun.

Caitlin's riding an ascending wave of MAOs and can't stop asking questions. I prefer her in one of her depressive troughs, but those generally don't last. Caitlin is a true chemical puppet, dancing between personae to a pharmacopic symphony of mood-altering drugs. I don't know where she gets the money for all the pills she takes—the so-called insurance Ron doles out to us just gets laughed at in pharmacies. I wouldn't bother trying it out in a hospital, which was another reason I jumped at the new job, since I want that back door ready on the day my pain gets too much for me to handle.

—Is your boss hot? Caitlin trills.

—I don't know that, either, he wasn't at the interview, I reply gently, checking the parboiled portions of tonight's pastas. Caitlin needs to be handled with kid gloves at the best of times, but when one drug starts making headway against all the others in her system, it's time to be extra careful. Caitlin has been known to talk for an hour and a half nonstop, to erupt in screaming fits of incoherent rage, and to lapse into half-hour crying jags. Exactly what triggers her violent mood shifts is a mystery to all of us, but I'd put it down to a latent fear of confrontation, one that's blown completely out of proportion by the antidepressants she gobbles like candy.

—So who hired you? Caitlin forces through a trembling smile, her eyes beginning to moisten. If she's about to blow, I hope it's a short episode. I'd like to get out of here as quickly and quietly as I can tonight. I hope Richard's not feeling randy. I just want to get a good night's sleep (if my pain allows it) so I can be ready for my first day tomorrow. I've never worked in a place with as much security as Mr. Redhawk's penthouse. Other restaurants I've worked at usually had two doormen at the most. The bouncers Ron hired from one of the bars up the block didn't last a week, since Ron conveniently forgot to pay them. That was about the time Ron became permanently invisible. Nadia's already been held up once, but we had so little traffic that she wound up talking the guy down and buying him off with a bottle of tequila. (I won't miss working here one bit.)

—It was the head of house staff, an older man, I say to Caitlin, surreptitiously making sure she's not within reach of any knives. He seems to run a pretty tight ship.

—Well, you're sure to get the boss's attention with that hot yoga body, Caitlin says, smirking. I know she's not really gay; this is just another direction the drugs throw her in. She must have been checking me out, though, since my baggy kitchen whites and checks hang on me like burlap sacks. Nadia has never given me a second glance; then again, I don't have any tattoos or piercings.

—Your new boss is a pretty fat cat, some kind of fund manager or something, says Kev's measured voice from the floor. He may be a junkie, but he likes to keep up with the news. I guess it gives him something to do between nods.

—Maybe he can bankroll Ron's next restaurant, Nadia sings through a cloud of pungent smoke, while her girlfriend giggles in her arms. The others join in with a chorus of boos, laughs, and profane suggestions, which come to an abrupt halt when Josh, our lone male waiter, comes downstairs with a terrified grimace and exhales in a stage whisper: —Cavatelli Guy's here.

Oh, great. The one customer I most don't want to deal with tonight. Some restaurants have regular customers; others have problem customers. Cavatelli Guy is both. He orders it every time he comes in, and every time he finds something wrong with it. With our staff in this condition (Josh has been sipping all night from a pitcher of martinis Nadia mixed up at the bar for all front-of-house workers), an argument is inevitable. I need to defuse the situation before it comes to a boil.

I make my cavatelli by hand, using organic pea flour. Grabbing a skillet from the overhead rack, I set to work:

> —Over medium-high heat, grease a pan with the end of a stick of butter and drizzle in an ounce of olive oil, no more;

> —Flash-sauté one cup of mixed shellfish (in this case, diced scallops, shelled mussels, and rock shrimp) until golden, deglaze with fish stock, and set aside in a bowl, leaving the drippings in the pan;

> —Drop in one cup of a mixture of minced shallots, garlic, cracked black peppercorns, and nutmeg, stirring till translucent;

> —Return the seafood to the pan along with a half-cup ONLY of crushed and seeded San Marzano tomatoes and the juice of one whole lemon;

> —Add one serving (two cups) of the parboiled cavatelli, stirring evenly to mix and coat.

A quick chop of some fresh mint leaves to garnish, and I hand the plate off to Josh, who claps his hands together and squeals with porcine glee as he takes the dish and turns to run it upstairs, followed by Caitlin, Nadia, and Nadia's cackling girlfriend, none too steady on her feet. Evan has already cleared his sauté station. Wendy's back at her post talking to herself, and Payne is slamming pans around and cursing. Kev has come up off the floor and throws me a dreamy wink and a salute as he takes my place at the range. It's too bad. This place could be something really special, but the owner's AWOL, our vendors don't trust us anymore, and the staff, while not inherently bad people, are all broken, like this restaurant, this neighborhood, this city.

I can hear the argument building right through the floor. Caitlin is fighting a losing battle to calm herself, Josh, and Cavatelli Guy, who sounds like— Yes, he's just thrown his dish on the floor.

Payne roars out a great cloud of obscenities and storms up the stairs to the dining room with a meat cleaver in his hand. Wendy's hot on his heels, a marble rolling pin in hers. Evan looks questioningly at me, then grabs a cast-iron skillet and heads upstairs to the gathering fray.

Time to go.

Kev is giggling down into a pan of burning asparagus as I peel off my apron and toss it into a bubbling stockpot. Crossing the basement to the pantry, I grab my knapsack from one of the wall hooks. It's a military bag, meant for carrying one of those big field radios, long before anyone dreamed up cell phones. I've gotten my routine down to a science. In under ten seconds, I've got it fully loaded with the best picks from the pantry. All fresh stuff; we get enough dry and canned goods in bulk deliveries at the soup kitchen I run. What I steal tonight, I'll serve up tomorrow—I'm sure Ron wouldn't begrudge me.

I've been stealing for the soup kitchen since the day I started here a year and a half ago. How I'll keep this up at the new Redhawk gig is something I need to figure out. I can't afford to lose this new job—money aside, he's giving me *real* health insurance, the kind I can actually use, the kind that may put an end to my pain. But I can kiss it goodbye if he—or someone on staff in that big fortress of a penthouse—nails me doing it.

Getting the food down to the soup kitchen won't be a problem; there are so many people going underground to the bank these days, I won't be noticed. But I'll need to get it there from the market once I've used Redhawk's money to buy it, then cover my tracks with the receipts.

I'm already halfway out the basement door when the crescendo of shouts from upstairs becomes screams, accompanied by a cacophony of breaking glass and flatware ringing off bone. I look back just in time to see Uzhka moving silently up the stairs two at a time, machete in hand. My last glimpse of Le Tableau is of John, Miguel, and Osvaldo giving me a three-faced, childlike, tripped-to-the-hairline smile. Then the door behind me slams shut.

• • •

Alphabet City is reclaiming itself. Once it was a slum, full of drugs and domestic violence. Then it became a sort of dirty playground, a recreation zone for the young and the better off who lived among the original slum-dwellers and made light of the grime and the ugliness and eventually drove property values through the roof. It was like that when I got here, before the party ended, before the economy crashed and the city burned. There was still optimism then, a freewheeling sense of fun and possibility, when you could slap a restaurant together in the time it took for the permits to come through, and you'd have lines down the block the night of your soft opening. I hopped from one place to another, which was a good way to build a reputation. By my fourth year in town, I had more contacts in my phone than I could recognize; I had job offers everywhere I went; restaurants overbooked when I was in the kitchen; and food bloggers hounded me online. I even began to think of opening my own place, where I could cook what I wanted, how I wanted, and train my staff to work properly for once.

For a moment, it seemed like it could happen. That moment was gone years ago.

The crash broke over the industry like a flurry of rogue waves. The leveraged restaurants—the ones that came late to the party and tried to make up for it with heavy borrowing to buy ambience and talent for the crowd—they went first. Then the high-end places, the ones with esoteric menus full of overly expensive ingredients. That was when the real scramble began, as reality sank in and people and places relying on their reputations suddenly realized they couldn't anymore. That was when places with poor food-cost control were dragged under, when those that couldn't downsize and simplify their food to compensate for imploding customer traffic went bust. That was when I came down here, where people in the industry had experience operating on shoestring budgets, where the dirty playground, with its previous rowdiness, could allow niche joints like Le Tableau a dwindling survival as the neighborhood reverted to its primal roots.

From Avenue B through to First, East Fifth Street looks like a war zone's aftermath. Blackened hulks of burned-out cars provide shelter for the legions of cats that escaped or were abandoned by the former denizens of the dirty playground, now gone feral and able to stand up to the large, fierce dogs maintained by the original occupants of the neighborhood. The boutiques and cafés that once lined the street have long been shuttered or, in some cases, looted and burned. Besides Le Tableau, there's only one restaurant left, Lavagna, which managed to do well enough to buy security from the bars. I've worked there before, and I'll go back there with my hat in my hand if things don't work out with the Redhawk gig. But that's only a last resort. I need to move up from this level fast, or I'll be pulled down with it when it caves in.

The bars are the dominant business, having weathered the crash with their built-in cushion of the drug trade. Nobody bothers running speaks anymore. It's not the cops (although they did crackdown a few years back, when the body count got too high to ignore); it's more that things have settled into a new rhythm. The bar owners are making enough from legal and illegal trade to buy security to keep things (reasonably) quiet, not to mention any necessary permits. Today you can buy off a health inspector and make your money back the same night and then some. It's not pretty, but at least it offers some stability—there aren't bodies dropping every night, like they did when the speaks ran hot. Think of it as progress. I can walk from here to the subway stop on Houston with no problem, as long as I walk past the bars, with their well-lit entrances, CCTV cameras, and industrial-sized doormen. I'm just a cook, invisible.

Since I left work so early, there's plenty of time for me to take this last food haul up to the soup kitchen and oversee the prep for tomorrow.

Once I'm in the subway, though, that's when things get dicey.

• • •

Down here, we're all on borrowed time.

The security cordon around the convention area—which this year happens to be the exact part of the Upper East Side where my soup kitchen is—puts a chokehold on all deliveries to the city. Including food. Before, my stealing and smuggling was just to keep this place going. Now it's so my charges don't starve to death underground while the new party candidates are chosen up above.

Everyone who eats in my soup kitchen has fallen through every last crack there is. At one time, maybe years ago, they had family, jobs, real connections with real lives. Then, as their illnesses took hold, they became names on the patient lists of Metropolitan Hospital, 172 feet over our heads. Then, with the budget cuts brought on by the crash, they became human flotsam, loose silt washed away by the tide of deinstitutionalization.

Like mud in a river, they followed gravity down to a nadir of equilibrium: here, off the southbound platform of the Ninety-sixth Street station of the Second Avenue subway. The black line.

I'm told this tunnel was decades in the making. And I'm sure there was a lot of excitement when it was first being dug. But when the funding ran out a few years back, it became a curse, a toxic football no politician wanted to pick up. Until someone got a better idea of how to use the space.

That someone is the woman who runs the bank behind my soup kitchen. I've never met her, only seen glimpses of her behind the security men. The only name I've ever heard her called is LA. She's what my parents would've called a siren, with the sort of hard-case bombshell look that Hollywood actresses try for and fail. She must have serious political connections, though, to get this kind of real estate.

That's why I'm here. Apparently, some high-ranking members of the City Council thought it would be a good idea to have a soup kitchen here, serving the public in its time of need. I guess they didn't look too closely at the operation LA set up right behind us: the biggest bank you'll never see. Need a loan? A safe-deposit box? Long-term storage for all the worldly possessions you kept when the real banks foreclosed on your home after you lost your job and your adjustable-rate mortgage adjusted itself to bankrupt you?

See, nobody trusts the upstairs banks. Too many scandals, too many new fees, too many casualties. People are desperate to hold on to what they have. If it's cash, they'd rather have direct access to it, even if that means lining up in front of large men with guns. More and more, people just hoard hard assets—jewelry, art, deeds to homes they dream of someday reclaiming.

So they clamor through my kitchen, averting their eyes from my charges at the common tables, lest they see themselves there. And they may be, sooner than they think. LA might have clout at City Hall, but I seriously doubt her operation is any more legal than mine is. And I steal to keep my place running; I wonder sometimes if her subway bank isn't the same thing on a larger scale.

Speaking of which, scale has become a problem, as I'm now being told by Jonah and Helm. Jonah is my manager, my right hand—he runs the kitchen when I'm not here. A high school dropout with a good heart, Jonah can't stand by idly and watch people suffer any more than I can. Helm is called Helm because that's the noise repeated most often in the cloud of gibberish he continually spouts. He's one of the colony, the group of mental patients evicted from the hospital overhead in the wake of the crash that now calls these tunnels home. Jonah is the only one who can understand him.

Through Helm's frothing rant, Jonah is able to fill me in. Apparently, the hamburger stand on the far end of the platform, serving the bank's customers, is doing more volume. It's far enough from the bank that LA seems not to notice or care about it. But nobody can ID the two big hairballs who run it, and nobody knows how they're being supplied. With the security cordon in place for Convention Week on the streets above, no deliveries are being allowed in anymore. Unless you smuggle food in like I do, it's not long before there isn't any. Stores are going bare, the few surviving restaurants in the area are cutting back to single-service schedules, lunch or dinner only. Manhattan's an island; we import our food supply. When that gets cut off, people get hungry fast.

So the hamburger hairballs are doing a brisk business . . . just like LA.

—Norm borm warm kjorm, Helm babbles.

—And there's been two more, Jonah translates.

This is troubling, at least to me. Helm is talking about the disappearance of colony members, a development since Convention Week began. Since there's never been a formal head count, only longtime members—like Helm—would notice when others had vanished. Even I wouldn't know if they were gone.

We're all on borrowed time.

And the clock's ticking.

I'm damn lucky to have found the job, for the food as well as the health insurance. I know I need a doctor for my condition; I've been putting it off for too long now, the episodes are getting worse. The health plan at the restaurant was a joke, even pharmacists just laughed when I showed them the card.

—Ponker hasa floo? queries Helm.

—Who's your new boss? Jonah translates.

—His name's Alex Redhawk, but he wasn't there; the house manager interviewed me, I explain. Their blank faces tell me the name means nothing to them. That's good, because I don't want to them to know I'm working for someone who's directly involved with the absurd political theater taking place right over our heads.

With dinner prepped and ready to serve, I need to get back downtown.

I carefully pack my knives. I need them out of sight to get through all the gun-toting guards and cops deployed for Convention Week. But I want them within reach while I'm on the subway.

• • •

The city ran out of money for the station renovation years ago. Add in the municipal layoffs, the union strikes, the power outages, and the general lack of maintenance, and the system crumbled from within. When subway crime spiked after the riots, the city increased the police presence in the core stations. But the layoffs and early retirements took too big a bite out of the force, so the city used what funds it had left on electronic surveillance, thinking that cameras alone would make an effective deterrent to criminals.

That was the wrong bet.

I don't look at anyone in the subway. I say nothing and show less. Anyone looking at me sees a working cook, grease-stained and broke—not an inviting target. For a woman, there's always another risk, but I've never encountered it (maybe rapists know that cooks carry their own knives). The subways are full of broken cameras and overflowing trash barrels and cardboard colonies of homeless people—hardly a lucrative area for robbery, although an excellent arena for spontaneous violence. The subway system has become a place for the practice of self-encapsulation, the art of disappearing in a crowd, knowing that even fragmentary contact with another could invite mortal danger. A place where the screech of brakes and rats gives way to the endless sound of dripping water.

Or, some say, of loud chewing. Through human flesh and bone.

This is how things are in most big cities now, and this is why Convention Week is going to wind up being a referendum on those new National IRA bonds. I haven't seen people so worked up over a political issue here in years. The guy sitting next to me is watching a debate on his phone. A couple of drunks at the far end of the car are arguing messily about it. I wonder what Mr. Alex Redhawk, my new boss, my new source for swag food, and provider of my first real health insurance in years, has to say about it.

I have my own way to practice the art of subway survival: my pain. It always kicks in as I descend the stairs from the street, into the wafting fumes of mud, wet power lines, and shit. Its burning ache provides the beacon on which to concentrate all my attention, my energy, my self-discipline.

My new health coverage won't kick in for at least six weeks. So we'll stay together a bit longer, my pain and I. I've grown used to it. It gives me focus; it sustains me on the perilous subterranean commute home.

Well, not my home. Not exactly.

Richard's apartment.

• • •

Richard was a customer from two restaurants ago who fell for me through my food; I live with him out of necessity. When I first came to the city, it was still possible for a young person from the Midwest to set up house here and live independently. Those days are long gone.

We have an understanding, Richard and I: He provides the shelter, I provide the food. Richard does freelance IT support for Urbank, and it made him enough to buy a one-bedroom place in one of those luxury conversions that went up all around Murray Hill and Chelsea just before the crash. Once the five-year abatement expired, Richard's property taxes jumped, which would have had a serious impact on his standard of living had he not found a stopgap measure.

Me.

Catching sight of Richard's building always brings mixed emotions for me. First, there's the immediate relief that I've survived the subway and gotten back aboveground in one piece. This is followed by the resignation of going home to Richard, whom I do care for, but from whom I necessarily keep my distance. I could probably maintain our status as is for years to come, and if I really had to bite the bullet I'd marry him, but our relationship is based on common requirements and limited possibilities. I need him not for who he is but what he provides: shelter, stability, someone to trust. I work in an industry that offers none of these things, that is in fact crumbling away, just like the city that spawned it.

You might ask why I don't up and leave. The answer is simple: Any place else would be worse.

When I let myself into Richard's apartment, he's on the couch with an old Pixar movie on the giant OLED monitor that doubles as a TV. A laptop is on the couch next to him, its screen filled with the sort of technoglyphics only computer geeks understand. He's also working on a bowl of my lentil soup. I keep jars of it in the fridge for quick comfort food:

—In a high-sided saucepan over medium heat, brown a pound

and a half of andouille sausage in its own fat. When done (about four minutes), set aside, leaving the drippings in the pan.

—Chop one whole white onion, one clove garlic (you can use more, I just don't like too much in mine), and one large carrot; toss into the pan with one ounce olive oil, and cook until tender (about eight minutes).

—Deglaze once with a cup of white wine. When this cooks down, add one pound of lentils (rinsed, drained, and picked over), return the cooked sausage to the pan, fill with enough chicken stock (I make my own, but you can use the premade stuff if need be; try to stick with organic) to almost completely cover the mixture, and cover the pan with a lid, turning the heat down to low.

—Simmer, stirring occasionally, for two hours. Keeps a week in the fridge, a month in the freezer.

Richard looks up from his electronic runes and smiles. It's not his fault. He's a good man, and I don't know where I'd be right now without him. But tomorrow, or wherever I'll be years from now, I don't see him in the picture.

—Hey, babe, he says, sighing. His eyes are red and he's slouching. Guess he had a long day, too. How'd it go?

—The wheels came off tonight.

—Yeah? he says with no surprise.

—Le Tableau is history.

—Well, you timed that new private-chef thing just right.

I kick off my shoes by the front door (locking all four locks), then stash my loaded knapsack in the back of the hall closet. I head for the shower, out of ritual more than habit; I didn't work a full shift tonight, so I'm not as rank as I usually am, coming from work. I strip down and crank the hot water at full blast. Home is where I draw the line on the city's grime. The bathroom also gives me the privacy I need to monitor my pain and, if necessary, apply my ayurvedic treatments. It's not at all bad tonight, but I'm worried about the soup kitchen, and about starting my new job, and I need to sleep. I dry off with one towel and wrap my freshly washed hair in another, then don my nightshirt and pad back out to the living room and curl up with Richard on the couch.

—Onward and upward, babe, he says, putting his laptop aside, allowing me to settle on the peritoneal bulge of his midsection. Ready for tomorrow?

—As ready as I'll ever be.

—Nervous?

—A little. I've worked with in-house staffs on a few catering gigs, but this is a full-time job. The chief of staff is this tough old guy, and I don't think he likes me. Plus, there are all those bodyguards. I've never seen so many guys with guns in one place.

—What does Redhawk do, anyway?

—No idea. Some big-time finance guy, that's all I know.

—He was on the news tonight.

—Really? For what? I say, feigning curiosity. The news about Mr. Redhawk will come out soon enough. I don't like playing dumb with Richard, but I also don't feel like talking about a job I haven't started. It occurs to me that I'm about to go to work in this man's house, and I still don't know what he looks like.

—Something about the election. Seems a lot of people want to see him run on an independent ticket, and they're wondering if he'll announce during the conventions, Richard murmurs. Almost absently, he's moved one hand to my bare thigh, close to the hem of my nightshirt. Bad sign. I try to keep him talking.

—You think I should make something special on the first day? I put my hand in front of his to block its progress under my nightshirt.

Richard turns to me with that warm gleam of genuine affection in his eyes, which I dread. —Babe, he's getting you to cook for him. That's special enough.

He kisses me on the forehead and then on the mouth. I was afraid of this. One of the worst things about being with Richard is that he truly adores having sex with me, while what little interest I had in him waned long ago. Keeping Richard's well-intentioned ardor in check takes some doing. I'm in no shape for intercourse tonight. But I can deflect that. I know what he wants.

Richard's cock is of unremarkable length and, as I learned early on, quite lacking in girth, enough to be a drawback when it comes to internal sensation. Not that he can help how he's built. He has other good qualities. Since we've been together, he's been good enough to take my grooming hints to heart. Now he carefully shaves his groin, liberally applying skin emollient (unscented, at my insistence) to counteract razor bumps. He uses cornstarch in his shorts every day and showers as soon as he gets home. (Mornings I leave up to him, as he's usually gone by the time I get up, though with the new job, I may have to recalibrate.)

Since he's circumcised, it's easier for me to focus on the key areas—glans, meatus, corona, and posterosuperior shaft, always know your ingredients—with my mouth. Using just the tip of my tongue along the outer rim of his aperture, I gently tease him to full hardness before taking the head in my mouth and shifting the blade of my tongue to the ventral realm of the crown of Richard's cock. The corona, where the head flares out from the apex of the shaft, is highly sensitive to planar friction, so I form a loose-fitting seal with my lips around the head and slowly work it back and forth in my mouth. I know he loves this, though it's not so easy to notice from my point of view—Richard's penile vascularity can sufficiently stiffen his cock, but there's little discernible throb within. I know only from the length and depth of his breathing what kind of effect I'm having on him and how soon it will be over. Using the tips of my fingers on the sharp stubble over his balls (one thing Richard won't do is wax, and really, I can't blame him), I work the base, shaft, and head in time, opening my mouth wider on the downward stroke, closing partially on the return, keeping my tongue in full contact with the opening and ridge. Richard is arching his back and raising his hips toward my face—he's never had any stamina—and taking my cue, I loosen and extend my jaw just a bit. Richard is as predictable as boiling water, and thanks to his hypospadias, his semen pools uneventfully behind my lower front teeth, nowhere near enough to spill out or trigger my gag reflex. Swallowing his easily manageable deposit (I wouldn't sleep with him until he got tested, a practice I've made him regularly continue), discerning as always those curiously bland notes of vanilla bean and chalk on the finish, I release him with a few desultory licks. Richard's head flops back on the cushions, his wide dreamy smile fixed in place. Now I know he'll sleep. What I don't know is whether I will.

No passion here, but no surprises, either.

Dependable. Predictable. Stable. Dull.

Safe.

WARRIOR THREE

"Inhale, arms reaching overhead to their fullest extent, arch the back, and allow a slight forward pelvic tilt . . ."

Santiago's eyes were half-closed, his mind focused on powering his movements with breath. He wore only a pair of loose black cotton drawstring pants, his feet bare on the mat. The windows were down and locked, the blinds drawn against the city light pollution. Nearly every appliance and light in his apartment was turned off, the only illumination coming from the soft glow of the television's OLED monitor. The front door was locked, bolted, and chained. His .45 Glock 21 lay holstered on the butcher block, at rest.

"Exhale slowly, dropping down into a forward fold, hands flat on your mat . . ."

The muscular topography of Santiago's belly rearranged itself with the reversal of airflow, while his lateral obliques fanned downward like slowly furling wings. His biceps and triceps remained outsize even as his arms telescoped toward the mat. His torso was a solid wedge of muscle flaring out from a trim waist and flat stomach. Since he'd begun his yoga studies two years earlier, he'd brought his body fat index down to nearly three percent. He'd started the practice to calm his nerves and reclaim his shattered sleep after going on a raid of a midtown hedge fund that went sideways, leaving him with a double-digit body count, a pair of frothing investigators from the Internal Affairs Division, and a stack of confiscated yoga DVDs.

". . . left leg stepping backward, weight forward on the hands in lunge pose . . ."

Since then he'd made steady progress as the city deteriorated. The IAD probe had gone nowhere, as the feds had invited his unit to participate in the raid, and he hadn't even discharged his weapon in the ensuing firefight. The firefights during the second and third raids—on one street gang and one Italian Mafia stronghold in the Bronx, respectively—had generated some flak. But for once, the shrapnel had hit his former partner, Everett More. Which suited Santiago just fine.

"Now inhale and transition to plank . . ."

It seemed like a lifetime ago. He hadn't been on a raid since. He didn't get out to crime scenes much anymore. The last one he'd visited—where a student in an Easter Bunny costume at a Queens elementary school had shot thirty of his classmates and teachers before turning the gun on himself—he hadn't even ducked under the yellow tape. He was no longer an Anticrime knuckle-dragger. He was Lieutenant Sixto Fortunato Santiago of the NYPD's elite Organized Crime Intelligence Division (OCID), and he hadn't had a partner in two years.

". . . now go into your cobra . . ."

Inhaling, he pushed back the concerns of the workday, willing the transition to a more tranquil zone. This was the high point of Santiago's day. No noise, no stress, no groups of bitching cops corralling groups of bitching civilians in the logistical free-for-all that defined NYPD security procedures during Convention Week.

He had eased into the administrative role surprisingly well. He loathed the bureaucracy of his position, as would any former street cop who'd seen real action and cracked real cases. Still, he had to admit that getting away from the Citywide Anticrime Bureau and behind a desk at OCID had probably saved his life.

After the last shootout, which had separated him from More, Santiago had been sidelined until the storm blew over. Both his former Anticrime boss and his current one at OCID had given sworn depositions declaring their utmost confidence in his abilities. In time, he was cleared by Internal Affairs, promoted, and relegated to administrative duty, and the team he and More had headed up was disbanded. Happily ever after.

Santiago knew this was an elaborate smokescreen orchestrated by his former partner's *real* boss, a CIA officer named Devius Rune. Everett "Ever" More was a government plant inside the NYPD, and Santiago couldn't imagine a more horrific choice. More was active-duty Marine Special Forces, with a long dark history in Afghanistan that had left him with a scarred voice and a penchant for blowing things up with impunity. Why More had been embedded in a civilian police force—which was wildly illegal any way you looked at it—lent a heavy irony to the term *intelligence,* military, political, or otherwise.

On paper, More had been thoroughly vetted by Internal Affairs, relieved of his weapon, and restricted to a desk job at a police motor pool in the Bronx. In reality, he was gone; Santiago neither knew nor cared where. He conceded that the sham was a small price to pay for getting More the fuck out of his life once and for all.

Shortly thereafter, he'd started on the yoga.

". . . exhale back into down dog . . ."

With More gone, Santiago felt as though a massive weight had come off of his shoulders, his mind, and his heart. Managerial duty seemed to come naturally to him. Maybe it was his age—he was now thirty-seven. Or maybe it was his degree; with his police career on a less demanding, more predictable track, he'd been able to finish his coursework, pass his finals, and get his criminology degree from the John Jay College of Criminal Justice. And with school out of the way, he'd thrown himself into preparing for the lieutenant's exam and aced it. In two years, he'd obtained a graduate degree, jumped two steps up the NYPD ladder (with corresponding salary hikes, a windfall in this day and age), and hadn't been shot at once. Santiago was a rarity in 2016: an upwardly mobile cop with an expanding pool of career options in a city that devoured them.

"Inhale, bringing the left leg forward. Now exhale and straighten the left leg, then bend it forward again, inhaling, and bring the arms up into warrior one . . ."

He did occasionally miss the thrill of the hunt. He now oversaw investigators rather than handling cases. He rationalized that by giving logistical support to the men under his command, by scraping together funds, he was doing his part to keep at bay the more or less constant anarchy that was New York City life.

". . . and exhale, extending the arms and pivoting the trunk into warrior two . . ."

There was one ongoing OCID investigation that stayed just over the horizon of his consciousness without fully disappearing. Probably that was because it was the Narc Sharks' case.

OCID Detectives Liesl and Turse, aka the Narc Sharks, were an inseparable army of two undercover detectives who would stop at nothing to close a case. They had been Santiago's peers at Anticrime and had—

somehow— managed to follow him to OCID, nearly getting him killed in the process. They had jubilantly morphed into the unit's fiercest attack dogs, using their own nefarious policing techniques to set a new clearance record. Santiago gave them a fairly loose lead, with the caveat that anything they did had to be fully documented. They cheerfully told him to fuck off. Frequently. Captain DiBiasi, the head of the unit, did not seem to mind their insubordination, occasionally even grunting in agreement. The Narc Sharks' reports came through OCID's computers with clockwork regularity, which made Santiago guess that they'd strong-armed a civilian departmental employee into being their private secretary.

For his part, Captain DiBiasi (who'd been stuck with Santiago on a bad case two years earlier) seemed content to keep a distant, everybody-play-nice-and-don't-fucking-bother-me attitude about the whole thing. Santiago toed the line, and life at OCID ground on.

But the invisible money the Narc Sharks were chasing intrigued him. It was SOP for drug dealers to move cash offshore as quickly as possible, or at least through a domestic laundry. But the Narc Sharks claimed they'd found a pattern of disappearing money—cash from drug deals that vanished without a trace. In off-street deals, the Sharks had put out nearly fifty grand in used bills with chemical markers, none of which returned to circulation, rang a bank's currency alarms, or prompted calls to police from irked retailers. Santiago knew the Sharks weren't stealing—Liesl and Turse might be mercenary in their tactics, but if they'd wanted to skim, they'd had years in the no-standards Anticrime unit to do it. They could score dealers for cash any time they pleased, and as far as he knew, they didn't. Santiago suspected they would rather kill suspects than steal from them. And the dealers they had under surveillance weren't putting the cash back into circulation themselves.

So where was the money?

"And now virabhadrasana three. Exhale right leg back, lean the upper body forward, arms extended. Make sure both your extended leg and standing leg are straight. Direct the energy in a straight axis through the body. Breathe. Feel the pose—warrior three . . ."

Sweat beaded the length of his body and dripped onto the mat. Santiago wavered slightly on his standing leg, his outstretched fingertips quivering as he sought the balance demanded by the pose, always a problem given his size. *Breathe, breathe.* He calmed his limbs, the tremors faded.

"Bring the leg down, feet together, with the arms stretching vertically overhead—"

And back to center. He brought his hands together, gently exhaled, calm. Opened his eyes.

And saw Everett "Ever" More sitting on the back of his sofa, the caked soles of his desert boots flat on the cushions, glaring at him like a demonic refugee from a Henry Fuseli painting.

More croaked: "Your warrior three's weak."

Santiago felt his equanimity pulling away, taking with it the room, the building, the whole city, leaving a maelstrom of fire and rubble in its wake. He closed his eyes again and desperately tried to regain a hold on the tranquillity that had been his just seconds ago.

In his gnurled, granular, disaffected voice, More gubbled, "We need to re-form the team."

This wasn't happening. It was a hallucination born of stress, sleep deprivation, and questionable take-out food. But Santiago no longer qualified for these. This wasn't one of the Narc Sharks' sick pranks. It wasn't DiBiasi taking unprecedented revenge on him for landing in OCID and making it more effective than ever. No, this was a malevolent gift, a present from the deranged, sadistic fucking pilot of the universe, who'd apparently grown bored with all the other mayhem he'd been causing and felt compelled to revisit the worst torment imaginable upon him. Santiago could feel his ataraxy wearing thin, actually fraying, like the fabric in a favorite old shirt.

"Devius thinks there's going to be trouble during Convention Week. He thinks there's funny money between the parties that's outside of the banks. He's suggesting we look into it: you, me, Liesl, and Turse. He's got Marrone working the money angle, too." More's tone was ragged but conversational, in the manner of a toad reciting scheduled stops over the PA system of a commuter train.

Suggesting. Might be. Think. It was happening again, the neatness and order Santiago had worked so hard to achieve being swept away by the man in front of him, who looked like a bum or an NYU student. It was happening again. Tranquillity was extinct, centeredness blown asunder.

"You have to take point on this," More went on detachedly, "because legally, I'm not supposed to be here."

Santiago couldn't believe it. More was back. Which meant Devius Rune. Which meant the CIA had decided to join in on the Convention Week fun. For some unholy reason far beyond Santiago's understanding,

Washington had decided to fuck New York yet again.

"Plus, I thought we could fix up our old cab," More offered, as though commenting on the weather.

This was the last straw. More wasn't just unapologetic about showing up for what promised to be an apocalyptic errand; he actually thought he could win Santiago over by playing sentimental.

Santiago felt his joints stiffening. In desperation and futility he could feel in his bones, he tried to shut out the terrible image that had already seared itself across the insides of his eyelids. Fuck More. And Rune. And all this Washington bullshit.

"More," he began with his eyes still closed, "I'm guessing you have a valid reason for showing up unannounced after all this time. And," he continued with increasing difficulty, "you might even have an explanation for breaking into my crib instead of sending an email, like a normal person. *But*"—Santiago's voice cracked, his eyes opened and bulged, his hands clenched into fists so hard the pain shot all the way up to his elbows—"no matter what the situation is, no matter who's planning what, you will GET YOUR FUCKING BOOTS OFF MY FUCKING COUCH RIGHT FUCKING NOW!"

(OBSERVATION)

MEL CORDRYCEPS'S AIDE SHIVERED, but not from cold. He stood just inside the Massachusetts Avenue entrance to Union Station, by the curved wall in front of Thunder Grill, waiting for the second call, which would tell him where to make the drop. He was no slouch—six-two, 205, played defensive end straight through high school and college—but he was out of his depth here, and he knew it. He wanted to make his new boss happy, make a career for himself in Washington; he'd never thought it would come to this.

As most men in their early twenties do to allay fear, he turned his mind to women. He sifted through the memories of those he had slept with, then through those he had yet to, mostly like-seeming archetypes dotting the landscape of his brief working and longer academic lives. Friends of friends, relatives of roommates. Staring at the Center Café kiosk in the middle of the Main Hall, he was struck by how identical all the shadow women of his mind were, how congruent in their projected personae (while all of them endlessly trumpeted their individuality). He was in a plain-vanilla sea, a disappointment to any man in his prime.

But now his consciousness took one of those unexpected turns upon which great chains of events are set in motion. It cast a sideways glance through his daily contacts on the Hill and fixed upon Caduta Massi's new aide, who had rudely pushed her way past him earlier that day.

Now, *she* was different. Hair short but growing out in a way that suggested it was previously much shorter, perhaps mowed with an electric razor. Piercings, little colonies of them, through nostril and eyebrow and tragus. Tattoos, to be sure—he remembered seeing a set of thin lines at the base of her neck, just above the collar of her blouse as she bent over a stack of manila folders: Of course he'd been looking. He wondered what other imagery she had on her body, how her mouth tasted—she was a smoker— what sorts of sounds she made at critical intimate moments (she had cursed at a snide reporter outside the House Chamber, with a sharp inventiveness that had amused and aroused him).

His cell phone buzzed. He couldn't place the voice—it was electronically shrouded, which jarred him out of his reverie—but he assumed it belonged to the man called Hurt. The metallic speaker directed him to make a withdrawal from the ATM in the West Hall and leave the package on the floor beside the machine, closest to the First Street exit. The line clicked off.

The aide took a deep breath, squared his formidable shoulders, and hoisted the blue Eastpak gym bag that held the first payment. He crossed the Main Hall with the Alamo Flags store on his right, buoyed by anxiety but also excitement. He resolved to introduce himself to Caduta Massi's aide that very afternoon, as soon as he returned to the Hill. His fear was subsiding, replaced by the promise of novel female contact, a panacea for almost any ill in a man of his age.

The aide followed his instructions to the letter and left the ATM whistling. He never noticed that the blue gym bag had disappeared before he crossed the threshold of the exit to the sunlit street.

• • •

Irukanji called the Behr on the same iPhone he'd used to call Mel Cordryceps's aide, turning the QOS setting back on Phonecrypt so the Behr would recognize his voice. The line remained secure.

"Sharpen your sweet tooth," Irukanji trilled into the phone. The Behr grunted—which comprised most of his conversational stock while he was operating—and cut the connection.

As Irukanji rose up the escalator past the Lucy store to the mezzanine, he slowly and deliberately raised the bag's shoulder strap to its full extension and laid it diagonally across his right shoulder, so the weight of the bag rested on his left hip. The move was a signal to the man watching from above. With his right hand, he slid the spool back in his right hip pocket.

The spool was what Irukanji referred to as a tick—a telescoping filament of synthesized biopolymer that could retrieve, store, and transport a zettabyte's worth of data in a strand of artificial DNA. The filament itself was nothing, invisible to all but enhanced and practiced eyes. The housing for the device—the tick's carapace—was the only part that took up any room, and very little of it. The tick could be concealed in Irukanji's palm, its filament deployed in a heartbeat to steal data from card swipes, computer drives, and any dock for wireless devices.

Irukanji was the lone civilian member of the team, as well as its youngest. He was a hacker in his mid-twenties, hired by CYBERCOM after an exhaustive background check turned up no red flags. Uncle Sam was behind the curve on cyber talent and needed all the help he could get. Data was the raw material of the twenty-first-century economy, and the initiated few—like Irukanji—were its purveyors. He'd pulled everything on Cordryceps's aide from the ATM card slot, from his personal cell phone number to the PIN for his online bank account, while simultaneously hoisting the bag. It was perfunctory; Irukanji stole data as a matter of course, just second nature now. He was unfettered by anachronisms such as privacy, secrecy, law. Armed with his tick, as well as his TS/SCI/TK/HCS security clearance from CYBERCOM, Irukanji could pull and sift the stored information on countless individuals, not to mention corporations, government branches, and the supposedly secure systems of the defense and intelligence agencies. His clearance gave him nearly unlimited access to DoD's 512-bit super-servers, which enabled him to rapidly sift through vast amounts of information to extract one glimmering bit of target material. Not for nothing had he been handpicked for this team. Data was the blood of the new world order, and Irukanji was an information vampire.

● ● ●

Mel Cordryceps's aide never noticed the nondescript, slightly disheveled man maintaining a precise distance behind him until he left the station. We are often closest to death when we think it furthest from us.

Nor did the aide see the nondescript man fluidly slip into the maroon Ford Taurus with its enormous driver and smaller man in the backseat, holding the blue gym bag.

And the aide could not have seen the smaller man in the backseat pass the blue gym bag to the nondescript man, who could have fit into the background of a Norman Rockwell painting except for the disconcerting coldness of his eyes.

And since the bag's zipper had been padlocked, there was no way the aide could have known its contents: a large holiday box of Perugina Golds.

And while he may have wondered about the parcel's weight, the aide had never been told that instead of chocolates, the box was packed with platinum wafers, each a Troy ounce of 99.5 percent purity, with a total net worth of three quarters of a million dollars.

If Mel Cordryceps's aide had known that the nondescript man and his team were watching him in the station, he would have broken for the exit at a dead run. Screaming.

The nondescript man glanced at the Behr, who was far and away the largest member of the team, with hands that could shatter a human skull. He was ODIN's right arm and had been with him since the early years in Iraq. He didn't talk much. He didn't have to.

The nondescript man said something Irukanji could barely hear.

The Behr grunted again, fired up the Taurus, and hung a left on G Street, heading toward I-395, fading quietly out of sight.

With two words, ODIN was deployed.

New York.

• • •

And in that august city, 102 feet beneath and slightly west of Second Avenue, just off Ninety-fourth Street, more or less under the Carnegie Park tower in all its cordovan hideousness, lies the subway bank at the center of this tale.

A newcomer to the bank would have quite a memorable journey to make.

First, at the edge of the platform, he would have to push his way through the soup kitchen, past the hordes of New Yorkers clamoring for the bank's safe-deposit boxes to secure whatever hard assets were left to them, as well as those incautious seekers of yield maddened by its offers of 20, 30, even 50 percent on its unique certificates of deposit.

Then, escorted by a troupe of mesomorphic behemoths—all wide crew necks and earpieces and lug soles in black—the visitor would be rather awed by the complex geometric ballads rising over, around, and beneath him, giving the impression of walking through a vast machine stopped temporarily for the sole purpose of his transit. And it is a bit of a hike, for the bank lies deep within caverns both natural and man-made, just as its CEO intended.

The first tunnel through which the visitor passes is a high rectangular passage lined with I-beams joined by riveted gantries, some bearing sprocketed wheels bound with chain falling away to unguessable depths. Latticework stanchions stretched and crossed themselves overhead—perhaps once a maintenance tunnel? The conduit ends in a massive disk of steel, with visible gears and pilings going directly into the walls, floor, and ceiling holding it firmly in place. Now one of the massive guardians speaks into his shoulder, a momentary screech of metal on concrete, leading to—

The second tunnel is uncomfortably round, ribbed, and railed. The curved walls are finished in metal, a sequence of vertical ribs projecting down the shaft's length to distant lights, many more horizontal ribs linking them up the walls, across the ceiling, and over the floor. In this passage, the only overhead light comes from a single fluorescent vein running down the shaft's length just slightly off-center from mid-ceiling. Twin support rails run down the ceiling and are paralleled by an identical set along the floor, as though for mirror-image industrial trains. An unfinished construction site? There is no way to tell. But the tunnel's irregular shape, its semi-finished feel, and cold off-kilter lighting may give our visitor the slightest urge to squirm.

Roundness begets rectangular once again at tunnel's end, and after perfunctory manual and electronic body checks, the visitor would be admitted to the bank's main office. Here, if he were lucky, he might chance to behold its chieftain in the lair where she holds court with those seeking her secretive services, financial and otherwise.

Said chieftain, known only as LA, is at this instant leaning against one edge of her massive desk, a hideous thing cobbled together from pilfered pieces of steel, concrete, and glass. There is no understanding the American aesthetic; they are a people who eagerly embrace ugliness.

LA is anything but ugly. Her visage and physique are all smooth angles and planes, the result of a consistent and varied workout regimen. Her bare arms are threaded with smooth twined bands of muscle and laced with a prominent venous tapestry. Her hands are hard, but her movements are delicate and controlled as they slowly trace the contours of her confidante's faceplate.

This other woman is visibly younger than LA, tawnier in coloring and slightly leonine in countenance. Her name is not as important as her role here. Let us call her N. She is LA's employee, a member of her innermost circle, her lover, yes, but more crucially one of the very few LA might possibly trust. N's role as LA's confidante is anything but skin-deep.

And while ripe of curve and contour, N does not possess the hardness, the tangibly cold discipline of her boss. So she knows to keep rock-still while LA's callused fingers form triskeles on her face. N is well versed in this activity, a form of meditation for LA. The boss is thinking out loud and hands-on.

—It's all led up to this, LA murmurs.

—What has? N knows she has only to make the ghost of a reply. She is an innately accomplished reader of others, a trait that has kept her alive and prosperous in a dark time.

—Convention Week. All this, down here, this rats' life of ours, now's the payoff.

—How so? N knows she has a limited window for questions, but it's all part of the ritual.

—Building the bank up to the point where *they* come to *us*.

—Who? N breathes.

The woman called LA draws her right hand back and softly, almost gently, raps N on the cheek. —You know who. Them. The politicos. Our ticket out of this cave.

N takes the slap in stride; it's nothing compared to what else has and will be asked of her. —Do we have enough?

LA is stroking the area she struck. —There's never enough, not really, but this meets the goal. We gave them a place to park their off-book slush funds, and they did. And that's our investment capital.

—How so?

—The money's ours. Those assholes are really stupid enough to think we'll just hand it over to them whenever they ask for it, like a real bank. They still don't get what it means to have this kind of privacy. They actually think they can work with us with no consequences.

—And what are those? N's eyes are closed; her breathing is shallow. She is at her best right now, alluring and self-effacing all at once. She learned this art over a decade ago, a lifetime for someone her age.

LA contemplates the younger woman she holds by the face, as though deliberating whether to strike her again. But instead she exhales:

—Getting caught.

N knows her employer has set up a large, complicated scam, one involving millions she made with a hedge fund that might kindly be described as crooked. She knows that LA, with the reptilian foresight N has come to admire and fear, got out of the fund just before the cops and feds staged a raid that culminated in a bloody shootout in the Bronx two years ago. N was puzzled by her employer's subsequent course, planning the bank, scouting the space, dispatching N and her peers to succor the favors of carefully selected members of the city and state legislatures.

How LA orchestrated all this, N does not fully understand. But she has enough common sense to know when things are accelerating.

—Convention Week is our endgame, LA says, cold stone and pipe in her voice. We take everything they pile up with us, we bolt, and then we splurge.

N is having some difficulty concealing her emotions. On the one hand, there is complicit joy in their shared endeavor. On the other is the raw anxiety that comes from the realization that what they are doing is incredibly, undeniably dangerous, with death or life in prison very real possibilities. She knows she has to say something, but what?

—On what? N breathes.

LA smiles, a most unwholesome sight for our visitor, and returns to tracing runes on the younger woman's face.

—On them. The city council, the state assemblymen, the governor, senators, the whole gang, right up to the White House. We're in business with the whole government. In one week we'll do more than the Mob pulled off in a century. And the best part is we're gonna do it with *their* money.

N is nervous—no, more than that. But LA's flexors, palmars, and pronators are tensing, pulling her close, and N knows the time for talking is over for a bit. In the best tradition of disciples, she will do her best to offset her fear with admiration for her patron.

What follows is not for our visitor to see, and so he must take his leave. Now.

PART II

TOUCHDOWN

GROCERY SHOPPING

SORTING THE LOGISTICS OF STEALING food for the soup kitchen from my new job was nothing compared to going grocery shopping with Caitlin.

I don't know what she's on at the moment, but it's turbocharged her mouth. I swear she hasn't stopped talking since we first met at the Greenmarket in Union Square half an hour ago. I'm trying to make the best picks, but even with my vendor contacts, it's hard to concentrate with Caitlin talking a mile a minute. I don't think she even knows what she's saying. But I have to put up with her to keep the food going underground. They'd starve without me.

I've tried to keep track of the regulars the last couple times I've gone down there, but their attendance is so sporadic, it's hard to get a firm head count. The only commercial food deliveries getting through are for convention events, and these come in convoys with armed guards. No way I could get near those. So many guns. And the guards don't seem shy about pointing them at people.

The city didn't used to be like this. I've never seen so many automatic weapons on the street. I see plenty of them inside the penthouse—with all the security guards and cameras, that place really is a fortress. On my first day, when I broke the plate, I thought *I'd* be gunned down. Until Alex—Mr. Redhawk—stepped in to save my clumsy ass.

—Because I really can't believe this is happening just too much all at once it isn't fair and you know just because someone leaves you a voicemail saying they're going to kill themselves it isn't necessarily a cry for help as much as for *attention* because if they . . .

For all the pills she's downing, Caitlin came through in the clutch. The scheme was her idea. I do all the shopping with the debit card given to me by Mr. Chiroptera, the house manager. I thought he'd take it right back when I broke the plate that night, but that was when my new boss showed me he might not be such a nightmare to work for.

His girlfriend, though, *she's* the nightmare.

The way she looked me over that first day, walking all the way around me to check the angles, it was like the ranchers back home do with heifers and broodmares. It gave me chills. She has this smile, it's not subdued but it's not overt, you can't really tell if she's happy or amused or something else. Her eyes gleam and give nothing away. And she's so deftly polite, so completely at ease verbally and socially—this is not the kind of woman I've met in my profession. Even her name is enigmatic but sensuous: Ing Kan.

The toughest, most stuck-up Ladies Who Lunch I've had to put up with over the years would be mere potstickers to Ing Kan. I feel like I'm a mouse and she's a cat just *toying* with me while she decides my fate. I'll have to keep my guard up.

Which is redundant, given my new job environment. I am literally surrounded. There's a small army of burly security goons with neckties and earpieces carrying every kind of weapon short of missiles. I don't know if they're stationed there overnight, but it wouldn't surprise me. I must be getting used to them, because they were a comforting sight after I had to push through a crowd of protesters outside the building a few days ago. The goons got me into the elevator while the cops broke up the crowd. Mr. Redhawk must be some kind of prominent person in the financial world after all, like Kev said. The cops were there in minutes and jumped all over the protesters and broke up the crowd quickly. I guess they don't want a repeat of what happened in Gramercy Park a couple years ago.

Neither do I, at least not until my health insurance card comes in a week or so. Pinnacle POS Gold! I've never had anything close in terms of health coverage. Maybe soon I can finally stop worrying. Maybe soon I'll finally be able to put an end to my pain.

But that will take some very careful moves. Besides the goons, there's Mr. Chiroptera. Now, *he's* there overnight, all right. In fact, he never seems to leave the penthouse. This man is the definitive house manager: Nothing goes into, takes place in, or leaves the penthouse without his express permission and laser-like scrutiny. I don't know where he sleeps or *if* he sleeps—it wouldn't surprise me if he stowed himself away in a closet at the end of each night and waited until whatever ungodly hour he gets the house stirring in the morning. It's probably pretty early, because he told me Alex—Mr. Redhawk—gets up early to catch the market action in Asia, so I have to shop for two different breakfasts, one for him and one for Ing Kan. I basically have to shop for individual menus, with a ton of Asian ingredients for hers. It's a minor nuisance, but it facilitates my system for fudging the paperwork from the Greenmarket to cover the food I hand off to Caitlin to deliver to the soup kitchen.

Here's how it works. I go to one of my Greenmarket vendor contacts, like Michael Ferro, the guy I'm buying from now, Chef Mike. He cooks on the underground restaurant circuit that survived after the cops closed down the speaks. He looks like a former hockey player or construction worker, thick fingers on big hands you would never think capable of making arguably the best soufflé in the city. You'd walk by him at the Greenmarket without a second glance. But he's my go-to guy for the best of everything: produce, game, even the precursors for making Asian condiments. That's a huge plus, because without him, I'd have to go all the way over to Sunrise Market off Stuyvesant Street to buy prepackaged stuff. I may have to do that anyway, but the more receipts I can generate through Chef Mike, the higher the premium he can tack on to cover the food I'm buying for the soup kitchen—not to mention for his own compensation. I plan on doing up an inventory spreadsheet at the end of every month to justify my grocery expenses. I can legitimately claim extra requirements for the separate menus. I can also point out how I'm saving the client money by making a lot of the hard-to-find ethnic items myself, from *balachan* to *kaya* to *shottsuru* (this is where those Sunrise Market receipts will come in handy, for price comparisons to support my swindle).

Mr. Chiroptera is a sharp, nosy old bird, but he's strictly a front-of-house man. The kitchen is *my* domain, and I've worked in enough of them to find ways around every bean-counting manager I've ever met. And at least Mr. Chiroptera can stand up to Ing Kan. Whatever his opinion of her—and I'll bet it's not a favorable one—he keeps it to himself. He's found a way to serve her courteously without letting her boss him around the way she does with the Filipino housemaids, Dalisay and Laarni, and even the security goons, though to a lesser extent. I get the distinct impression that the maids work more for her than for Alex—Mr. Redhawk (why do I keep *doing* that?). I'll have to watch myself around them, too. Mr. Chiroptera is definitely Mr. Redhawk's man. There's politics in every palace, even if that palace is a penthouse.

But the cameras are immune to human foibles. They just see—and record—*everything*. I've never seen this kind of surveillance. Living in the city, you get used to being on-camera, at high-traffic intersections, in stores, riding mass transit. But even then there are dark zones, everyone knows them. That's where the hand-to-hands are made and where people silently disappear into tenement vestibules and where illicit lovers embrace—away from the electronic eyes. There are no dark zones in this penthouse. I can't see all the cameras, but I can see where some of them are watching; there's a bank of monitors here in the kitchen. I'm guessing it's so the chef can monitor the progress of meals in the dining room and traffic in the adjacent wine salon. I've read about some of the wines Mr. Redhawk has on his shelves—it looks like he bought out all of Grey Stack's last vintage before the crash took them down, along with almost every other California winery; those bottles go for four figures apiece at Christie's. While the dining room is stunning—muted gold sponge-painted walls, rose base table and chairs for twelve under a mother of a Baylar chandelier—it's the wine salon that really drew me in. All Shanghai and Louis XVI chaise longues with low-lying tables and ottomans, dark reds and greens, velvet and silk, with subtle accents of that same muted-gold motif offset by mahogany so deep you could fall into it. The walls are made of wine in cherry honeycombs with a climate-control system I know must be there but haven't been able to see.

I guess this bank of monitors in the kitchen is here so that I can get food or drinks out to where they're needed at just the right time, without ever having to leave the kitchen. I'm surprised we don't have more staff back here, but we haven't had a big function yet. Dalisay and Laarni are my runners, and Mr. Chiroptera doubles as the house bartender. It's a small, efficient arrangement for the house; Mr. Chiroptera told me we'd hire vetted staff from outside for large events.

I learned about that my first night, when I dropped the plate. I have dropped plates before, just not an antique Chinese Famille Verte porcelain charger that Mr. Chiroptera later told me cost a grand. A thousand-dollar plate, and I dropped it because I was so nervous when I served her. Ing Kan's eyes were— I can't describe them. She was right in front of me, and I felt like she was looking down on me from a high cliff, even though she was smiling that damn could-mean-anything smile, with her chin on one delicate fist, a perfect arc from her jawline to her magnificent neck to her shadowed cleavage. I swear it wasn't my fault—it was *her*. But that moment was lost when the guards charged in with guns drawn, Mr. Chiroptera came flapping and scowling into the dining room, and my new boss waved them off, saying, *It's all right, it's just a plate*, and then Ing Kan barked something at the maids and the mess was cleaned up in about three seconds like it never happened and I was apologizing and trying not to lose it and of course at that moment my pain gave me a jolt that nearly brought me to my knees. In front of *her*. And from the way her smile changed, the way she seemed to find my predicament . . . *charming*, I think this was exactly what she wanted.

I've never felt like this. I've never been in a situation like this. I'm not sure I can handle something like this.

—Beth? You okay?

Caitlin has apparently run out of chemical wind. She's looking at me in a surprisingly lucid way that doesn't come around often. I need to get us both back on track. Ing Kan is out for the afternoon—she does something with the Chinese embassy, I'm not sure what—but I'm still on Mr. Chiroptera's clock.

—Sorry, just a lot on my mind. Have you got everything?

—Yeah, all set.

—Know where you're going? Once you're inside, you find Jonah. He'll get the crew started on dinner prep. Don't talk to anybody but him, and make sure you ask for a head count, got it?

—Yeah, Beth, I got it.

—Don't forget, ask Jonah for the *head count*.

Caitlin doesn't know about the disappearances. It's better that she doesn't.

She's doing me a huge favor. If anyone catches on to the little operation I've set up here at the Greenmarket, I'm done, and maybe Caitlin and Mike are, too. I'm working for powerful people now. I'll bet Richard would put his apartment up as collateral to get me out of jail, but I don't think that would be enough to save me if this doesn't work.

And the insurance—God, I *need* that insurance, I think about that magic little card every time my pain gives me a twinge to remind me it's still there.

By the time I walk Caitlin and her groceries over to the subway entrance for the 6 train—it's early afternoon, still reasonably safe to travel underground—her mouth is off and running again. I give her a hug. She gives me a wink, dry-swallows two tiny pink tablets, hoists her shopping bags, and trundles downstairs to the train.

I hope she remembers my instructions.

The colony's getting smaller, and no one knows why or how.

And the crowds at the bank next door just keep getting bigger.

Those must be good burgers the hairballs are serving.

Most people in the colony have been institutionalized for a good portion of their lives; they can't survive in the outside world. When the hospital's funding was cut, they all drained down into the tunnels.

I saw it happening from the Yorkville Common Pantry around the corner, which I was supplying with food from another restaurant job. I saw it happening, and I had to *do* something, the city damn sure wouldn't. No one was going to help these people, there was no money left, and who'd help a bunch of homeless crazies?

I would. I did. I still do. Where I come from, you don't let suffering rule, whether it's people or animals. You do something about it, and you keep at it until it's gone or you are. Otherwise, there's no hope for you or anyone around you: Once the suffering takes root, it spreads like cancer or a fungus and consumes everything in its path. You wouldn't let blight or an infestation ruin your crops, or you and the livestock wouldn't eat.

The suffering of others becomes your own. I was raised to believe that, and I still do. I can't let the colony go hungry, and it'll starve for sure with the security cordon in place for Convention Week.

Chef Mike has worked his magic with the card receipt, so it's time for me to take my groceries back to the penthouse and get started on dinner.

• • •

Back at the penthouse, I hand my doctored paperwork and house card to Mr. Chiroptera, who takes them with a silent hand and dour countenance—well, nice to see *you*, too!—and vanishes from sight. I haul my groceries to the kitchen, tonight's menu in my head.

First Ing Kan's meal, to show off my chops with seafood: fresh kingfish and tuna squares with citrus and ginger. This is just to stay on her good side. Really, that's all it is:

—Trim six ounces of sushi-grade tuna and an equal amount of same-quality kingfish into equilateral squares.

—Mix together one teaspoon each of ginger juice (one of the first things I found in my new kitchen) and orange oil (that was the second) and a dollop of grapeseed oil.

—Arrange in a checkerboard pattern on a plate, lightly sprinkle with coarse-ground sea salt, and serve. For a shared vegetable side, I'll give 'em my asparagus-bean salad, never misses:

—Lightly brown half a dozen prime sea scallops (thank you, Chef Mike!), then slice thinly and chill in the fridge until serving.

—In a bowl, mix a teaspoon each of mirin, sesame seed paste, low-sodium soy sauce, and a pinch of minced garlic, and set aside.

—Diagonally slice eight butter beans and five asparagus stalks; julienne one leek and a dozen green beans (the mandoline and food processor here are better than any I've ever used); then finely chop one plum tomato and enough fresh chives and tarragon to fill one teaspoon each.

—Just before serving, toss together all ingredients and season with one pinch each of sea salt and white pepper; add a drop of olive oil and a generous handful of fresh baby mâche or watercress; and squeeze one eighth of a freshly sliced lemon over the salad, being careful not to drop in any seeds.

As for Alex—sorry, Mr. Redhawk, why do I keep *doing* that?—I'm going all-out with my chicken gnocchi dumplings with lentil sauce (trust me, lentils go with everything):

—Cut a roasting chicken in half, season with freshly cracked pepper and kosher salt, and place the halves in a large ovenproof sauté pan with two tablespoons olive oil over medium heat until golden brown on both sides. Set chicken aside and place three sprigs each of fresh rosemary and thyme between the outer skin and the flesh—add a pinch of crushed red pepper if you like. Do not clean pan; add another two tablespoons of oil, half a dozen seeded and chopped plum tomatoes, four crushed garlic cloves, and a cup of dry white wine over medium-high heat. Cook until the broth is halfway reduced, then return the chicken to the pan along with three to four cups of organic chicken broth or stock until the pan is nearly full. Cover the pan and place in a preheated 325° oven for two hours (I did all this before I left to meet Caitlin at the market).

—Boil four pounds of unpeeled potatoes (I siphoned these off of the huge sack Caitlin took to the soup kitchen) in salted water for thirty minutes, rice them into a bowl, and set aside until cool.

—Thoroughly mix your spuds with one large egg and another large yolk and a teaspoon of kosher salt in a bowl. On a well-floured surface, knead in a cup of AP flour and half a cup of finely grated Parmigiano-Reggiano (they had maybe a pound of premium aged Parmesan in the fridge, I've never seen this quality, the rind alone will make a sensational sauce!), and start rolling into dumplings.

—Place a cup of lentils du Puy in a medium saucepan with enough water to cover by two inches, along with two teaspoons of kosher salt, bring to a boil, then reduce heat and simmer for twenty-five minutes and drain. In a separate sauté pan (you would not believe the flatware they have in this kitchen), place two tablespoons olive oil over medium-high heat, then add two finely chopped shallots and one finely diced carrot along with half a cup of tomato puree, the drained lentils, and one tablespoon finely chopped preserved black truffles (my third find in this wondrous kitchen). Cook no more than five minutes, then shut off heat and let rest in pan, stirring occasionally.

—Fill a stockpot with well-salted water (you must think I'm trying to give my new boss high blood pressure) and bring to a boil while shredding the chicken with your fingers. Fill your dumplings with the chicken, then drop them into the boiling water for no more than five minutes. Plate each serving, drizzle slightly with truffle oil, and sprinkle with a handful of chopped fresh chives. Reheat the lentil sauce and coat each serving to taste. (He'll love this. I just *know* he will.)

The penthouse kitchen has all the latest cooking gadgetry: probeless meat thermometers; plasma cooktops that can boil water in ten seconds and change temperature in fractions of degrees; digital dispensers that can powder or liquefy nearly any ingredient you can think of and distribute them in portions measured in cubic centimeters. If my restaurant had a kitchen like this, I'd be rich. Well, I'd *have* to be rich just to afford this kind of gear. It makes even a four-star feast like tonight's dinner a breeze to whip up.

That was the plan, anyway.

Until I burst into the kitchen with my shopping bags and see Ing Kan sitting sideways on one of the barstools on the far side of the center island opposite the range, one magnificent leg crossed over the other beneath a sprayed-on pencil skirt that reveals much of one perfect haunch, a glass of rosé in one elegant hand, a cell phone the likes of which I've never seen in the other, speaking in a language I cannot identify, her unknowable smile beginning to curve her delicious mouth upward, looking at me with those gleaming, unreadable eyes I could fall into and drown.

Shit.

Ing Kan's tongue is dextrous and animate as it curls around a series of lachrymose syllables that apparently signal an end to the conversation in whatever language she's using. An incongruous sequence of finger motions appears to deactivate her strange phone, which quickly vanishes into a Golgotha purse that's worth more than three months of my salary. I can't take my eyes off her hands as her fingers entwine themselves around the stem of her fifty-dollar Rosenthal wineglass. My knees feel fluttery, then my pain gives me a jolt, and I turn away from her and make an elaborate show of putting the groceries on the counter. I am so not ready for this. The kitchen is *my* lair, and she's invading it, but I don't know how to make her leave. I go into Prep Mode, hoping she'll get bored slumming with the help and look for someone else to toy with. Maybe the guard who stands outside Mr. Redhawk's home office. The one with the machine gun.

—I've been meaning to tell you how much you've raised our standard of living since you've joined us, Ing Kan says in dulcet tones behind me. I swear I can feel her words on the back of my neck, which gets hot. She hasn't moved from her perch, but her voice is encircling me; I can feel its pull. I want to get out of here. No. No, I don't. I can't.

—You really are quite talented. It's pleasurable, watching someone who's very good at her work.

—Thanks, I think, I manage. I'm in trouble. *Come on, Beth, focus.* —I've never seen a phone like yours, I say, trying to stall her while I unwrap the groceries. A woman like this probably doesn't cook much. I figure she'll take off once I break out the raw materials.

—Oh, that's for the embassy. My callers are far away, and they require a great deal of privacy. Men are so touchy about that sort of thing, don't you think?

The fish. Where the hell is the fish? I already don't like where this conversation is headed. Raw fish is a good deterrent.

—I suppose that depends on the men, I say evenly. I have no idea where those words came from, nor the calm voice uttering them. It sounded like me in ordinary circumstances, and these are anything but.

—Indeed it does, Ing Kan replies in four evenly spaced syllables. Beneath the thunder of paper shopping bags and the jagged dissonance of plastic ones, I hear the whisper of silk on skin. She's gotten up. She's walking over to me. It's a good thing I'm not holding a knife, because I'm having trouble keeping my hands as steady as my voice. —Big-city ministers are always more of a nuisance than the small-town ones.

Something in me chafes under that. I'm from a small town. —How so?

Her heels tap out a slow, measured rhythm on the floorboards as she walks toward me. *Tock.* Pause. *Tock.* Pause. *Tock.* Pause. —The village ministers worry over trivia. A foreign car, perhaps, or they need me to get a Cartier watch for their wives or mistresses. Their urban counterparts have greater concerns: One of their wealth products sours, or a real estate deal turns into a financial sinkhole.

Ing Kan's voice is getting softer, her footsteps getting closer.

—Or maybe they have a mistress at a large international bank who does special favors for them, channeling bribes for them, laundering money for them, she says in a voice that's more exhaled than spoken.

I'm gritting my teeth.

—Or maybe, she hisses, they're high up enough in the government or the army that they've stolen more than they can conceal, and they need someone on the outside to help them hide it.

My mouth is dry, yet my tongue feels large and wet. —That sounds naughty. I don't know why I say it. I can't afford the stakes in this game. No matter whether I want to play or not.

Ing Kan's steps come to a stop, and she emits a delicious little chortle I can taste in my mouth. The fish is cold in my hands, but there's warmth on my back.

—You see, they're under constant pressure to maintain the appearance of frugality, but once they have a taste of what real wealth brings, they can't give it up.

She's standing just off my left shoulder, close enough for me to feel the warmth of her body, apparently looking at the fish I've unwrapped on the counter. She leans forward for a closer look, giving me a vista of her right ear, her jaw, her neck. I hear the pronounced inhalation of a sniff, and I have to close my eyes and flex my toes inside my shoes to stay steady on my feet.

—The fish is fresh, Ing Kan says in a near-whisper. —Most people don't realize that good fish should smell sweet.

She's close enough for me to smell. There is sweetness in her scent. And heat.

Right then I am saved by the scowling countenance of Mr. Chiroptera, and Ing Kan is gone, and I am weak and breathless and utterly lost, the fish cold and firm in my fingers.

What is Mr. Red— What the hell is Alex *doing* with this woman?

And what is *she* planning to do with *him*?

Or me?

ESPRIT DE CORPS

". . . AND YOU DON'T LIKE IT." McKeutchen's voice grated through the phone, followed by a peculiar percussive snap. Santiago knew that sound. It meant pastrami. Captain McKeutchen, Santiago's former boss from the Citywide Anticrime Bureau, his NYPD "rabbi" or protector, and his closest friend on the force, was picking his teeth while on the phone.

"I don't like *any* of it! First he breaks into my crib. I almost shot him. Then he says we gotta bring Liesl and Turse—and Marrone, you remember her, the chick from Treasury?—in on this. On top of it, he asks about our old cab. That's when I called you." McKeutchen had been Santiago's boss when he worked Anticrime, performing the police equivalent of sanitation work with the worst human flotsam sloshing around street level, his office an undercover taxicab. Where he had first met Everett More and his world had been dropped into a washtub full of chaos, blood, and fire. More's absence the past two years had been a period of tranquil prosperity for Santiago; his former partner's sudden reappearance could only bode ill. And there was the shadow behind him—Devius Rune, More's handler, the CIA hyper-spook. No, Santiago did not like things one fucking bit.

"Tread lightly, kid, that's all I can say." McKeutchen chewed noisily into the phone. "If More's back in town, it means Langley's on our turf, too. Uncle Sam wants you. Where are you guys now?"

Santiago lowered his voice and looked over both shoulders before replying: "Shea."

The disgusted hiss of McKeutchen's sigh said it all. Santiago was calling from the no-man's-land near Citi Field in Queens, home of the

New York Mets; the ghost of its predecessor, Shea Stadium, lay beneath the cracked pavement of the stadium parking lots.

But just beyond lay an automotive thieves' bazaar. The pirate garages (advertised online as "refurbishers" to lend an air of legality) sprang up during the crash in the wake of Shea's demolition; none had a license, all took cash only, and each one offered a unique range of car modification services to discerning clients who did not ask questions.

Santiago found himself in the uncomfortable position of double abettor. His first partner in crime was More, the root of all evil, who had "asked" Santiago to bring their clapped-out old Crown Victoria taxicab from the Anticrime motor pool in Manhattan to this godforsaken patch of Queens, far from prying eyes.

His second was his father, Victor.

Santiago's pulse had been elevated since More's initial manifestation; it had lowered (marginally) only when his father, to his surprise, had agreed eagerly to come along on this insane ride with a jaunty *"Conozco a un tipo."* I know a guy. With his father on board, Santiago felt just slightly less paranoid about undertaking this absurd errand.

Santiago's heart rate had surged again upon his return to his old home unit of CAB Group One, smiling through the backslaps and handshakes, laughing at the good-natured jeers and insults, praying that all his former colleagues would keep their fucking mouths shut long enough for him to get his old beater taxicab across the river to the pirate garages. Before Captain DiBiasi found out just what the fuck he was doing and at whose behest. DiBiasi considered More the equivalent of walking uranium and would just as soon see him buried—maybe along with Santiago—beneath the Hudson River.

Ironically, it had been DiBiasi who'd first backed the scheme to excise More from NYPD active duty two years earlier, to keep the dogs at bay while Devius Rune got him out of the country into something else that Santiago didn't know about and didn't *want* to know about. DiBiasi and *his* boss, Deputy Chief Randazzo, had given Santiago vital cover with the mandarins of One Police Plaza, exonerating him from the mess in the wake of the twin shootouts that ended the GC Piso case of 2014. Where Santiago had first met DiBiasi. And Liza Marrone.

There was no easy crosstown route from the CAB Group One station house to the Queensboro Bridge. Gingerly steering his coughing old cab through the hellish traffic clogging the Fifty-ninth Street on-ramp, Santiago had plenty of time to recall the day he was shanghaied into the Undying Lie two years ago.

• • •

It had been a day full of suits, lots of them, which was Santiago's first clue that he was out of his element. There was a horde of reporters waiting outside the commissioner's office, so the meeting was convened in room S-20, the Office of the Property Clerk. Santiago knew the room well and took some small solace in the familiar racks and rows and shelves full of the detritus of open and pending cases. But where the evidence stopped, where people replaced objects, was where Santiago's comfort zone ended.

Due to the vagaries of political scheduling, the mayor and district attorney were behind closed doors at City Hall; still, the meeting was comprised of more high-level city and state officials than Santiago had ever seen in one room.

DiBiasi and Randazzo were huddled with DC Devaney, the NYPD's chief of Operations. Also in the huddle were DC Derricks (NYPD Counterterrorism) and McKeutchen, who periodically glanced Santiago's way to give him a frown of encouragement. DiBiasi, too, glanced at him periodically, but his look conveyed a seemingly intense desire to drown Santiago in a septic tank.

Then there were the staties, Deputy Superintendent Bergstrom (one star) and Captain MacReady (two bars). The latter was the head of Troop NYC's Criminal Intelligence Unit (NYSP Counterterrorism); he and DiBiasi glared good-naturedly at each other from time to time. Bergstrom was the bad news—he was second in command of the entire state police force, and his boss answered directly to Governor Mansoni in Albany.

Forming a negatively charged ionic bond between the first two groups was the fed huddle, composed of agents Santiago had often prayed he would never see again. There was a tall, cadaverous SAC from the local FBI field office named Totentantz, whose saturnine scowl seemed to draw air out of the room. Next to him was a fuming TFI director named Reale and a pair of T-dogs named Gilliard and Rondo, with whom Santiago and More had locked horns more than once. Reale was angrily muttering to Liza Marrone, Santiago's only friend in the fed group, a FINCEN investigator who'd originally been detailed to the Anticrime Bureau as a bad joke. Now she was trying to get in on one of the largest and most convoluted financial crimes in city and national history, and Santiago knew her closest comrades at Treasury wished her the worst. Next to her was a middle-aged geek with a book under his arm, some muckety-muck from the Treasury's Office of Terrorism and Financial Intelligence. Santiago didn't know his name, but he seemed to be making what Santiago deemed excessive casual body contact with Marrone for a guy wearing a wedding ring. Santiago once kindled a small torch for Marrone, but his ardor was another casualty in the firestorm that was GC Piso.

The fourth huddle in the room stood on its own. This was comprised of black-clad Isabella Trichinella, the mannish, leather-vested council speaker whom nearly every cop on the force hated for her ceaseless public cries for an independent civilian oversight committee for the NYPD. Beside her was her omnipresent aide, Tsetse Fly, whose wasp-waisted jacket and short tight skirt over ivory-colored stockings and garters revealed a magnificent figure that did nothing to assuage Santiago's anxiety. There was Peter Fasciola, the city's public advocate and lord of glen plaid, dispatched posthaste from City Hall in the wake of the raid and subsequent shootout. There was the short but vivacious attorney general for the Southern District of New York, Alphonse Alstromeria. And then there was a short, pallid guy wearing a stained and rumpled suit and a cold-looking sweat whom Santiago had never before seen.

"That's Necator," McKeutchen explained after peeling off from the NYPD brass huddle. "He's the Dems' bagman between here and Albany. Your little stunt apparently raised a hurricane of shit in Washington. They're closing ranks on us up here." On one side of him was Devius Rune, the CIA officer who held More's leash. On the other side was More, still reeking of cordite from his most recent slippage of said leash. He had just visited a small taste of Afghanistan upon a quiet wooded section of the Bronx, leaving a slew of bodies in his wake, some of which would be identified later through DNA testing, so extreme was the tissue damage. The Office of the Medical Examiner was screaming for an explanation, which could be a problem. The NYPD had no weapons in its arsenal that matched what the pathologists were pulling out of More's latest victims.

Devius Rune seemed maddeningly composed to Santiago. He stood placidly alongside More with a thick folder stamped DEPARTMENT OF DEFENSE under his arm. Periodically, he would mumble something to More out of the side of his mouth, just low enough that Santiago couldn't catch it. Santiago's pulse was pounding in his wrists and temples, and his stomach felt like congealed lava. His mind was overloaded with images from the shootout, along with fun-filled potential outcomes like termination, criminal charges, and prison. Room S-20 was full of agitated bodies throwing off heat, but Santiago shivered through his sweat, just like that wormy-looking little Necator.

After a short eternity, the huddles began to break apart, to sift and rearrange into a line that ran more or less down the middle of the open space. On one side of this line stood Derricks, Randazzo, McKeutchen, DiBiasi, More, and Santiago. On the other side stood everyone else. Santiago experienced that strange truncation of time he always felt under extreme duress, like he was watching events unfold through the wrong end of a telescope.

AG Alstromeria made the first *attaque*, spikily addressing Rune but gesturing at More: "Your boy's in serious fuckin' trouble."

"I don't think so," replied Devius Rune smoothly, brandishing his folder in a neat *passé-arrière*. "DoD directives 5240.1 and 5525.5 clearly state—"

"Don't give me that shit," Alstromeria snarled in mid-*balestra*, "you two are in gross violation of Posse Comitatus on multiple counts—"

Now it was *corps-à-corps*. "If you'd let me finish—"

"You *are* fucking finished, in this town *and* in Washington, when the SSCI gets through with you, you'll be—"

"—incidentally acquired information pertaining to a direct threat to U.S. national security by groups that have been deemed terrorist or criminal organizations, in which lives are endangered, falls within the purview of DoD directive 5525.5, reference I, which you should know—"

"—fuck that, you can't just open fire with machine guns and bazookas in the middle of a residential neighborhood without even informing other law enforcement agencies of the kind of threat you're describing—"

It was a real donnybrook, the politicians and half the feds rallying behind the AG with accusatory screams, and the cops hurling profane retorts. Santiago had never watched a tennis match, but he felt like he was at one now, one in which teams of players simply hurled their rackets at each other.

Devius Rune and More were silent amid the din, and slowly, Santiago discerned that FBI SAC Totentantz was, too. The wraithlike fed moved his bloodless jaws around, bruxed his big bovine molars, and said something. He had to repeat himself twice before the AG heard him: "I said it was an interagency operation. The FBI had the lead, fully within PCA parameters. We were approached beforehand with intelligence procured by the—by Mr. Rune here. Information was disseminated between federal, state, and local law enforcement agencies as per Title 10, Section 371, of the U.S. Code." Totentantz shifted his deathly gaze over to the AG. "With which I'm sure you're familiar."

Santiago caught a glimpse, just the faintest motion out of the corner of his eye: More stirring. It was a shift so imperceptible as to be picked up only by someone who'd rolled with More six nights a week in a taxicab for six months. But Marrone's reaction to the bombshell was bigger—her jaw dropped, and her eyes widened at Devius Rune. Santiago chanced a glance over at DiBiasi and Randazzo, but they stood stolidly mute. So did MacReady and Bergstrom, although the deputy superintendent flicked an uncomfortable glance at the pols' huddle, also not lost on Santiago.

For their part, the pols and feds were visibly flummoxed at this *battement,* as concisely evinced by the council speaker's querulous "What the fuck is he talking about?" leveled at the AG. The public advocate was dumbstruck, Necator mopped sweat from his glistening forehead, and Tsetse Fly's luxuriant locks sagged pitiably toward the floor. The Treasury men seethed. Clearly, they had not expected such treachery from one of their own.

AG Alstromeria regained his composure long enough for an *esquive* directed at the police brass: "So you were informed *before* the raid?"

Derricks and MacReady in tandem: "Correct."

Randazzo: "That's right."

DiBiasi: "Asshole."

Santiago's mind was churning. If true, this meant that Devius Rune had tipped the heads of the various departments before they'd raided the Piso offices, before their star witness made a run for it that ended in a bloody shootout in one section of the Bronx, leading to the interrogation of said witness, which led to *another* bloody shootout in *another* section of the Bronx, where More had rained down death from above.

"So you were simply overtaken by events, is that it?" Alstromeria, the veteran trial lawyer, twisting *in quartata* to try to land the killing blow.

"The University Heights shooting was the endgame of a high-speed pursuit of a key witness in the prosecution of the GC Piso case, as you know," Randazzo offered with surprising gentility. "That it took place inside the clubhouse of a gang that OCID had already infiltrated during a separate long-term investigation was pure coincidence."

"What about the Fieldston shooting?" Public Advocate Fasciola chimed in.

"A joint CT operation to apprehend the head of a foreign organized-crime syndicate well known to international law enforcement agencies, including the Office of the District Attorney of the Southern District of New York," DC Derricks offered in a smooth *coup fouetté*.

Visibly stung, Alstromeria paused before snarling, "So you just went in, guns blazing?"

"The Organized Criminal Intelligence Division, in conjunction with uniformed officers from the Fiftieth Precinct on nearby Kingsbridge Avenue, evacuated all residences within a three-block radius of the target address prior to the raid. The only casualty was an elderly man with a preexisting heart condition, who was taken immediately to Bronx Montefiore Hospital and stabilized. He was discharged this morning and returned to his home by a police escort," DiBiasi gnarled with not so veiled sarcasm.

"Asshole," added Randazzo. The AG's teeth clenched, and he seemed on the verge of a retort, but given that Randazzo was about the size and weight of a Kodiak, he found the means to hold his tongue. Others were less courteous.

"You mean this fucking bloodbath was *legit*? That these pricks can just show up and shoot up our city whenever they fucking feel like it as long as they call the right people first? What kind of bullshit is this?" Speaker Trichinella shouted, waving an accusatory finger at Devius Rune, More, the cops. Tsetse Fly was trying to calm her boss, whispering to her, stroking her hand. Reale was shouting louder but less intelligibly. Marrone was trying to settle him down to no avail. She and Santiago looked helplessly at each other across a chasm of professional animosity.

The triangle of Devius Rune, FBI SAC Totentantz, and AG Alstromeria was the center of gravity in room S-20. It was Rune who delivered the *coup-lancé* to the AG: "You'll be getting two calls later this afternoon. One will be from the National Intelligence director, who will inform you that the GC Piso case constitutes an emergency circumstance under Title 10 of the U.S. Code, sections 371 and 374. The other will be from the assistant secretary of defense, who will explain why the Posse Comitatus Act does not apply to the GC Piso case under the Military Purpose Doctrine. Sergeant Santiago here will see that the operative surrenders his weapon and police identification to the appropriate office. I will then take the operative into my custody and back to Washington for a full debrief. We're done here. Have a nice day."

The results were mixed. Totentantz held his deathly glower but said nothing. The staties pressed their lips together and clenched their jaws. AG Alstromeria uttered a repetitious epithetic crescendo as he stomped out the door ("Bullshit! *Bullshit!*! BULLSHIT!!!"), flailing his arms and spitting. He was followed at a sanitary distance by Public Advocate Fasciola, who only glared at Devius Rune. Speaker Trichinella was a bit more blunt, hissing "Cocksuckers" at Rune, More, and Santiago. Tsetse Fly followed mutely, patting her boss on one leather clavicle. DiBiasi blew her a kiss. Devius Rune smiled beatifically and said nothing.

Santiago felt like he was attending a grotesque parody of a wedding, where the guests filed past bride and groom to deliver good wishes, only here they spat venom. Reale and the T-dogs lingered just long enough to pay their respects to Santiago, More, and Devius Rune ("*Fuck* you, fuck *you,* and FUCK YOU") before leaving in a cloud of muttered profanity. Santiago could hear the council speaker, the public advocate, and the AG screaming at one another out in the hall by the elevator.

"Well, we've had dinner and a show, now for the rape in the backseat." DiBiasi sighed. Glancing at Devius Rune, then at Totentantz, he voiced the question that Santiago yearned to: "Would you care to enlighten us poor local law enforcement peons as to how we might resolve this little debacle?"

Deputy Superintendent Bergstrom made what might be considered, in different circumstances, a valiant attempt to represent the state of New York's opinion on the matter. He was prevented from elaborating on his point by Chief Devaney, who suggested, "Shut the fuck up, Don."

"OCID gets the collar," DiBiasi stated flatly. Randazzo grunted in agreement.

That stirred Totentantz from his torpor. "In this investigation, the Bureau will—"

"In your mother's cunt," DiBiasi snarled. "Your team did tech support and crowd control. *My* men hit the doors, *my* men were under fire. I'm not out for glory. I want an umbrella for when the shit rains down on us from Albany. And shit it surely will." He cast an evil eye toward the staties.

This time, when Bergstrom tried to put in his two cents, it was DC Derricks who laid down the Susan B. Anthony: "Shut the fuck up, Don." Now the Stetsons were adjusted. "Fuck all you assholes," offered Deputy Superintendent Bergstrom in a gesture of police fraternalism. Captain MacReady rolled his eyes to the ceiling, shook his head, and followed Bergstrom out of room S-20.

Chief Devaney's posture was a perfect isosceles triangle: head slightly tilted toward the floor, both sides of his mouth pushed down, hands in pockets, floorward-ho. Without looking up, he muttered, "Jesus H. fucking Christ." He raised his head and took a deep breath. "This is a fuckup of biblical proportions. Here's how we can fix it. OCID makes the collar and gets city charges on the books. Get a list of state charges from MacReady; Bergstrom's just gonna run to the governor. You charge whichever mopes are still breathing, no thanks to him"—a quick flick of the eyes to More— "then turn 'em over to the feds. Between the three of us, we can pin a few centuries on these scumbags; they'll never get out. I'll make a statement to the press fucks that it was a joint operation resulting in an unprecedented success that—" He paused, looking around.

"Foiled terrorist plots in our fair city?" offered DC Derricks.

"Prevented international organized crime from taking root on our fair shores?" suggested McKeutchen.

"Highlights the smoothness of interagency cooperation between federal, state, and local law enforcement," Devius Rune finished.

Devaney nodded, chewing absently on the inside of his cheek. "Randazzo, you work out the handover with him." He tossed his head at Totentantz. "Sergeant, relieve that one of his weapon and get the paperwork going with MELD," he grunted at Santiago. Leveling his finger at More and Devius Rune, he intoned, "I want you both fucking gone in one hour, gone, beyond the city limits, and don't ever come back." He held the finger and the look for a long moment, then put his hand back in his pocket and shuffled out of the room.

"I figured that's how he'd play it," DC Derricks murmured as DiBiasi, Randazzo, and Santiago exchanged puzzled glances. McKeutchen chuckled obscenely and Devius Rune smiled, not an entirely pleasant sight.

"More signs out on extended military leave. He hands over his gun and badge, with Detective-Sergeant Santiago here supervising. I'll have him on a plane to Washington in half an hour. But his name stays on the rolls."

"Why?" Randazzo asked with a frown.

"In case he's needed here again," Devius Rune replied matter-of-factishly.

"Fuck you, Secret Agent Man," DiBiasi growled, stepping in close enough to Devius Rune that More turned his cold piscine eyes toward him. "And fuck you, too, whatever you are. We need you here like we need Ebola. Get the fuck out of New York and stay the fuck out of New York." Randazzo put a hand—a very large hand—on DiBiasi's shoulder.

"The politicians won't go after you because they need you," Devius Rune counseled. "And someday you may need More."

"Bullshit," Santiago sputtered. He'd been quiet long enough. "After what he just did? How the fuck you know the council won't hang us all out to dry? Or City Hall? Or fucking Albany?" He was closing in on Devius Rune. "I'm fuckin' low man on the totem pole here, I got a fuckin' bull's-eye on my ass! They're gonna—"

"No, they won't," said every other man in unison. Except More.

"Kid, no cop ever gets prosecuted on an interagency case gone even half right, especially not one this big," McKeutchen rumbled. "The feds'll dine out on this one for years. So will OCID." He tossed his great fat head at DiBiasi and Randazzo. "Not to mention the medal the mayor's gonna pin on Derricks for keeping city buses bomb-free. If you get anything outta this, it's gonna be a promotion." He swiveled his suet toward Devius Rune. "In fact, I insist on it."

"I'll see what I can do," Devius Rune said evenly.

"Fuck you, Secret Agent Man," McKeutchen growled, also moving toward the CIA man. "Your walking disaster here gets a pass, then Santiago gets his stripes."

"Asshole," added Santiago.

"Captain McKeutchen's right," More croaked, and they all turned to stare at him. "Santiago's done enough."

Devius Rune exhaled audibly through his nose and nodded once at McKeutchen. Santiago felt just a little bit of air creep back into room S-20.

"But you're More's liaison," Devius Rune said with a sudden grin for Santiago. "You'll see him off, you'll issue a written statement saying More's on indefinite leave, you'll file and maintain the necessary reports with NYPD, and you'll be the first person More contacts if—and when—he returns to New York." He turned to face the captains and chiefs. "Agreed?"

They all nodded, and Santiago felt the floor go rubbery beneath his feet. He would not face criminal charges. His fate would be worse. He would still be tethered to More, albeit at a distance. *I am fucked beyond all understanding,* he thought. *Check, mate, and sodomy. New York, New York, the great sausage factory.*

The meeting broke up amid sighs and scuffles of feet. Santiago heard only McKeutchen speak briefly, to DiBiasi ("Lemme talk to you"), as they filed out to the elevator.

Devius Rune closed his folder and checked his watch, a big black Tawatec H3. Without looking at More, he muttered, "Three minutes." Pivoting smoothly on one heel, he left the room, giving Santiago a parting glimpse of a ghost of a half-smile. Then he was gone.

Santiago made a grand show to no one in particular of escorting More to room 1008, where More went through the motions of surrendering an NYPD-issue Glock .45 he'd never used, along with the badge he'd never used. More silently filled out the MELD paperwork (in handwriting superior to Santiago's, which set his teeth on edge) that officially put him on extended leave without pay. *This is all it takes,* Santiago fumed silently, *this is how they do it. They turn bodies into paper.*

He managed to hold it in until they were outside, walking toward Pearl Street, where a pair of huge black armored SUVs stood waiting. Devius Rune stood in front of the rear one, along with two men in dark suits who were only slightly smaller than the trucks beside them. But Santiago knew he couldn't let More go without it: "Did you know?"

"No," More clacked, "but it makes sense. This way Justice and Treasury will get the credit, but we'll still be able to get all the data they pull up on GC Piso. We'll be able to work the overseas connections better than they can. And you'll be protected."

"My ass," Santiago shot back. "You're the one who's protected. *I'm* completely fucked!"

"No, you're not," More replied in the abruptly clear voice he could summon on command. "I'll see to it."

And then More and Devius Rune were in the back of the SUV and it was pulling away and Santiago was left alone on Pearl Street with his eyes on Chinatown.

This is how they get away with bringing the devil to New York, he thought. *Because our demons here can't keep their shit together.*

A mad thought struck him at random and he hurried back inside, toward room S-20, to the evidence lockup for the GC Piso case, where a stack of yoga videos lay interred.

• • •

Now, two years later, with More riding shotgun beside him, Santiago drove them to the "shop" owned by Victor's "guy" out near Shea, in a part of New York that looked more like an East L.A. barrio.

Everywhere were cars, guns, graffiti from half a dozen gang names Santiago recognized and many more he did not. As soon as Santiago and More drove up in their old Crown Vic, a pair of heavies with shotguns bookended them in front and behind, one pulling the shop's iron shutter down to the floor with an alarming crash. More was out of the cab before Santiago got his door open, hands out of sight behind his back, presumably within easy reach of the arsenal he always carried, in the event that any of the *vatos* in the garage got fatally stupid. *There is no God,* Santiago mused morosely as he climbed out of the cab, keeping his hands in plain view. Back in town under a day, and already More was looking to get them both killed.

The first thing Santiago noticed was the enormous (and enormously illegal) stash of gasoline barrels stacked floor to ceiling at the back of the garage. Gas hoarding was nothing new in New York City in 2016. Wild price swings from market gyrations, along with rampant gouging by filling station owners and fuel shippers, as well as periodic pump shutdowns due to overstrain of the power grid, had led to widespread popular mistrust. Hence home fuel caches. The inevitable explosions and fires had nearly broken the back of the NYFD, already reeling from budget cuts and numerous station-house closings. There was at least one five-alarm blaze per borough on any given night of the week; the cops referred to them as hot flashes. Santiago figured the guns in the garage were mostly for show, as a single stray round would put the entire place into orbit and likely incinerate any adjacent ones. He fervently hoped More wasn't feeling trigger-happy, but he was actually glad the crazy bastard was there. More had his own methods for gang control, and Santiago felt the particularly ironic twinge he experienced when forced to concede that More had his uses, chaotic and destructive as they were.

Santiago had barely cleared the driver's seat before More was leaning inside to pop the hood release. The armed face-off was forgotten as everyone gathered around the taxicab's engine bay for the new class project. First to stick his head nearly into the dilapidated Ford's ventricles, fluorescent angle light in hand, power cable spooling over his shoulder, was Victor's "guy," Odilàn. He was a compact, nutmeg-skinned Mexican with a mane of raven hair slicked back from his forehead and two tiny tattooed tears in jailhouse teal beside his left eye. Odilàn was Victor's solution to More's idea for beefing up their old hack.

The proposal had played out between the former partners in typical fashion.

More: "This car has always sucked. We're going to fix it."

Santiago: "Oh, really, Commander Psycho? And just how are 'we' supposed to pay for that?"

More: "I know a guy."

That had ended the conversation and caused Santiago to write himself a note in his phone to stock up on Tums again. More's guy would undoubtedly be Devius Rune. Santiago did not want to think about what sort of expense account More had with the CIA. He was certain his own NYPD superiors should never, ever know about it. Santiago could not bring himself to trust a man like Rune, who struck him as having the omniscience of a god and the morality of a scorpion. Rune was More's handler; when he let the demon off the leash, parts—and people—of New York City tended to explode.

Odilàn was checking the length and width of the cab's engine bay with a yellow tape measure, jotting notes on a brown paper sandwich bag with a two-inch nub of a pencil. More had his face in the engine bay, too, and the two of them were muttering inaudibly to each other. Santiago had no beef with his father's friend, whom he silently hoped would lean back long enough for Santiago to slam the hood on More's head. They were wasting time. Certain key people would have to be informed of More's reappearance, quickly and quietly, as much for Santiago's own protection as for any legal reason. More was military; for him to jump back in with civilian cops meant he was operating off the books, on Rune's orders. But Santiago was More's contact (read: accomplice) inside NYPD. Santiago knew he owed Rune for protecting him from the shitstorm that followed their last operation together, but he couldn't trust him. Everything about More's return smelled wrong to Santiago, who intended to insulate himself with as many layers of police bureaucracy as possible. He knew, deep in his bones, there was another cataclysm coming. More's presence guaranteed it. Nor could Santiago stifle the upwelling of questions flooding his mind since More's reappearance. Why now? What demented shit had transpired to bring More out of hiding? And was it a cover story for another search-and-destroy mission More was supposed to carry out in violation of every law on the books?

What did More need with him?

Or with OCID?

Or Marrone?

More had specifically asked Santiago to bring her in. But why her? Marrone was a fed, an investigator for the Financial Crimes Enforcement Network division of the Treasury Department. Marrone chased fraudsters and money launderers and counterfeiters and anyone else who broke rules with money. She was an accountant with a gun, someone who should be riding a desk but kept jumping into field investigations. She had a habit of pissing off nearly everyone she worked with. She was also a hazel-eyed, aquiline beauty for whom Santiago had decidedly unprofessional feelings, which never quite died, even when he had learned what a pain in the ass she could be. Since the last time they'd worked together, Santiago had kept up intermittent contact with Marrone, mostly by email.

But what he really wanted to know was what More—which, by extension, meant Devius Rune and the CIA—wanted with a U.S. Treasury agent and the Organized Crime Intelligence Division of the NYPD. Had their separate investigations somehow popped up on Devius Rune's radar? Jesus, were they *all* under CIA surveillance? And why the fuck were they huddled around this beat-up old yellow—

Oh, *that* was why.

More had slammed the hood shut and spread an oversize color printout across it. Being the son of a machinist, Santiago knew enough about engines to know that the one described on the spec sheet in More's hand wasn't stock. It had a name: ROUSH 427 IR. It was huge. It was menacing. It was pretty.

"*Coño.*" Santiago exhaled at the engine schematic, and everyone in the room save More nodded agreement. In Spanish, he asked, "Is it blown?"

"*Se podría pensar así, de mirarlo.*" Odilàn said in Mexican street Spanish: You'd think so, from looking at it.

"What's it put out?" Santiago asked.

"560 horse, 540 torque," More scatted. "That's a proprietary fuel injection system you're looking at. I've driven vehicles with this engine. It's fast and it's dependable."

"How much?" Santiago hoped the answer would never leave this room.

"Thirty grand," Odilàn immediately replied in perfect, unaccented English. "Cash."

"We'll have to upgrade the exhaust and suspension, reinforce the chassis and body, maybe a few other things," More gubbed. Odilàn nodded.

Santiago rolled his eyes at More. "So how the fuck—"

"I know a guy," More quacked. "Now we've got the car settled, let's go get Liesl and Turse. You call Marrone, have her meet us."

Santiago thought: *And we're off.*

• • •

They found the Narc Sharks, Liesl and Turse, hard at work on their missing money case, the Mavridez operation, at 500 Amsterdam Avenue on the Upper West Side of Manhattan.

In their years in the Narcotics and Anticrime bureaus, the Narc Sharks had rewritten, thrown out, and burned the book on dirty tricks. When he was in Anticrime, Santiago was their peer; during the transfer to OCID, he had been promoted to sergeant, thus becoming their superior and earning their undying disrespect and ill humor.

Santiago had always tried to keep his distance from the Narc Sharks, largely for reasons of self-preservation. He did not want to be too close when one of the corners they always cut turned around and cut them back. Nevertheless, Santiago grudgingly admitted that if anyone could survive the high-risk, long-odds MO of being undercover narcs in New York City, it was Liesl and Turse. A truce of sorts existed between Santiago and the Narcs, who bore his command insofar as he didn't do anything to curtail their hobbies, such as turning the Mavridez operation into their biggest slam dunk for 2016.

Santiago figured there were three reasons the Mavridez case was a Big Deal for them. One was it gave Liesl and Turse a valid excuse for avoiding numerous pain-in-the-ass details that were becoming the norm for an understaffed, underfunded, and overtaxed police force, like the logistical nightmare that was Convention Week.

Another reason: It was galling to the Narc Sharks that they were now lower in rank than Santiago, whom they deemed a pussy and a sellout and unworthy of their subordination. They were obviously frothing for promotion, and cracking a big case was the best way to get one.

But Santiago thought the main reason Liesl and Turse assigned such importance to the Mavridez case was its potential for serious blowback, on OCID in general and the Narc Sharks in particular. The two detectives had spent over *fifty grand* of the department's money buying Mavridez narcotica, and thus far, none of the bills had been recovered through the usual money-laundering channels. The marked currency had not turned up in banks, wire-transfer stations, or even local businesses. The money simply went into the building housing the Mavridez operation and disappeared. Leaving the Narc Sharks on the hook for the cash.

Which carried serious consequences if they couldn't recover it.

Captain DiBiasi, OCID's commanding officer, had told the pair of Narcs on their very first day in his unit that he would nail each of their fucking livers to his office door if a single one of their cases was ever blown because of planted evidence, inadmissible surveillance records, witness tampering, or any other "abortions." Not that DiBiasi had any problems with said illegal activities—he just didn't want the Narc Sharks (who knew a thing or two about such nefarious doings) getting caught and smearing OCID's name with their shit.

As he parked his unmarked OCID cruiser a block away from the target, Santiago realized the Mavridez operation could literally make or break the Narc Sharks' careers. He was uneasy getting out of the car; More, on the other hand, made hardly a sound as he glided from the car to the street, his eyes already locked on the Mavridez building.

500 Amsterdam Avenue was not, despite its central location in Manhattan's prestigious Upper West Side, considered a *bonne addresse*. It was one in a trio of tenement houses left over from another century, given a new lease on squalor by the political insistence that subsidized housing would keep the neighborhood in balance (thus buying more votes to support and sustain that view for decades to come). In exchange for keeping their properties in a social-support role instead of selling them to predatory developers who would turn them into luxury housing at sky-high market rates, the owners of these properties had received huge tax breaks from the city for years. Little effort was made to maintain the buildings and none at

all to monitor the inhabitants. Thus it was not unusual for prewar co-ops and brownstones with selling prices between seven and nine figures to rub shoulders with halfway houses, SROs, and 500 Amsterdam Avenue.

According to records wrung out of the building's management company, Manolo "Manlo" Mavridez, the listed tenant of apartment 3R, paid $698.17 a month in rent. He collected Social Security (fraudulently, as it was later discovered), a small pension from an automotive body shop in Queens (also bogus), and a federal tax credit for having "bought" an all-electric vehicle (stolen), the phony title and bill of sale secured with his Akoya Pearl credit card (which managers at Urbank outlets all over town had been giving away in a desperate attempt to win back fleeing customers).

Meanwhile, Manlo made mad money, working with his son Pavlos and nephew Eladio. The Mavridez operation had been grossing an estimated three hundred grand a week in sales of heroin and crack cocaine, volume enough to bring them onto OCID's radar.

The Narc Sharks (with an undercover detective on their field team called Rouse) had made some preliminary surveillance and some low-level street buys—around the corner, never inside the building, in the shadows of nearby brownstone stoops, after making a coded request inside the deli on the corner of Amsterdam and West Eighty-fifth.

Santiago knew the Narc Sharks had been exceptionally thorough and careful throughout the course of their investigation. They had cut no corners and overlooked no procedural details. In theory, the final bust looked to be a smooth and almost routine affair.

Except they hadn't taken into account the all too human element, which had manifested in the mind of one Braulio Casta, aka Brownie, the Mavridez operation's chief enforcer.

Brownie was not a member of the Mavridez family. He was tall, dark, and handsome in the brutal manner of large apes. That he had maintained his good looks to the ripe old age of thirty testified to both his fighting skills and propensity for violence. He had been on the books as a violent offender since his teens. In the late nineties, he had narrowly avoided a life sentence when an attempted murder charge was commuted to aggravated assault on a technicality, and Brownie had wound up sharing a cell in Attica with a boyishly cute Eladio Mavridez, who at the time was serving a sentence for drugs and weapons possession. Within the confines of their cell, the boy and the ape had bonded. Eladio won an early release and told Brownie exactly how and where he should make contact with the Mavridez clan when he got out. Seven and a half years into a ten-year sentence, Brownie made parole, followed Eladio's instructions, and found himself standing on the stoop of 500 Amsterdam Avenue.

Eladio recruited Brownie to manage security procedures for his family's thriving drug operation. Business was so good following the crash that revenues began to outpace inventory. A logistical solution was needed, and the job was outsourced to Brownie. Who quickly developed a network of paid neighborhood informants reporting on all movements of the local Twentieth Precinct cops, especially the School Squad, which deployed twice a day every weekday and camped out on the corner in front of the deli. Brownie distributed disposable prepaid phones and SIM cards to neighborhood locals and soon had a steady stream of electronic intel on the local movements of all law-enforcement and municipal employees. He even had two junkies who were regulars in the precinct holding tanks as his eyes and ears. It was a simple, effective operation, and as such, it prospered. Until Brownie decided to part ways with the Mavridez clan.

It wasn't because of the overbearing manner of the senior Mavridez, who was always suspicious of Brownie as an outsider and let him know it with regular, if restrained, affrontery. It wasn't Manlo's son Pavlos, either, who stank up his bedroom and the adjacent outer hallway with the reek of weed, sweat, and sex from marathon sessions with his nymphomaniac girlfriend, Orquidia, who kept giving Brownie the eye whenever Pavlos had overexerted himself with his indulgences.

No, it was Brownie's recruiter and cellmate, Eladio, who made him conclude that the Mavridez boys were unworthy of both his invaluable services *and* their hard-earned drug profits.

The idea came to him when Eladio broached the notion of sending their greenback flow underground into the subway bank. Ever since then, it had gnawed at Brownie's mind like a termite.

Initially Brownie had thought Eladio's grand plan was a joke—move tons of cash into the fucking *subway*? Brownie was pretty good with his hands, a blade, and a modest array of firearms, but muling sacks of money into the tunnels was like swimming in shark-infested water with bleeding hemorrhoids.

But Eladio said: —No, homes, the way we do it is a little every week, like we're working stiffs, okay? We get one of those super-size safe-deposit boxes they got down there, the high-security ones people are using now instead of in regular banks, *me sigues?* I heard they were supposed to be lockers for fuckin' transit workers, can you beat that? So here's the play: Each of us gets two boxes, but we only use *one* till it's full, right? We use a different name for each of our boxes. Then the *bank* puts the money out on the street for us through its own customers, okay? It's like a big loan-sharking operation, only no loan sharks, just the bank and the customers standing in line, see? The bank's offering fifty, sixty percent interest. Who's gonna say no to that when all they can get upstairs is one percent on a three-year CD, you know? And here's the best part, homes—the bank handles all the collecting for us, you don't have to get your hands dirty. They'd even spot us five percent for write-offs, *conseguirlo?*

Brownie nodded periodically, pretending to follow along with Eladio's ravings, the termite manifesting in his mind with each passing sentence.

Eladio continued excitedly: —We take the repaid loan money and put it back into a different set of safe-deposit boxes squeaky clean, man, we don't have to do a thing, the fucking city washes the cash for us! As long as we go low and slow on the flow, we won't get no heat on us. C'mon, man, this is how we set ourselves up for life!

Brownie was skeptical. —Don't you gotta fill out forms and shit to get a box there?

But Eladio smiled the cute little grin that Brownie remembered from jail and replied: —Hey, this's a fuckin' bank for fuckin' street business in a fuckin' subway tunnel, they don't give a shit about your résumé, *estafador.*

Eladio had quickly won the group over, and the profits from the Mavridez operation began to pile up in an empty bedroom closet in Manlo's apartment. On the day the cash reached the ceiling and the door could no longer be closed, Eladio took it off the hinges. Then he took the hinges off the wall, and the wood slats surrounding the doorframe, spackled away any trace of their existence, and hung a slab of Sheetrock in the doorway. More spackle, a fast hand-sanding, two coats of quick-drying primer, and the doorway to the cash stash had vanished.

Brownie had watched from the hallway for a while, the termite chewing away inside his head, then turned away and padded quietly down the hall. As usual, Manlo was in the living room watching TV. On-screen, another ridiculous reality show was playing out in night-vision green. A man holding some sort of electronic device was stumbling around in a pitch-dark room

of an apparently abandoned building, tripping over things and calling out
to unseen conversants:

> MAN: (crashing through wooden latticework in the dark)
> Do you hear me, spirit? I want—no, I *command* you to—
> (stumbling over an upturned chair) (BLEEP) Oh my—(BLEEP
> BLEEP) I'm being attacked, the spirit is actually making physical
> contact with me (tripping headlong over a discarded water heater)
> (BLEEEEEEEEEP), the attacks are coming from all sides, oh
> my God I'm bleeding, I can feel blood on my face, the attacks
> are getting stronger now (tripping over a broken pipe protruding
> from the floor), ow ow my ankle, I think the spirit just broke my
> ankle, oh (BLEEP), it hurts like (BLEEP BLEEP), Dave, guys,
> help, help, I lost my EVP recorder, we have to find it to analyze
> the evidence—(tripping and falling face-first through an old
> windowpane, shattering it—BLEEEEEEEEEEEP)

The camera cut to blackness, in the middle of which slowly appeared
a glowing caption: *GHOST D.W.E.E.B.S.*

Catching sight of Brownie in the doorway, Manlo scowled, so he
continued down the hall to the window by the fire escape by Pavlos's room.
As usual, it reeked of ganja; and as usual, Pavlos's moans emanated from
within. But this time the door was ajar. Brownie stopped to peer inside, if
only for a moment. But he was transfixed by the sight of Orquidia using
her lips, tongue, and mouth on Pavlos's cock with a mastery Brownie had
never experienced himself. She was doing things with her upper lip that
didn't seem possible. When she saw Brownie watching through the door
(which obscured the rest of Pavlos, who was too preoccupied to notice),
she did not stop, say a word, or move to close the door. Instead, she looked
directly at Brownie, holding his tormented gaze, while she slowly intensified
her movements, adding an array of nonverbal sound effects for his benefit.
Pavlos kept moaning, arching his hips toward her face, one hand on the
back of her head.

Brownie stood rock-still, hearing his pulse in his temples, watching
Orquidia do that thing with her upper lip for him. He thought about the
closet, packed floor to ceiling with cash, which Eladio was sealing up at that
very moment. He thought about that asshole Manlo watching that stupid
GHOST D.W.E.E.B.S. show and scratching his nuts. He thought of that

stoned moron Pavlos, who even now, as he was coming in her mouth, didn't realize how good a thing he had with Orquidia. Brownie felt a single bead of sweat trickle down the center of his chest, directly above his thundering heart. He could hear the termite working in his ears, chewing away at the makeshift barrier between him and a whole closetful of cash.

Watching him, on the bed, Orquidia expertly collected Pavlos's semen in her mouth, using her unbelievable lip to cull the final drops cleanly off the tip of his still-pulsing cock. She raised her chin so that Brownie could see her throat, swallowed slowly and visibly, then smiled warmly at him, lips shining, eyes bright.

And Brownie put a 147-grain Remington Golden Saber JHP round right through her talented upper lip.

When Pavlos sat bolt upright in reflex, Brownie shot him, too, through the right temple.

Then he was moving down the hall with silent, seemingly huge strides to the living room. Manlo was still on the couch, but twisted halfway around, his right arm outstretched, scrabbling for the Mossberg 12-guage they kept behind the sofa. Brownie shot him four times through the back, and Manlo stayed twisted in place.

In the far bedroom, the stash room, Eladio had been preparing the first coat of paint. He stood motionless and wide-eyed, staring down the barrel of Brownie's Beretta 92FS with a paint roller in one hand, the other raised to the ceiling. He said something like: —What the fuck you doin', homes? Brownie was looking at his mouth, remembering that cute little smile from jail but seeing Orquidia's amazingly agile lips, smelling the cash behind the Sheetrock not four feet away, the termite's jaws clicking, and he shot Eladio right between the eyes at point-blank range, blood spraying out the back of his skull all over the new primer.

As Brownie went to work on the Sheetrock with a hammer, it occurred to him that maybe he should've used his silencer. But fuck it, there was no way the cops would get here in time, he'd just fill one big trash bag and split, and besides, he had his people looking out for him, and they hadn't texted him anything for the past half hour.

Except that all of a sudden there were shouts in the hallway right outside, and then he heard the front door caving in and saw one long-haired freak in black and another with sandy blond hair and a mustache above a weird purple T-shirt with red on it, beneath a shiny gold badge on a chain, and heard FREEZE MOTHERFUCKER and snapped off two wild shots at the mustache and then he was running, running, running down the hall to the fire escape and ramming the window up with one hand and firing another blind shot back down the hallway with the other and then he was out on the fire escape but tripped over the laces of his goddamn Barabbas high-tops and then an incomprehensible force slammed him over the railing with a clatter of metal and he was falling, falling, falling . . .

"Got 'im," yelled OCID Detective Sergeant Liesl.

"The fuck you did," OCID Detective (first grade) Turse yelled back. "*I* got 'im."

Clearing the apartment yielded one bizarre result after another. First there was the couple on the bed, apparently shot midcoitus (quoth Liesl, "They *both* got the custom lip treatment"). The living room had another stiff twisted into a half-pretzel, four entry wounds in his back, his front a ragged red ruin, a Mossberg shotgun just out of reach. The TV was on.

"Is that *GHOST D.W.E.E.B.S.?*" Turse asked his partner.

"Yeah."

"What's the name stand for?"

"I think it means—"

"Yo, check *this* shit out," yelled Rouse from the other bedroom. The one with a head-shot corpse on the floor and a freshly sealed door to a closet packed to the ceiling with cash.

They were still there when Santiago and More arrived fifteen minutes after the shooting. The cops from the Twentieth Precinct had shut down Amsterdam Avenue between Eighty-fourth and Eighty-fifth, and cordoned off the side streets. Traffic was being diverted with much difficulty and profanity, the press was caterwauling around the building entrance, and Captain DiBiasi was on-site and in vile humor. To Santiago, the situation did not look promising.

The Narc Sharks were ebullient from their kill and the excavated cash stash, which had yet to be counted but looked to be in the millions. Best of all, they could see the marked bills from Rouse's most recent undercover buys in the stacks of currency. Hence DiBiasi's silent, if smoldering, restraint.

"It's a match, Cap," a giddy Turse bubbled, pointing to one of the bundles with a Luma penlight, which unveiled a handwritten number sequence across the top right corner of the bill. Turse was checking the number against a list of serial numbers in his phone. He and Liesl had accounted for every marked bill they had put toward the Mavridez operation, scanning each serial number into an app called iScore, specially designed for OCID the previous year by a convicted hacker in exchange for a reduced sentence.

Turse was on a health kick; he wore black Sugoi ventilated running gear over a pair of black and yellow Via Dolorosas. Liesl, in more traditional garb, wore jeans, boots, and a lavender T-shirt with crimson letters spelling TRIBBERS GRIND IT OUT across the front. Both he and Turse wore flak vests underneath their clothing. Around the OCID locker room, it was said that even if they shot at a suspect and missed, the smell would kill him.

The icing on the Narc Sharks' cake was More's return, as Santiago had known it would be. Both OCID investigators revered More, something both Santiago and DiBiasi tried to discourage. It was More who'd gotten them to ditch their regulation 9mm Glocks in favor of high-capacity .45-caliber variants; it was More who'd recommended loading them with powerful Winchester PDX rounds, half a dozen of which had blown Brownie off the fire escape.

While the Narc Sharks were jabbering excitedly to More, DiBiasi fixed his withering gaze on Santiago, who started laying out his defensive spiel as calmly as he could.

"Cap, More just showed up outta nowhere. I called you right away, nobody else." He edged a bit closer to the captain and dropped his voice. "More says his boss is worried about Convention Week. Says there's weird money shit going on and he needs our help with it."

"Our help," DiBiasi echoed in a monotone, the first words he'd spoken since Santiago and More had popped up at the crime scene.

"Look, Cap, he says this shit is for real. If it is, we gotta inter up like before," Santiago flustered, referring to the interagency operation—or fiasco—that had been the Piso case two years ago. "If we come up dry, if there's nothing there, or we miss, our asses are covered. If we play solid defense, nobody'll fuck with us." He didn't seem to be breaking through DiBiasi's odd detachment. "The press'll eat it up, maybe keep the ME off our backs this time." This got the slightest flicker of attention; Santiago knew the Office of the Medical Examiner would go ballistic when they heard More was back in town. He was gambling that this sore spot would rekindle DiBiasi's usual rancor and get DiBiasi out of the Twilight Zone. But the OCID captain seemed to be looking far beyond Santiago, Amsterdam Avenue, Manhattan, Earth.

DiBiasi jerked his head for Santiago to follow him out of the building. The Narc Sharks brought up the rear with More, talking a mile a minute. They were living a dream: a monster bust with a clean kill. The perp had fired first—the Narc Sharks had half a dozen NYPD witnesses, and the Crime Scene techs had already found three spent shells they would later match to the Beretta lying on the fire escape three stories above the corpse on West Eighty-fourth. Internal Affairs could go jump in the lake. The shooting was clean.

Right around the time the black Lincoln bearing Deputy Chief Derricks, head of NYPD Counterterror Operations, pulled up in front of the building (Santiago was surprised to see him at a drug bust), as they were all clustered outside Eddie's Bicycle Shop on Amsterdam, with the Narc Sharks trying to get More to come see the body to show him just how "fuckin' awesome" those PDX rounds were, a short, pudgy Crime Scene tech came running up with something in a clear plastic evidence bag.

Whatever was inside not only made the Narc Sharks shut up but, worse, it got More's attention immediately. Santiago knew instinctively this was a bad sign. More's interest meant someone else was going to die, very soon, and Santiago found himself praying to a god he did not believe in that it wouldn't be him or any of his team.

What was in the evidence bag was an old-fashioned clipboard almost never seen anymore, holding a pad of old-fashioned graph paper, also on the wane. There was a hand-drawn diagram showing what looked like instructions into a building, or maybe through it, Santiago wasn't sure. He saw two small paths filled with vertical lines bracketing a long straight segment with some shorter routes off one side, and a series of longer, larger runs with lines off to the top edge of the paper. It seemed too abstract to make sense, even less so considering where it recently resided.

"Where'd you find this?" Santiago asked the fidgety tech.

"Living room. We already got photos and prints, so I thought you might want to see it," the tech replied, nervous in the presence of the Narc Sharks and More, who could make a glacier feel uneasy.

"Was this with one of the stiffs? There's no blood on it," Santiago pointed out.

"It was on the TV in the living room, body on the couch, four rounds through the back," the tech said, fidgeting.

Which reminded Turse: "You watch *Ghost D.W.E.E.B.S.?*"

"Sure," said the nervous tech.

"What's the title mean?"

"It stands for—"

DiBiasi seemed to snap out of it. His glower went from Derricks to More to Santiago, then back to Derricks, though still he said nothing. More pointed at the clipboard, shaking in the mitts of the jittery tech. Derricks relieved him of his burden, and the tech scurried back inside the building.

"This was at the crime scene, we don't know what it is," Santiago exhaled, frustrated with the effort of keeping one eye on DiBiasi and one on More. "Make any sense to you?"

Derricks studied the clipboard, frowning. He worked his jaws, pensive clucks emanating from his closed lips, then uttered one word: "Shit."

More and the Narc Sharks crowded in closer, DiBiasi hissed an irritated snort through his nostrils, and Santiago eased out his phone, one finger already on the speed-dial button for McKeutchen. "What?"

"It's the subway, Second Avenue Line, Ninety-sixth Street station. This is the north end. Metropolitan Hospital's up these stairs here." His fingers moved over the graph paper, and Santiago saw the stairways and signs of the station in his mind. "Up here's the Lexington Avenue line; these little things must be service conduits. This would be the mosque over here"—Santiago saw Derricks's eyes flick briefly up to More's, then back to the page—"so this should be the Ninety-fourth Street entrance over here."

"And these?" More pointed to two large squares on the diagram joined by a narrow set of lines. One of these squares was clearly marked SOUP KITCHEN; the other was marked with a large black X.

Derricks frowned. "Dunno. We've got some stationary cameras covering the entrances, put 'em there soon as the tunnels were finished and open to the public. Thought it was a good idea with the mosque so close by. Had some chemical-sniffing equipment in place for about a year, then had to yank it. Budget cuts." He snorted. "We never got anything unusual at the main entrance. Ninety-sixth Street got a lot of inbound traffic, weird hours, looked like a lot of homeless people. The soup kitchen makes sense."

"In a subway," DiBiasi grunted absently. Santiago was chewing on that one, too. A soup kitchen underground made sense in winter, out of the elements where many homeless slept already. Between a hospital, yeah, that made sense for those mooching bathrooms, food, or meds.

But the mosque . . .

"Oh, shit," Santiago muttered. Now he saw why Derricks had been summoned. The Second Avenue line didn't run directly into Grand Central the way the Lexington line did, but the diagram clearly showed several conduits linking the tunnels. If someone were hiding a bomb in the mosque and wanted to send it downtown to GCT, all they had to do was get it underground.

"We'll need a warrant to search the mosque, and we'll need to see if it has any underground connections to the subway tunnels. We need to get with MTA, DEP, Con Ed, everybody." Santiago's blood was pumping, but his head was clear and his mouth was under control. Derricks was nodding, fucking More was, too, even the Narc Sharks were grinning.

The only one not saying a word was DiBiasi, and that made Santiago nervous. By now the captain should have been positively fulminating, between the Mavridez mess, More showing up out of the blue, and now a terrorist plot. By rights DiBiasi should've been cursing out everyone, shouting into a phone or a radio, taking charge. But he wasn't. He was standing on Amsterdam Avenue with a thousand-yard stare aimed out at the street. Santiago heard additional car doors slamming behind him.

DiBiasi intoned: "And I beheld, and lo a black horse; and he that sat on him had a pair of balances in his hand."

Liesl looked over at him with a grimace that said: *What the fuck?*

Santiago turned to look for the cause of the captain's disturbing non sequitur. And saw her standing in front of another black Lincoln with Treasury plates: Liza Marrone. *Jesus, she looks good,* he thought. *Why's she have to be a fucking fed?*

Treasury Agent Liza Marrone, FINCEN Analysis/Liaison Division, posted to Treasury's New York City USTRAC field office, took in the assemblage, her eyes lingering on More, then flicking over quickly to Santiago, whom she greeted thus: "What the fuck?"

DiBiasi tolled: "And I saw, and behold a white horse: and he that sat on him had a bow; and a crown was given unto him: and he went forth conquering, and to conquer."

Turse looked at Liesl and inquired: "What the fuck?"

Santiago turned back to see a white SUV disgorging the long, cadaverous frame of FBI SAC Totentantz, head of the Bureau's local field office, who looked his usual terminal self. Striding directly up to More, he said, "I just knew this would involve you."

Apropos of nothing, Liesl queried aloud: "What the fuck?"

DiBiasi swiveled his face away from Totentantz's deathly pallor to More's slightly more vivid one and uttered: "And there went out another horse that was red: and power was given to him that sat thereon to take peace from the earth, and that they should kill one another: and there was given unto him a great sword."

Now genuinely afraid, Santiago looked imploringly at his boss and asked, "Cap, what the fuck?" as he heard yet another door slam. He turned to see Devius Rune, his right hand still holding the handle of the street-side passenger door of a New York City taxicab, a Ford Crown Vic, like the one they'd dropped off at the pirate garage in Queens, no suit this time, just jeans and a windbreaker to hide the gun Santiago knew he was carrying, a pair of pale yellow Rothco aviators not quite obscuring his locked gaze upon DiBiasi.

Santiago and Marrone had their mouths agape, their eyes canted slightly up beneath their dropped heads, waiting to see who did what. The Narc Sharks looked befuddled; Derricks and More stood silent. Devius Rune broke the tableau first, addressing DiBiasi: "I'm here under Title 10, Chapter 18, and Title 18, Section 831 of the U.S. Code, authorizing the secretary of defense to provide assistance to both the Justice Department and to local law-enforcement agencies in emergency cases involving chemical, biological, or nuclear weapons of mass destruction, the Posse Comitatus Act notwithstanding."

The grizzled Pakistani cabdriver, who had been waiting for Devius Rune to let go of the door handle so he could drive away, looked querulously at the CIA officer and politely asked, "What the fuck?"

DiBiasi returned Devius Rune's stare and replied: "And I looked, and behold a pale horse: and his name that sat on him was Death, and Hell followed with him."

And the crime scene techs began bringing the body bags out of 500 Amsterdam Avenue.

GETTIN' OUT THE VOTE

THE NEW YORK STATE CAPITOL in Albany had taken twenty-eight years, five architects, and one structural failure to complete. And that was before telephones.

The Red Room: domain of mahogany wainscoting, realm of coffered oak ceilings, land of bands of gold and bronze leaf. Sunlight poured through the high Moorish windows, imbuing the crimson drapes and carpet with the hue of freshly spilled blood. From on high down the walls of the Hall of Governors leered the visages of ghosts who long ago haunted the Executive Chamber: Roosevelt, Rockefeller, Van Buren, Cleveland, Morton, Flower, Tilden, Glynn . . .

Through the hidden door to the service elevator originally commissioned by FDR in 1929 came Deputy State Comptroller Anthony Ascaris, talking rapid-fire into a cell phone he thought secure.

". . . so the new legislation will be item one at the next convening of the assembly. We'll see that it has the votes to pass. The new issuance is all revenue anticipation notes for the Stability Reserve Collection. These good-faith bonds already have city sponsorship. They should be triple-tax-free with a maturity of no more than two and a half years max . . ."

Ascaris's trajectory took him between one desk, along the wall between the windows, and the main desk in the center of the chamber. The downstate contingent huddled at the former. The New York City delegation, having surreptitiously arrived on separate trains, consisted of Peter Fasciola, the public advocate, and the heads of three of the most powerful unions in New York City and state, to wit: the Federated Union of Certified Teachers; the New York State League of Unionized Teachers; and the Services Collectivized Restaurant and Entertainment Workers Union. Since they shared a first name, the union heads were commonly known around Albany as the Three Pauls—Falciparum, Ovale, and Vivax. Fasciola was addressing the Pauls in low, measured tones.

". . . and we want the attack ads to focus on how Mayor Baumgarten's opposition to the new bond program is already causing severe pain to middle- and low-income New Yorkers. Two million jobs lost. Three million adults on some form of public assistance. Young working people leaving the state, welfare rolls spiking. The tax burden for city support services jumped eight percent last year. And what does Mayor Baumgarten want to do? Cut jobs. Slash spending. Impose draconian austerity measures to repair the city's finances and bail out the bankers while the average New Yorker has to put up with higher taxes, fewer services, a bankrupt police force that can't handle the crime wave, and a health care system that's stretched to the breaking point by budget cuts, a sharp rise in the homeless population, and rampant disease. Mayor Baumgarten wants to make all that worse . . ."

Meanwhile, at down desk center, resplendent in all his three-piece cream-on-cream worsted majesty, sat Governor Mario Mansoni, enthroned. His audience, Senator Theodore Usanius Rickover Davidson III, sat across a river of mahogany from him.

The governor was saying: "So I can issue a message of necessity on the SRC bill. That'll let us fast-track the vote instead of having it sit on every desk in the Senate for three days, waiting for someone to oppose it."

The senator was nodding. He added, "I'll put the word out to our side of the chamber to convene in the conference room when the vote comes to the floor. Since absent legislators automatically get a yes vote, the bill should sail through the Senate, no problem."

"The problem's not with the Senate, it's with the assembly." Mansoni steepled his fingers. "Terry Saginata's the Rules Committee chair, and he's the fucking king of all budget hawks. If he votes no, the committee could stall this bill, maybe even kill it. We need to get him on our side."

Ascaris, done with his call, had drifted over while the governor was speaking. Senator Theodore Usanius Rickover Davidson III slowly smiled at Governor Mansoni, who turned and smiled at Deputy Comptroller Ascaris, who turned to smile at Public Advocate Fasciola, whose eavesdropping ability was legendary—it was said around City Hall that he could hold one conversation while listening in on three.

Fasciola smiled back, dismissed the Three Pauls with a wave of his hand, and pulled out a cell phone he thought secure.

• • •

Steinway Hall on West Fifty-seventh Street in midtown Manhattan was closed on Mondays, which made it an ideal location for much-needed afternoon trysts between the City Council speaker's special aide, Tsetse Fly, and her inamorato, Trey Panasome, a junior budget analyst from the city's OMB.

It was a tough job, being the speaker's assistant in these turbulent times. Grueling Board of Ed meetings. Shouting matches with other council members, union reps, aldermen. Threatening calls from lawyers of every stripe. She was overworked, underpaid, and not appreciated, but having worked so hard to attain this position, she found herself incapable of leaving it. Izzy (the speaker insisted on casual first-name usage when they were alone but, in contrarian passive-aggressive fashion, would scold her if she did so in public, especially in front of the press) wouldn't last a week without her, and so made it exceedingly difficult for her to leave. Thus, as a small but satisfyingly rebellious treat, Tsetse Fly would occasionally make room in the day's crammed schedule to slip away from the grinding maw of municipal affairs, to seek release and solace in the embrace of her paramour.

The city afforded many enclaves rich in possibility for ardent young lovers, but Steinway Hall was her favorite. She knew nothing of the firm of Warren and Wetmore that had designed the venerable space, but she adored its magnificent rotunda and the domed ceiling adorned with the paintings of Paul Arndt, of whom she also knew nothing. Nor did she recognize the works of Wyeth, Seyffert, Chambers, or Kent, but that did not prevent her from enjoying their paintings through a warm erotic mist. And she had no idea who Mia LaBerge was, nor that she had painted the one-of-a-kind art case piano that stood resplendent in the center of the rotunda's ground-floor gallery. All Tsetse Fly knew was that here, bent over the key frame, her knees on the cushioned bench, her nipples gently sliding over the polished wood of the action, was where she felt safe. Safe from the clawing, maddening demands of the city, as she slowly rocked back and forth, impaled on the thick, pulsing phallus of her Lothario, which filled and stretched her rectum as no other had. That they had found each other amid the rush and danger of the city meant that neither vocation nor protocol should keep them apart. Tsetse Fly *needed* Trey Panasome, and she knew, deep in her bowels, that Trey Panasome needed her. Beneath the Swarovski chandelier, spread-eagled over the piano case, with outstretched fingers moist and trembling on the stretcher bar, she felt completed, the void left in her core by the ceaseless demands of her station integrated anew into a solid, throbbing whole.

"What the FUCK are you doing?" City Council Speaker Isabella Trichinella screeched from beneath the colonnaded arch.

There was nothing, nothing she could do, nowhere to hide or run. It had all been a dream, these lustful, life-affirming moments with Trey, moments of sweetness stolen among the crumbling ruins of a once-grand metropolis. Her clothes were on the floor, along with scattered sheets of Beethoven's Thirteenth Sonata. All that was within reach was her purse, into which she hastily slipped a small pump bottle of Liquid Silk; Trey Panasome, who was fully clothed, hurriedly shoved a tube of Mandelay into his fanny pack.

"Get the fuck out of here," Trichinella growled murderously at him, "I'll deal with you later."

It was difficult to tell whether he looked at her or at his lover, owing to the Kangol ball cap and bulbous Gucci sunglasses he had on, but Trey Panasome must have heard the speaker's tone right through the Beats buds in his ears, for he made a manly display of disappearing fast.

Tsetse Fly had one foot off the bench and one hand outstretched, within inches of her panties, when her employer rasped: "Don't." Chancing a look over her left shoulder, Tsetse Fly could see that the speaker had come in alone. That meant the security detail would be outside. Trey would run right into them.

The spike heels of the speaker's stilettos—manta ray slingbacks; Tsetse Fly *loved* those shoes—were muffled by the baize carpeting as she walked toward the piano.

"Please don't hurt him," Tsetse Fly pleaded, ashamed at her weakness.

"I don't intend to," replied Isabella Trichinella in a flinty voice. "He'll keep his mouth shut if he wants to keep his job. Besides, OMB doesn't have the budget for new hires. I'll scare him a bit, maybe get some of his pay docked. He won't mind." The speaker was standing next to her, one hand on the piano's music shelf, her face close and her eyes hard. Tsetse Fly was still on her knees on the bench, but she instinctively drew her arms over her breasts, her lips parted and trembling.

Trichinella snapped her fingers, the sound loud and harsh in the marble chamber, and pointed at the soundboard bridge. Tsetse Fly immediately uncrossed and extended her arms and leaned forward, assuming her former position.

"Your boyfriend's going to have to do without you for a few days," Trichinella said in a more neutral tone. "They're getting ready to fast-track a vote in Albany on our new SRC bonds, and they want to lock in a yes. With our budget shortfall here, there's bound to be resistance from upstate as well as the mayor's office. So we need Albany to muscle City Hall. Our team's working up a plan to tilt things our way." The speaker was absently untying the belt of her raincoat as she talked.

Tsetse Fly chanced a question. "What about the underwriters?"

"They'll play ball if the state's behind the issuance. The wards will be circulating attack ads, TV and online, with union backing. They'll focus on the layoffs, the budget cuts, the lack of services, the rising number of New Yorkers on public assistance, homelessness, crime, the usual." Trichinella shrugged off her raincoat. She sported her trademark men's button-down, leather vest, and trousers, black on black. "No bank wants to look like it's starving the population. Besides, they need the revenue they'd get from the service fees. They're all drowning in red tape from Dodd-Frank. And they've been losing retail customers in droves for a couple years."

"Why?" Tsetse Fly asked, playing for time.

"Don't play dumb with me," the speaker barked, and Tsetse Fly dropped her head between her elbows, her eyes locked on the pedal box. "You know why, and we don't need to call attention to it. The banks will go along if Albany and Washington lean on them enough. Besides the mayor, the only one who might make a stink is Julius Exmoor, and the public already thinks he's Satan. The banks aren't the problem; the problem is Albany. We've got the Senate covered, but we need to swing the assembly." Trichinella wore no jewelry save for a man's tank watch on her left wrist. It glinted coldly as she unbuttoned her right cuff and began rolling up her sleeve.

"How do we do that?" Tsetse Fly whispered to the sostenuto pedal.

"That's where you come in," Trichinella replied with an unpleasant smile. "Terry Saginata is the Rules Committee chair. You remember him from that cancer fund-raiser last year? He couldn't take his eyes off you, and he's brought up your name every fucking time I've talked to him since. He's known to have very particular tastes—you two have a lot in common. You've got the rest of the week off, starting now. You're on the seven-fifteen out of Penn Station, gets into Albany Rensselaer at nine-forty-five tonight. He's staying at the Desmond. There's a committee hearing tomorrow morning. We should know by noon whether Saginata's backing our bonds or not." Trichinella finished rolling up her sleeve halfway up her right bicep; the contours and vascularity spoke of strength and disciplined training.

Tsetse Fly's eyes, which had slid closed as she savored the cunning and power in the speaker's voice, snapped open. "What will you do without me?" she whispered.

Trichinella leaned her head in closer so that her lips nearly touched the helix of Tsetse Fly's left ear, her breath hot on the scapha. A shudder that Tsetse Fly could not suppress ran down the length of her body, making her waver slightly on the bench.

"Giardia will take your place for a while," the speaker hissed, and Tsetse Fly could hear the malicious grin in her voice. This was meant to sting, and it did. Giardia was a hot young eager beaver under a year into a new post as a councilman's aide. A competitive swimmer with the body to prove it, she was known to pursue any opportunities for climbing the municipal government ladder with feverish abandon. Pain, jealousy, and rage swirled like windblown leaves within Tsetse Fly's mind; she bit her lips and squeezed her eyes shut, fighting back tears.

Then Trichinella leaned forward a bit farther, so her lips brushed the shell of Tsetse Fly's left ear, making her inhale sharply. "When you get back to town, go to your safe-deposit box in that subway bank. I know you have one," the speaker whispered throatily. "Take It Back has one there, too. Washington's okayed the release of the funds pending a yes vote. Necator will meet you there with the cash."

Tsetse Fly's purse still lay open on the piano's side arm. Trichinella reached inside with her left hand as she sibilated into Tsetse Fly's ear, retrieving the lubricant without looking. Gently but firmly, she rested her right hand, palm down, between Tsetse Fly's scapulae, with just the slightest insinuation of force.

Tsetse Fly looked up over her shoulder at her boss with gratitude and without fear, a wry smile drawing the left side of her mouth up. Trey could wait. There were times her job was unbearable and times when she wouldn't trade it for the world. Like right . . . *NOW*—

THE WINE TASTING

ING KAN ISN'T HAVING A GOOD DAY.
I'm guessing this from the aggravated tones coming from the living room, where she lays coiled on a butter-soft Italian leather divan, barking angrily into that weird-looking phone of hers. Damned if I know what she's saying, but you can bet she's not happy with whoever's on the other end of the line. Her perfectly painted mouth is twitching, her free hand playing with the hem of her immaculate white silk robe, her hair (pulling back when she remembers she's had it done for tonight's event), her nails (stopping short of chewing them when she realizes she just had a manicure). She has been acting awfully strange lately, even without these tense calls.

Ing Kan cuts the connection and throws her phone across the room onto another couch just as I come in on my way back to the kitchen with some champagne flutes. Maybe it's because I'm enjoying seeing her keyed up like this that I think I can talk to her on a level playing field.

—Bad day? I ask breezily.

When Ing Kan turns her eyes to me, I realize instantly how big a mistake I've made. Her eyes seek, grab, hold, and throttle mine. I try to maintain forward momentum to get me back to the kitchen, but it's too late. She says icily:

—I'm sorry you had to see that. Would you be so kind as to retrieve my phone?

My mind rummages noisily through three possible responses: I could do what she asks and not makes any waves (most likely); I could try to verbally backhand her by claiming I wasn't hired for that sort of thing, which would inevitably get back to my boss (most problematic); or I could tell her to fuck off (most desirable). I settle for the first option, carefully shuffling flutes between my fingers to accommodate the phone—it really is a weird little gizmo. Seeing as I've just been demoted from chef to maid, I figure I should try to save face.

—Man trouble again? I say, a little more quietly and delicately.

Ing Kan seems to appreciate that I'm showing her the proper deference. Or maybe she just likes watching my reaction when she takes the phone from my hand, when the contact with her planate skin sends a visible tremor up my arm. Her eyes seem to catch the ambient light in the room and amplify it with some inner voltage. She is clearly delighted by my discomfort. Damn her.

But her glee doesn't last; the wattage in her eyes goes cold. Whatever that call was about, it's really rocked her boat.

—I tried to help a man, a very powerful man in China, Ing Kan says distantly, her eyes sliding from me to her phone. —He and I have had business dealings for several years. Recently, he has run afoul of men more powerful than he, men at the very center of the government. He asked for the kind of help that is not mine to give. He sees my reluctance as a form of betrayal and is threatening to implicate me in his troubles.

She blinks languidly, once, and seems to come back to her surroundings. Her eyes unexpectedly dart to mine in a shift I feel in the small of my back.

—I imagine you of all people can comprehend the potential difficulties that can arise from helping others, yes?

Holy shit.

She knows.

Ing Kan knows I've been stealing.

She's not saying it, but she knows—she has to know.

And she's letting me know that this knowledge is hers to deploy at a whim.

My knees feel weak. I've just gone from being a gainfully employed private chef to a possible prison inmate in the space of a phone call I didn't even understand.

Ing Kan, damn her, is taking power and joy from watching the truth dawn on me. She's recovered her poise and equilibrium at the expense of mine.

And then she hits me with the *coup de grâce*. In one fluid motion, she stands and turns, pirouetting toward the bedroom she shares with my employer and possible chief accuser. Her robe, which apparently was untied, parts widely and silently so that I may behold Ing Kan's transcendent naked body for a window that will never close in my mind. In an instant I drink her all in, from the impossibly elegant promontories of her breasts, to the golden roadway of her belly, to the glabrescent pulchritude of her vulva, to the delicate pearl stickpin in her labia, exquisitely crafted to nearly—but not quite—match its surroundings.

And then the window is closed, and Ing Kan is gone. All that remains is my trembling. I can hear the tinkling of the flutes in my fingers and, just at its edge, her laughter.

● ● ●

Mr. Chiroptera, the house manager, was kind enough—if you could call it that—to bring me a bottle of each of the wines being served tonight, but apparently, he forgot the champagne. Ing Kan has confined herself to her bedchamber to prepare for this evening; it's safe for me to move around the penthouse. So off I go into the magnificent wine salon, a room I could happily die in, to fetch a bottle so I can complete the evening's menu for Mr. Redhawk's interview.

The salon is set for a seduction: silk and velvet and brocade everywhere, in red and gold habiliment. Ing Kan must really want this coverage badly. Since it's Convention Week, there must be some political slant, though far be it from me to fathom what it is.

Heading back to the kitchen, I catch a fragment of something so incongruous it stops me in my tracks.

Someone's singing.

In *this* place.

I stop and strain my ears to make out the words:

I am the Moosie Moose.

I have a big caboose.

And if you put it in your mouth

I'll sing and dance for you.

What comes next sounds even more out of place.

It's laughter.

A *child's* laughter.

Now, that is not the sort of thing you hear in Castle Redhawk. This whole place screams CHILDREN KEEP OUT.

It sounds like it's coming from the office. Wait, the tone has changed, now it's more declarative, like someone practicing a speech:

THE CLOSING OF THE CHARITABLE CONTRIBUTION TAX LOOP-HOLE HAS DIRECTLY CONTRIBUTED TO THE RAPID DECLINE IN OUR OLDEST AND MOST VENERABLE EDUCATIONAL AND CULTURAL INSTITUTIONS. THERE IS NO DATA AVAILABLE TO QUANTIFY THE AMOUNT OF REVENUE RAISED, JUST AS THERE IS NO WAY TO QUANTIFY THE DAMAGE DONE AND THAT WHICH WILL BE DONE BY THE SHUTTERING OF YOUNG MINDS TO THE RICH TAPESTRY OF CREATIVE ACHIEVEMENT. AT WHAT POINT IS THE IMAGINATION SUBORDINATED TO THE BOTTOM LINE? THERE ARE OTHER WAYS TO MAKE A BUCK THAT DO NOT COME AT SUCH TERRIBLE EXPENSE.

I'm at the door of the study. It's open and unguarded, which is yet another weird thing about today. I hadn't noticed it before, but the guard who usually stands here is gone.

In fact, *all* the guards are gone.

Not only that, the staff is gone. The house manager, the Filipino maids Ing Kan lords over, and the goon squad—everyone else who usually works here is gone.

I've been standing too long in the doorway. Alex Redhawk is looking at me with a slightly bemused smile.

—Et tu, Chef? He smiles. He has such a disarming, boyish grin. Five-star teeth, of course. A jawline I could chop onions on. These alone make him the polar opposite of Richard, my boyfriend. My mind takes a mad fleeting swerve into the realm of the improper before I manage to recover.

—Hi, uh, I, just had to get one last bottle for tonight's tasting menu, I manage. *God, Beth, get a grip. You don't want the boss to think he's hired some flake.*

The office overlooks Bryant Park, looking north up Sixth Avenue. There are two huge monitors on a gargantuan desk behind him. One has the grinning, squealing visage of a teething toddler. I must have a really stupid look on my face because Alex—stop it, Beth, *Mr. Redhawk*—says:

—My nephew. Jack. Just turned three. I was supposed to spend Labor

Day with my brother and his family, but I've been tied up with all this Convention Week stuff, and I'm trying to make up for it. He turns back to the monitor and makes a few cooing noises at the kid, who laughs and squeals and cries, "A-wekk, A-wekk."

The other monitor has a block of text on it, including the lines I must have heard earlier. For the first time, I notice Alex is wearing a headset with a lip mike, like the kind Richard has at home for using voice-recognition software. As though he can read my mind, Alex says offhandedly:

—I'm supposed to give a speech at a fund-raising party next week. At Julius Exmoor's house. You know, the old Frick museum? Allegedly, it's for me to lay out my plans for deficit reduction, foreign direct investment, taxes, stuff like that. But everyone really wants to see where I stand on the National IRA bonds.

It finally hits me. All the hints I've been getting, from Jonah to Richard and even Ing Kan—Alex isn't just a rich businessman, he's a rich businessman who's getting into politics. No, wait, he's already *in* politics, he's . . .

—That's what tonight's tasting is for, right? That reporter, I blurt. Oh God, I just cannot stop putting my foot in my mouth in front of him. What is *wrong* with me? Whatever the boss wants, the boss gets, it doesn't matter what it's *for*. I really have to watch myself. If I'm this antsy around Alex, how am I going to get through an evening of Ing Kan and obscenely expensive wines?

Alex, damn him, just chuckles through his nose at my evident distress. Something like that. She wants to ask me if I plan to run for president.

I nearly drop the bottle. Which is easily worth fifteen hundred bucks. And I say the one thing I definitely should NOT say:

—Are you?

I'm practically whispering. The kid on-screen is cackling like a hyena at me.

Alex's handsome smile fades; his eyes lose focus and move down. *Oh no, oh shit, oh fuck, oh now I've done it, I am so sorry, Mr. Redhawk, please just forget any of this ever happened, I'm going back to the kitchen this instant and I'll never—*

—I don't know, he says flatly.

What do you say to that? To someone who *might* run for president, who actually *can* but *won't*?

—To tell you the truth, I'm not really interested. The presidency's just a front for whichever party controls Congress. Politicians bore me. Given my standard of living, the thought of a drudge job in public service is less than appealing. Don't get me wrong. I hate things the way they are, and I have some pretty strong ideas about changing them, which is what tonight's interview is all about. But personally, I'd rather spend the evening with Jack here. His grin returns, and he makes some faces at the kid, who goes berserk with glee.

I can only stand in the doorway with a fifteen-hundred-dollar bottle of wine in my hand, in stunned silence.

My boss.

The Man Who Would Not Be President.

Who is a billionaire.

And almost criminally handsome.

Who is also good with children.

And just happens to be shacked up with the most exotic, mysterious, alluring, and unsettling woman I've ever met in my life, who makes me feel like a mouse being toyed with by a leopard.

I'm not going to think about this anymore.

—Beth? You okay?

Goddamn him, he actually sounds concerned.

I need to get out of here.

—Yes, well, I'm sure you'll know what to do, I stammer, nearly smashing the bottle on the doorjamb as I spin away and almost gallop back to the kitchen, the only place in this surreal castle in the sky where I feel safe.

● ● ●

Alex—more likely, Ing Kan—pulled out all the stops for this wine tasting. Naturally, I've been tasked with creating a suitably spectacular tasting menu:

> —Beluga caviar (actually, Kaluga caviar, mistakenly known as River Beluga caviar "Malossol," wholly illegal in the U.S.) Pairing: *1979 Veuve Clicquot La Grande Dame champagne.*

> —Butter poached lobster and *kumamoto* oysters with fresh *uni en coquille* with passionfruit tapioca pearls and *yuzu*-vanilla-bean foam (the butter for the poaching also has slabs of applewood-

smoked bacon to add a depth of flavor and more *umami* without it tasting of bacon).

Pairing: *1997 Domaine Ramonet Montrachet Grand Cru Côte de Beaune*

—Rare oolong-tea-smoked roasted duck breast and foie gras *roulade.* Crispy skin with five-spice oolong tea and Burgundy mahogany glaze. Burgundy-truffle reduction and fresh shaved white truffles, house-made rose petal and sour cherry conserve.

Pairing: *1969 Domaine de la Romanee-Conti La Tache Grand Cru Monopole Côte de Nuits*

—Pork belly, braised in white soy sauce, *matsutake* mushroom *jus,* and *sake* lees. The pork belly is pressed and slow-roasted until crisp, with a crackling, caramelized crust. Served over wilted pea shoots and roasted *matsutake* mushrooms.

Pairing: *1997 Domaine Armand Rousseau Pere et Fils Chambertin Grand Cru Burgundy*

—A duo of Kobe beef:
1) Raw sashimi-style carpaccio with shaved porcini mushrooms, wild baby arugula, and Paolo Bea single-grove olive oil
2) Seared filet mignon with seared foie gras, Bordeaux, cognac, and perigord truffle reduction with fresh black currants over a potato and parsnip puree.

Pairing: *1959 Domaines Barons de Rothschild Château Lafite Rothschild Pauillac*

Of course, Ing Kan laughed at my efforts:

—*Amuse-bouche*, merriment for the mouth. You've got to hand it to the French. They can't field an army or run a country, but they do have an unparalleled sense of linguistic irony.

Standing silently behind her in the kitchen, Mr. Chiroptera was a stone-faced golem, while the Filipino maids scurried this way and that, giggling quietly, their eyes flicking from each other to me and back. I could have found more sympathy in a microwave.

That was hours ago. Now I've gotten everything prepped, poured, and plated, and I'm hiding in the kitchen sampling the wines, only one of which I've ever tried before. Hey, I'm the chef, I'm *supposed* to make sure the food and wines are well paired, aren't I?

I'm starting with half a flute of the 1979 Veuve Clicquot La Grande Dame, savoring its notes of vanilla bean and orange peel while watching Alex and Ing Kan welcoming their guest on the bank of security monitors in the kitchen. Mr. Chiroptera told me to oversee the wine tasting from here but not to come out of the kitchen for any reason. Come to think of it, given the importance of the occasion, I can't understand why he's not working with me tonight. Where is everybody?

The interviewer has arrived. She's a TV anchor for one of the morning financial-news programs on the Baumgarten Network, which plays on several monitors around the penthouse all day long. She has this weird name, Stephaany, I can't even pronounce her last name, I think she's Hawaiian Chinese, and she's an absolute stunner. She's wearing a skintight Gethsemane dress that probably cost more than I make in four months; it broadcasts a figure that sculptors would die to re-create. When did TV personalities get like this?

Maybe it's my second glass of wine—the Burgundy, with its notes of burnt chocolate and freshly turned earth—that makes me notice something's not right. I'm watching Alex, Ing Kan, and Stephaany splayed out on the divans in the salon, chatting comfortably, Ing Kan making occasional body contact with Alex (bitch) when I catch it out of the corner of my eye. There's an extra camera—no, four of them, covering four new angles in the salon. It's my job to know everything in the kitchen where I'm working, and I know as sure as I'm standing here that those cameras weren't there last week.

The monitors have been carefully incorporated into the existing display so as to blend in perfectly. If I weren't me, if I weren't a little buzzed from the wine, if I didn't feel like I wanted to break a bottle over Ing Kan's head, I might not have noticed. But they're here, on the sly, and they're recording.

The new camera angles are much more close-up and high-resolution than the normal ones for the room. From here I can see the wet shine on Stephaany's lips and the warm brightness of her smile. From here I can watch Ing Kan's jeweled hand on Stephaany's clavicle, transmitting an almost imperceptible caress. From here I can see Alex crossing and then recrossing his legs.

Oh no.

I pour a full glass of the three-thousand-dollar Pauillac and knock it back in one gulp, notes of swamp gas and broken rusty pipe all the way from the nose to the finish. I clamp my eyes shut on the tears already welling up. I barely manage to get the wineglass back on the counter without crushing it and grinding glass shards into my hand. My throat is constricting, my pulse is pounding in my ears, and now, goddammit, of course, my pain hits me, an upwelling of agony that radiates from my core to my head. I have to steady myself on the edge of the counter to stand.

That's why I'm working alone tonight.

That's why I was told to stay in the kitchen, in front of the monitors.

This is all Ing Kan's doing.

She got Alex to dismiss the staff. She got the new cameras installed—I don't know how, maybe her friends at the Chinese embassy helped—and sure as shit, she set this whole scene up.

She set *Alex* up.

The Man Who Might Be President.

She'll have him on video.

Doing exactly the sort of thing presidential candidates should not be caught on video doing.

I pry open my wet eyes. What I see are not the motions of those supposedly engaged in an interview. Or, for that matter, a wine tasting.

The occupants of the wine salon are engaged in tasting each other.

One of the new cameras is positioned for a shot of the large divan in salon center, on which Ing Kan and Alex are languorously extricating Stephaany from her dress. The image clarity surpasses that of any surveillance feed I've seen on restaurant security cameras. Stephaany was not wearing a bra; her breasts are the exquisite ovate projections that are the goal of painters and gemstone cutters. The nipple that isn't covered by Ing Kan's mouth is sorrel-tinted and very hard, its prominent mount encircled and gently clasped in Alex's strong left hand. Stephaany's eyes are closed, her back is arched, her lustrous hair is flowing over Alex's now-bare chest and shoulders as she leans back against him, drinking hungrily from his mouth. Ing Kan's hands are busy below, separating Stephaany from a sheer black thong, her hands quickly moving back up to the smooth, hairless juncture of her thighs, fingertips moving in a rhythm echoed in Stephaany's undulating hips.

I need to get out of here now, right now, but I cannot move. I am transfixed by the scene unfolding on-camera, Alex gently levering the nude reporter to her feet and Ing Kan positioning herself between her legs, scarlet-tipped hands prising her thighs apart. There is audio feed for these new cameras, and the aural resolution is every bit as clear. Stephaany lets out a long, low wail of pleasure as Ing Kan deftly guides Alex's cock—a long, thick, smoothly magnificent specimen—up inside her.

I don't even see how I pour myself one more, the La Tâche this time, and drain it greedily, notes of molten lead and ground glass filling my mouth. My pain is reaching threshold. I need to get out of here.

On-screen, Ing Kan is kneeling between Stephaany's quavering legs, her tongue moving artfully from labia to clitoris and back. Alex is standing behind the reporter, thrusting into her very deeply, very slowly, drawing a loudening series of moans from her. On a backstroke, before his next thrust, Ing Kan skillfully withdraws his cock and directs it into her mouth, to check the fluid level of Stephaany's excitement.

I know this because she's watching me.

Every part of Ing Kan is focused on pleasuring her two partners, but her eyes are looking directly into one of the new spy cameras.

At me.

Ing Kan knows I'm watching.

She knows I can't stop looking at her as her lips and tongue expertly work Alex's cock, drawing shudders from him as he towers above her.

She wants me to see this.

So that I will know the full extent of her power.

And now I can see it all, in its horrible sprawling perfection.

Ing Kan has her hooks in a man who inhabits the highest tier of American society, who manages billions of dollars, who is contemplating a run for the presidency, whom she now has on high-definition video in a three-way with herself (a foreign diplomat and most likely a spy) and a well-known TV anchor (who, I notice for the first time, is wearing wedding rings). Blackmail doesn't get any better.

Wait, there's more. She has me by the nipples, too. She knows—I don't know how, but she does—that I've been stealing from Alex. If she can pull off this kind of stunt with cameras and reporters inside a high-security penthouse, she can certainly track my movements and discover my thieving. And she knows I won't say anything to anyone, ever, because I'll lose my job, my health insurance, and probably wind up in jail.

My pain flares up in such a bolt of white-hot excruciation that I don't see anything anymore. I don't see the hallway, the door, the elevator, the street. I don't see the stairs, the platform, the glaring headlights of the subway as it pulls into the station. I don't see the homeless I might well have fed, the evening commuters and partygoers and predators and freaks, New York's nighttime carnival retinue. I don't see Richard's building, I don't see his front door, I don't see him as he sees me and starts shouting, *Beth, what's wrong, what happened.* I don't see the bathroom door, the medicine cabinet, the emergency bottle inside. I don't see myself sinking to the floor, yanking my pants off over my shoes, tearing my panties to shreds, uncapping the bottle and shaking the droplets of neem oil onto my searing vagina, my groin, my whole pelvic frontage—anything, *anything,* to make the pain stop. I don't see the bathroom door shaking on its hinges as Richard pounds on it from the other side, calling my name. I don't see my reflection in the full-length mirror on the inside of the bathroom door, half-naked and crying, my face a contorted mask of fear and pain, my body wracked with spasms, twitching on the tile, helpless, broken, utterly lost.

I see only Ing Kan's eyes locked on mine, glinting with malice and exultant with victory, as I am reduced to a fading shadow in the gathering blackness that engulfs me.

(DETECTION)

DOWN IN THE BOWELS of the Second Avenue subway, behind a makeshift soup kitchen, inside the biggest shadow banking operation in New York's history, the governor's courier, the wormy man called Necator, is having a Bad Day.

Necator is Governor Mansoni's personal bagman. A veteran of many Democratic administrations in Albany, he is a government mule, hauling instructions and money that his superiors wish to keep private. The instructions form the nervous system of the Democratic machine in this part of the country; the cash keeps that machine well oiled and leaves no digital spoor.

He has been making too many trips down into the subway bank. There have been too many clandestine money runs, too many arguments and crossed wires happening as Convention Week oozes inexorably onward. A pallid, moist, frightened man by nature, Necator is worried that his repeated trips underground will invite unwanted attention. His business requires the utmost discretion.

His fear reaches new heights as he stands bookended between two massive guards, in front of the bank's would-be CEO, in her private chambers at the rearmost section of the bank complex, far out of sight of her customers.

This is no standard bank chief: She is the first criminal queenpin of New York City. She boasts the largest loan book in town. Her safe-deposit boxes (originally lockers meant for transit workers) are prized by commonfolk and crooks alike.

It should also be noted that she is an exceptional beauty, though one marked by a slight air of coldness, of toughness; this is a woman who takes what she wants. She has the physique of a dedicated athlete, all sharp angles and planes and veined muscle.

She would not have come this far up the ladder of criminal enterprise without possessing exceptional instincts. These are telling her that it will soon be time to step off this particular rung. The clock is ticking on her operation, which she doubts will last beyond Convention Week. In fact, she has planned for it not to. There have been far too many politicians for her to stomach, although they were contacts she had to make. But she has tarried too long with them. You lie down with dogs, you wake up with fleas.

This woman has immense ambition and no time for parasites.

She is known only as LA.

And at the moment she feels her time is being wasted by the fat courier whining in front of her.

—I'm telling you it has to be now! Speaker Trichinella's already sent her aide up to Albany to meet the Rules Committee chair! The vote's going to the floor by Friday! We need the cash now—

—So front it yourself, LA drawls. She knows well that buying politicians is a requirement of growing any substantial criminal enterprise, but she will never understand their assumption that the underworld is their personal ATM. She figures this is a reflex they developed from decades of squeezing money out of legitimate businesses.

—We can't, that's what I'm tellin' ya, wails the fat courier, Oversight's all over us, OMB, the independent inspector general, even some a those pricks from the comptroller's office who're supposed to be on *our* side! We can't make a distribution this big from a government account, it's gotta come outta the Take It Back slush fund! That's what it's for, ya know, *contingencies?* The wormy man is sweating and breathing hard, visibly unnerved at being a small, flabby body in a group of large, exceedingly muscular ones. He has no illusions about his place on the food chain.

LA shakes her head, wondering how these politicians could be so stupid as to think she would simply give back the money they funnel through her bank, no questions asked. She flicks her eyes to her guards, and the courier is hauled out, his protests ringing off the walls.

The courier nearly expires from his climb back aboveground. His heart is further punished by a message on his phone from an agency he wants no truck with: the NYPD. His worst fears are being realized. Sweating copiously, he waddles at speed out of the station's Ninety-fourth Street egress, rudely brushing past a young woman in chef's whites carrying a bulging military-style knapsack. Both are caught on a hidden surveillance camera that does not belong to LA. The courier never notices—he is too busy punching numbers into his phone, which he thinks is secure.

• • •

"Got something," Irukanji called out. ODIN, the Behr, and the rest of the team stopped what they were doing to listen.

"It's that Necator guy, calling the governor's private line," Irukanji went on, fingers over his earbuds as he eavesdropped on the cellular transmission. "He's all freaked out. Says he just got a call from NYPD. Says they want to ask him about subways—no, something in the subway, near the mosque."

"Plot it," grunted ODIN, frowning.

More tapping. "Manhattan, East Ninety-fourth Street between Second and Third avenues, heading west," Irukanji sang out.

ODIN's lips were pursed in thought. "What's the closest subway station?"

Irukanji's fingertips danced on his laptop. "Ninety-sixth Street, Second Avenue line, with egresses on Ninety-fourth and Ninety-seventh."

"The cops are onto the bank," the Behr muttered. This was not welcome news.

"Maybe," Irukanji said distractedly, still working. "He was asking for cover from Albany, right from the governor's office, no code, no bullshit. He's scared."

"So is he going to meet with the cops or not?"

Irukanji nodded. "The governor said he had to, no matter what. If he didn't, the cops would know something's up."

"If the cops knew about the bank, they'd have raided it already." ODIN exhaled. "Could be they were looking for something else and stumbled across him. Anybody in government would get their attention, but they probably haven't figured out what he's into yet. You get anything else?"

Irukanji was rolling now. "Yeah, Necator stalled them. The cops called a meet with him tomorrow, Morningside Park in Harlem, noon. Requested by a lieutenant in OCID," Irukanji added, his voice rising, "name of

Santiago."

The nondescript man code-named ODIN was at his "easel," a digital bulletin board that folded down to the size of a tablet. Extended, it was a six-by-six foot square of electromagnetic catch "paper" material now hanging from a nail in the wall. Using a specialized stylus that could transfer handwritten notes, audio, and image files, the nondescript man had worked up a hierarchical chart on his digital drawing board. The name at the top of the chart was MASSI, CADUTA; adjacent to the name were JPEG and 96-bit MP3 files (photos and audio intercepts, respectively) thoughtfully provided by Irukanji. Caduta Massi's name was connected by bright digital lines to several others: ASCARIS, ANTHONY; FASCIOLA, PETER; MANSONI, MARIO; TRICHINELLA, ISABELLA. Each name sprouted other connecting lines. Fasciola's name bore three links: P. FALCIPARUM; P. OVALE; P. VIVAX. Trichinella's name went first to a GIARDIA, L., then on to one FLY, T., which in turn linked to SAGINATA, T.

Two names were well off to one side of the chart. The first, linked to Caduta Massi, bore a photo of a young woman with short hair and multiple piercings. The second was linked to nearly all the others. This contact, accompanied by a photo of a pallid, wormy-looking man, bore only a single name: NECATOR.

The easel, stylus, and nearly all the software ODIN's unit was running had been acquired by Irukanji through Dark Web channels. Specifically, these materials were purchased through an illegal online exchange from a highly specialized purveyor of such goods, known only by his online moniker, the Khazar.

Another series of stylus commands conjured up a map of Manhattan on the easel. ODIN highlighted the area around Morningside Park and magnified it. A red dot from a laser pointer within the stylus stabbed out onto the easel, moving along Morningside Boulevard along the park's western border, lingering over several locations: Seminary Row; St. Luke's Hospital; Greenhouse Nursery School; the Cathedral of St. John the Divine . . .

ODIN's mission parameters were clear: His team was to illuminate and monitor the DNC network between Washington, Albany, and New York City, back-channeling all intel to Senator Cordryceps, who was particularly interested in all matters that pertained to funding. The senator suspected Democratic involvement with the subway bank but had no proof.

Cordryceps wanted to hit his opponents where it hurt them the most—in the wallet, where greed could turn each link of the chain into its weakest point—but needed more information.

ODIN's instructions were clear: Any and all law enforcement was to be kept out of the operation until the senator's trap was sprung. Above all, *nothing should happen to the subway bank.* ODIN figured the senator—maybe the GOP itself—had money there as well.

But that was irrelevant. Right now his main concern was that Necator was meeting an NYPD lieutenant named Santiago in Morningside Park tomorrow, to spill the beans about the bank.

The original plan was for ODIN to gather enough dirt on the DNC for Senator Cordryceps to go public; the ensuing media frenzy would upend Convention Week, and the Dems would be routed, resulting in a massive coup for the GOP.

If that approach didn't work, Cordryceps still had ODIN in place.

And ODIN had Bad Boy.

Which was the nickname for the weapons platform they were field-testing on this assignment, a prototype that would be piloted by the Behr. Officially designated the Mark III Combat Exoskeleton by DARPA, Bad Boy was a heavily armed and armored battle suit to be worn by Special Forces operators in high-intensity conflict zones. The initial concept of the suit was simple: Put the firepower and force protection of a tank into a single-man platform that could be transported in civilian vehicles. The Pentagon procurement mandarins had waved their magic wands, the wizards at DARPA had gotten a-conjuring, and with time and a black budget, Bad Boy's ancestors had taken shape, eventually bequeathing the Mark III. All that was needed was someone skilled and crazy enough to field-test it.

That ODIN was known in certain circles as one with access to such advanced, classified tactical gear was the reason Senator Cordryceps had contracted with him. ODIN was a master of military systems—their use, their strengths, and their weaknesses. In the years since his separation from the army, he'd done a lucrative business field-testing advanced weapons and equipment for a military that was constantly being made to do more with less, thus increasing its reliance on outside "contractors."

Two other former members of ODIN's wartime unit made up the team. Soffitt was seeing to the methanol cooling system attached to the barrel of the modified Mark 48 machine gun in the gauntlet surrounding Bad Boy's left hand; Tyvek was loading in the belts of SLAP rounds. The Behr was working on the stripped-down XM25 grenade launcher in Bad Boy's right-hand gauntlet.

ODIN had been calculating the team's insertion route to gain access to the subway bank as quietly as possible. Now his carefully laid plans had been blown to hell. Because of one fat loudmouth who had managed to catch the attention of the NYPD. Just what ODIN needed.

ODIN glanced at the clock in the corner of his easel, which read 1437 EST. At this time of year, he had about six hours of usable daylight left. And the clock was ticking. They'd have to move fast. But they were very good at that.

ODIN turned away from the easel for the first time since Irukanji had intercepted Necator's call. The others gave him their undivided attention as he spoke: "Necator doesn't talk to the cops. We know where he'll be tomorrow and when. We use the rest of today to recon the AO and set up an ambush site. I'll take him; the rest of you have security. You"—he pointed at Irukanji—"stay here and monitor all transmissions before, during, and after. I want to know where the cops are and who they're talking to at all times. Same with the politicos."

ODIN tapped his stylus, and the easel filled with the blues and greens of an urban map. "The park backs up against Columbia University, so we'll have campus cops to deal with. If NYPD shows up heavy, if anything goes sideways"— he glanced at the Behr— "then Bad Boy goes to college."

ODIN smiled, and now so did the Behr. It was an awful thing to see.

• • •

```
Prime Contract No: N0041756-07-C-4040
Subcontract No: WG-11-S-085
Security Clearance: DARK SECRET
Mandate: DISAGGREGATED PERSISTENT ENGAGEMENT
Area of Operations: DOMESTIC
Mission Profile: CLANDESTINE SR
ST/SO Solution (hereafter "Subject") Code Name: ODIN
```
Records from a now-defunct hospital in Lakeway, TX, indicate subject's birth on or around September 19, 1973. Father _____ and mother _____ both now deceased. No known siblings; an

aunt, _____, also in Lakeway, deceased on or around August 7, 2002.

Little is known of the subject's early years. First solid reference prior to enlistment occurs February 3, 1987, when subject received his first ham radio license (call sign K9ODN). During high school, subject belonged to several electronics and communications clubs, excelling in continuous wave (Morse code) and field-expedient antenna construction. Subject received several written accolades from faculty citing his "innate gift for understanding complex communications" (op. cit. March 7, 1989).

Subject (apparently in response to Iraqi invasion of Kuwait) enlisted in U.S. Army at age 17 (written consent from parents on file). Chose infantry. Arrived Fort Benning, GA, September 27, 1990. Graduated basic training (honor grad) December 1990, received first selection of assignment location. Chose Third Infantry Division at Fort Benning. (NOTE: This facility is home to the Infantry, Airborne Parachutist, Pathfinder, and Ranger training schools, as well as the elite 3rd Battalion 75th Ranger Regiment and Regimental Special Troops battalion units). Subject's mood described as "positive" and "upbeat" (op. cit.).

With the massive force buildup for Operations Desert Shield and Desert Storm, advanced recruits saw training school opportunities otherwise difficult or impossible to obtain. During Advanced Infantry Training (AIT) throughout January 1990, subject broke standing fitness and swim records. FITREPs from this period cite innate leadership, infantry, and field-craft skills. At some point during AIT, subject recommended for Ranger training by _____.

Upon graduating at the top of his class in February 1991, subject notified of his selection for Ranger training. First course (Airborne Parachutist) passed in 3 weeks. Subject began Ranger school March 1991 (Jungle, Mountain, and Desert phases, 90 days). FITREPs from 75th Ranger Regiment command highlighted subject's advanced technical skills with tactical radios, going so far as to call him "exceptionally gifted" (op. cit.). In combat skills, subject earned both the Distinguished

Pistol Shot badge and the Excellence in Competition rifleman's badge.

Once again, subject completed Ranger school at the top of his class (June 1991), earning both the prestigious Hall and Kelso leadership awards. (NOTE: These confer high status—subject passed all graded leadership positions and peer reports. He could not recycle, could not have retest on critical tasks, could not suffer any loss of equipment due to negligence.) In July 1991, subject tried out for the Regimental Reconnaissance Detachment (RRD); subject selected for RRD September 1991.

Subject's initiative (at a time of increasing strains on the military to meet force requirements) combined for a rare opportunity to volunteer for SOF training and deployment. Subject reported for Phase I SFQC training at Camp Mackall, NC, September 12, 1991. Subject's mood reported as "beyond gung-ho" [sic].

As subject went on to be selected for active-duty SOF, then by USARSOC regulations, the only available reports on his performance are prior to Phase V (Robin Sage). Phases I through III saw exceptional performance by the subject across the board, though with surprising breadth. For instance, in Phase II (Language and Culture), the subject evinced both the customary bookishness and a surprising intellectual elasticity; yet in Phase III (SERE), he displayed a record-setting propensity for endurance, stealth, and (during the interrogation module) the requisite coldness.

Subject completed Phase 6 of SFQC at Fort Campbell, KY, on March 15, 1992. One week later, subject was assigned to 5th SFG and shipped out on first operational deployment as an Echo sergeant with ODA 534 in Kuwait as part of Operation Southern Watch under the command of _____.

OSW proved largely uneventful thanks to U.S. enforcement of a regional no-fly zone. The deployment did, however, give the subject valuable in-theater time to acclimate to the demands of his post. According to classified interviews with former members of the unit, the subject acquitted himself well in his new surroundings, showing an affinity for the new (e.g., PRC-5 and PRC-37 satcoms, MBITR short-range high-band radio, TRQ-43 high-frequency radio, and HW/SW encryption systems). Anecdotal descriptions report the subject's mood as "stoked" [sic].

Again circumstances combined to afford the subject a most unique career opportunity. On the referral of Major _____, subject was temporarily (July 1– August 31, 1992) detailed as special communications adviser to TF Blue under the command of V. Admiral Marty Mayer during the naval exercise Millennium Challenge 02. As is well documented, the exercise simulated a regional Mideast invasion by USN assets against a smaller, less technically sophisticated foe (TF Red, commanded by USMC Lt. Gen. Paul Van Riper). TF Red demonstrated the effectiveness of UW tactics against the technologically superior might of the U.S. (swarming missile attacks by small-boat flotillas hidden in commercial shipping convoys, the use of ordinary commercial fishing nets as camouflage screens, the use of messengers instead of phones to transmit orders, the use of light signals instead of radio for field communications) to such a degree that 16 USN vessels were "sunk" during the exercise, and USJFCOM ordered TF Red to follow maneuvers allowing TF Blue to "win." In the ensuing media circus (alleging the waste of $250 million to stage "scripted" vs. "free play" battle simulations), the subject was visibly struck by the effectiveness of asymmetric warfare tactics in the face of technological superiority, as well as what he was heard to call the "blatant fucking hypocrisy" (op. cit.) of the commanders in charge of the exercise. Pleading the need to rejoin his unit for "real" military commitments, subject returned to 5th SFG on September 2, 1992, narrowly avoiding both USN debrief and clamoring media-outlet coverage. According to classified internal USN email correspondence from this period, subject's attitude "sucked" [sic].

With demand for SOF assets rising, 5th SFG was reassigned to Mombasa to provide security for humanitarian aid shipments bound for Somalia. Subject (posted to ODA 564 late 1992) tasked with acquiring intel on Somali clans and warlords that might pose a potential threat to Operation Restore Hope. From Beledweyne in the north to Kismaayo in the south, ODA 564 reported grim findings throughout its AO: Somali airstrips used by violent *qat* exporters (which perpetrated numerous crimes while subject's unit could only watch, the U.S. not being tasked with drug interdiction in the region at the time); cache after cache of heavy weaponry (which most likely made its way to Mogadishu the following year); even coming under fire from militia hidden within crowds of angry civilians (which, given contemporary ROE, subject's unit could not return even in self-defense). Numerous operational maladies plagued the deployment, such as the uselessness of SQTC-mandated Arabic in a linguistic area dominated by traditional African dialects, as well as the unsuitability of Humvees for Somali terrain. On March 3, 1993, SFC Robert Deeks was killed when his Humvee drove over a land mine. Judging by command dispatches, morale in the unit worsened steadily thereafter, and 5th SFG was pulled out of its AO on June 26, being stood down in Mombasa while other units were mobilized for Operation Gothic Serpent. When TF Ranger was mauled shortly thereafter during the Battle of Mogadishu (October 3—4), subject had to be forcibly restrained from boarding a QRF flight of supporting SOF from Mombasa. After a long private meeting with his 5th SFG commanders as well as _____ from USSOCAFRICA, subject was detached from 5th SFG to undergo OCS, returning to Fort Benning, GA, on October 9, 1993. Subject's outlook described as "darkening" (op. cit.).

By the time the subject completed OCS (graduating February 21, 1994), USSOCOM had stood up the SFAUCC to train future forces in specialized urban combat techniques to prevent another catastrophe like Mogadishu. In an unprecedented move, subject took both this course as well as the MOS Phase IV element of the SFQC (for which he had been ineligible as an enlisted man), as well as "fox" training for SF intel personnel. Once again the subject surprised his supervisors by graduating at the top of his respective classes and finishing out 1994 as a fully qualified USARSOF commanding officer. Subject reinstated to 5th SFG January 3, 1995, for immediate deployment to Kosovo in support of Operation Joint Endeavor. Mandatory psychological evaluation prior to deployment reported subject's mood as "vastly improved" (op. cit.).

For the first time, the subject was given a command of his own: ODA 666, which would become one of most arcane, highly decorated, and rightfully feared SOF units in the history of covert operations.

But not right away. From 1996—99, ODA 666 worked largely behind the scenes, building networks among local populations to counter friction between Serbian and Kosovar factions. This proved a fruitful period for the subject in terms of networking: The Kosovo post saw him building extensive contacts among international SOF elements then deployed in the Balkans, including British SAS and German KSK. Additionally, ODA 666 saw extensive deployments as "guests" of SOF aviation elements from both the 160th SOAR and French RHFS, wherein he also made numerous contacts. Also, for the first time, subject's unit tasked with a joint operation with U.S. ____/____, though only in a supporting role. By and large, the unit remained out of the spotlight, as per its mandate. It was not implicated in the '96 Sarajevo debacle, when Serbian forces targeting civilians in violation of the Dayton Accord lost several snipers to unknown countersnipers, all by exceedingly difficult shots made under adverse conditions. (NOTE: Shooters never identified; ballistics tests on recovered shell fragments proved inconclusive. See Memorandum _____.)

ODA 666 deployed everywhere in-theater, by aircraft, land-based vehicles, on horseback. The unit distinguished itself with an outstanding record of seized arms caches (both Serb and KLA), as well as CQ house-searching, signals intercepts, and urban SR. When a US OH-58 Kiowa helicopter went down in Serbian territory on August 8, 1998, ODA 666 was the first element in the QRF to arrive on-scene, securing the crew and destroying the damaged helicopter before Serbian paramilitary forces could close in. ODA 666 remained in-theater until 5th SFG returned to Fort Bragg, NC, mid-1999.

Within 48 hours of the 9/11 attacks, 5th SFG was tasked with standing up a SOF forward CP inside Afghanistan. For the remainder of 2001, ODA 666 lived on airstrips, first Karshi-

Kanabad in Uzbekistan, then the infamous "Motel Six," at Bagram
AFB in Afghanistan. Various undocumented deployments followed
throughout late 2001, in which ODA 666 worked hand in glove with
a host of other units, including U.S. and foreign SOF, OGAs,
and elements of the Northern Alliance.

In early 2002, ODA 666 was designated a forward SR element
of TF Rakkasan. On March 3, subject's unit was conducting a
clandestine cross-border recon of Sakesar peak in Pakistan when
USN SEAL teams were ambushed on Takur Ghar just across the
Afghan border. With all SOAR assets dedicated to QRF and TRAP/
CSAR duty, subject could only listen in on a covert frequency
as the TACP embedded with the Rangers called in "danger close"
airstrikes from F-16s on station, to no effect, as the troops
and crews of Razor 01 and Razor 02 were decimated. The attack
was repulsed only when another TACP called in a strike from a
Predator, the first UAV combat airstrike on record, which was
followed up with an obliterating hail of JDAMs from a B-52.
The enemy force was completely destroyed, and subject was left
holding a radio on a mountaintop 133 miles away.

Here a break in the subject's record occurs. ODA 666 was
sent back to Fort Campbell, KY, on May 5, 2002 (and officially
deactivated at the end of the month), possibly as part of the
reorganization that would add a fourth battalion to 5th SFG by
2008. While neither subject nor unit was censured or disciplined,
anecdotal reports from the period indicate subject's negative
opinions of military planning (especially of joint operations)
and growing disillusionment over the loss of his command. This
interregnum from May 2002 to March 2003 should be considered a
"cooling-off" period in which the subject immersed himself in
a host of new battlefield technologies, including the use of
high-speed data links for ground asset/UAV interface and new
real-time exploits for both cell phone and laptop intercepts to
be used in urban SR. Subject's mood described as "distant" yet
"highly focused on unknown objectives" (op. cit.).

Subject resurrected for the March 2003 "Scud hunts"
throughout western Iraq. Reinstated with command of 5th SFG's
ODA 523, subject instigated a series of combat innovations that

would be used by SOF throughout the war. First and foremost was communications: Working closely with embedded USAF TACPs, subject helped devise a grid system to prevent friendly-fire mishaps (including "black" no-go sectors for aircraft unless SOF units called in "sprint" CAS missions). 5th SFG personnel had trained directly with USAF pilots at Nellis AFB throughout 2003, and the subject helped design a front-line "joint-fires element" CP staffed by both SOF and USAF personnel, so air-to-ground communications were uniform and smooth. CENTCOM had already placed substantial air assets at 5th SFG's disposal; F-16s, A-10s, and B-52s remained on-station 24/7 during the Scud hunts. On the ground, subject forbade the use of Humvees in his unit, opting instead for Ranger Defender RSOVs. Subject also had input into the design of the M1078 "War Pig" long-range SOF support vehicle. Numerous 5th SFG units, including subject's own, trained extensively in the Jordanian desert with the new vehicles prior to deployment.

ODA 523 saw extensive action during the Scud hunts, during which subject and his XO (CW5 Mark Behr) utilized a new CAS technique that has since become known as the "get-and-grab" system, coordinating AWACS, strike aircraft, and ground controllers to direct precision airpower onto enemy targets. This system worked with surgical strikes (as at the battles of Ar Rutba and Ginz) but also with rapid strikes on multiple targets, as at Dewaniya, when the subject (using a single B-52 loaded with JDAMs under his direct control) hit 21 targets simultaneously. Under subject's command, ODA 523 achieved an unprecedented success rate in CAS missions; subject would soon be awarded the Soldier's Medal.

Soon afterward, subject was again given a fortuitous referral, this time by _____, to Maj. Gen. Stanley McChrystal, for Joint Special Operations Command (JSOC), which had been operating since 2001 between USCENTCOM, Afghanistan, and Iraq and adjacent countries. Unlike other SOF units, JSOC operated independently of SOCOM. It also utilized a new structure of small-team SOF backed by more conventional forces, especially Rangers, which may explain subject's suitability for the role. JSOC was first tasked with the manhunt for Saddam Hussein, but Gen. McChrystal envisioned a theater-wide deployment of the command to counter al-Qaeda and nascent insurgency forces. JSOC designated the unit tasked with this to be TF 16; standing this up required fast, efficient staffing. Once again, events aligned to give subject leverage, and he seized the moment to reconstitute a stripped-down version of ODA 666 within JSOC. Subject hand-picked his own small team: CW5 Behr; 1SG Michael Soffitt; and CSM Peter Tyvek. The unit was tasked with "optimized SR"— proactive intelligence gathering and counterintelligence, utilizing both ground and air assets—and was authorized for joint operations with British SAS. ODA 666 was given free rein to operate in-theater; this quickly escalated into cross-border operations into Iran.

Henceforth began ODIN's war.

ODA 666 made its bones while spearheading Operation Viking Hammer (March 28—30), following the infamous "Ugly Baby" insertion via Kirkuk. Working in tandem with Kurdish *pesh merga* subject's unit defeated an AQ force at the Sargat Valley. While the main enemy force escaped from Biyara across the border into Iran while ODA 666 watched (an event that subject would long remember), its abandoned HQ yielded a treasure trove of intelligence, including international contact lists for Hamas, Hezbollah, and Abu Sayyaf operatives. The men of ODA 666 all received Army Commendation medals, but subject's mind was doubtless turned toward Iran from this point forward.

Next, ODA 666 was at the top of the selection list for the covert raid on the al-Qadisiyah biochemical weapons facility in Iraq. (NOTE: Prior to this operation, subject should be considered "white" SOF; however, with his participation in this raid, subject crossed over to "black" SOF for the remainder of his military career.) This time, given his experience, subject was part of the planning process. His input showed in the seamless design and execution of the raid: two MH6 Little Birds loaded with SOF snipers; four Black Hawks full of Rangers to block enemy attacks from all sides; two Chinooks carrying the main assault force (including ODA 666); two more Chinooks on standby with GRF and CSAR teams; and four AH6 DAP gunship escorts overhead. A C-130 flying MASH unit was set down on a preselected airstrip nearby for immediate MEDEVAC. While several Chinooks were damaged by enemy fire upon infiltration, those of the QRF were able to safely exfiltrate the assault team (thanks to careful weight precalculation before the raid—also to the subject's credit). The extensive contingency planning paid off. The raid was considered a resounding success, and the subject was awarded the Distinguished Service medal.

Yet the subject's mood at this time was recorded as "less ebullient than expected—subject seems oddly detached" [sic]. Also noted was the unit's habit of eschewing contact with U.S. personnel while in stand-down mode, in favor of the separate "villa" housing UK SAS units.

Subject's technical skills were now put to use airing out Baghdad International Airport. Under then—Prime Minister al-Jaafari, in 2003 the first post-Saddam intelligence service was stood up in Iraq, with Shirwan al-Waeli appointed as its operational head. Waeli was already known to coalition intelligence as a Shi'ite nationalist and loyal follower of radical cleric Muqtada al-Sadr. On his watch, Sadrist operatives working in conjunction with intelligence operatives of the Mahdi army infiltrated the entire Iraqi transportation network. No coalition force movements in-theater passed undetected; Sunni officials and their families were watched, harassed, and even murdered as they moved about; elements of the nascent Iraqi SOF (being trained by some of the subject's own colleagues) were shadowed and ambushed; and men, munitions, and money for the Mahdi army moved freely into and out of the country via the airport, directly beneath the noses of U.S. and British forces.

Working with a small OGA unit headed by _____, ODA 666 conducted long-term covert electronic surveillance of senior airport officials, ground crew, and contract workers (June—November 2004). On the combined strength of cell phone intercepts, UAV tracking of vehicles, and countless man-hours of surveillance, ODA 666 identified a ring of 16 Sadrist operatives with direct connections to Waeli. On Christmas Eve 2004, ODA

666, backed by TF 16 air and ground support teams, sprang Operation Sigmoidoscopy. All of the ringleaders were arrested in raids around the airport and nearby Airport Village.

But the initial euphoria over the teams' success soon turned to frustration when Prime Minister al-Maliki quickly denounced the raids as excessive overreach; most of the ringleaders were released by February 2005, over the persistent and vocal objections from the CIA and JSOC. The operation was soon lost amid the rising sectarian violence around the capital.

However, some did not forget. Two of the ringleaders were killed when the car they were driving was hit by a Hellfire missile fired by a Predator drone near the southern Baghdad district of Abu Tshir on July 7. Authorization for the strike could not be confirmed, although at the time, ODA 666 was known to be operating in the area in support of ongoing JSOC operations.

From 2005–07, subject's focus shifted outside of the capital to the surrounding rings of small towns and villages known as the "Baghdad belts." These largely Sunni and near-lawless areas were seen as coveted real estate for Iraqi and Iranian insurgents alike, particularly for the movement of fighters and the fabrication of the occupation's most ubiquitous artifact: the IED. CENTCOM made finding and shutting down the supply and production lines for IEDs a priority; alongside SAS and Delta Force, ODA 666 was one of the lead investigative teams.

Going on early, hard-won intelligence breakthroughs, subject's unit cut a swath through the belts with fire and sword. Yusifiyah, Tarmiyah, Mahmudiyah, Salman Pak: All felt ODA 666's wrath. The unit set record engagement rates during this period, as subject honed his signature brand of Special Reconnaissance. By the time of the legendary Taji DOCEX intelligence haul (December 2006), ODA 666 had earned a fearsome reputation. Captured disk drives from this time contain numerous references to the "Devil's Double Cross," a bold CAS maneuver in which successive stacks of A-10 jets and AH-64D helicopters overflew each other at near-right angles, forming a low-altitude X with an enemy target at its center. After successive sorties overhead, fast-moving JSOC ground elements under the direction of ODA 666 moved in for mopping-up operations. The kill rate was astonishing, the intelligence gathered indispensable. ODA 666 was in top form.

Subject's innate battlefield creativity had repercussions beyond JSOC. When reconnoitering areas known to be rife with IEDs, subject devised a manned airborne ISR unit within army aviation elements (thus avoiding reliance on USAF for air support, a touchy subject between the services throughout the war) to provide real-time data on enemy snipers and IEDs to army air and ground units. This system was adopted full-time by the army for the war's duration, and subsequent units were deployed to Afghanistan. But while conventional forces adopted this system for an essentially defensive mandate (i.e., to protect ground forces), subject's aim was always to harness new technologies for prosecuting an ever more lethal air-to-ground offensive campaign.

With the advancement of CENTCOM'S "Contain, Protect, Deter" (CPD) doctrine to counter Iranian influence in Iraq in late 2006, JSOC's focus turned toward Iranian networks known to be operating in-theater. Naturally, ODA 666 topped the list of assets allocated to execute the policy, and it drew the plumb assignment: targeting Department 600, the RG Quds Force operations staff. Subject's unit went into confinement late in December; just before Christmas, QF officer Moshen Chizari and the station chiefs of both Baghdad and Dubai were tracked by cell phone exploits on JSOC helicopters to the SCIRI compound. With an AC-130 gunship circling overhead, ODA 666 moved in. There is a surviving fragment of a phone call to cancel the raid from SCIRI head Abd al-Azizi al-Hakim to Ali Khedery (a U.S.-Iraqi liaison officer since the days of the CPA); in the intercept, a frantic Hakim staffer is heard screaming that the compound is under attack, followed by an unmistakably American voice growling, "Drop the fuckin' phone or I'll blow your fuckin' head out the fuckin' window" (op cit.).

Once again the raid captured reams of intelligence implicating IRGC-QF forces operating against U.S. forces in

Iraq, and once again, the U.S. military bowed to pressure from the Shi'ite-dominated Iraqi government to release the Iranians. Subject's mood not recorded at this juncture; however, it is noteworthy that within two weeks, JSOC stood up TF 17, a unit tasked specifically with countering Iranian meddling in Iraq. Lead element in TF 17: ODA 666, which distinguished itself in short order with the capture of the "Irbil Five" (January 11, 2007).

Subject's reiterated focus on Iranian and pro-Iranian Iraqi elements harkened back to his earliest days in Iraq but added a dangerous new political dimension to ODA 666's activities. This was occurring during a fragmentation of the Mahdi army into splinter or "special" groups beyond Sadrist control, which activities ran the gamut from kidnapping and extortion to the smuggling of EFPs from Iran to Iraq. This last was a most sensitive item, as EFPs were a deadly Iranian development of IEDs that could destroy even the most heavily armored vehicles and MRAPs in coalition inventory. The fact that sophisticated electronic intelligence (provided in part by ODA 666 and some of its OGA contacts) illuminated members of the EFP smuggling network as no less than standing members of the Iraqi Parliament (such as _____ and _____) meant that any raids carried out by TF 17 could have high-level political implications. Subject's mood when he returned to the capital to be briefed on Operation Phantom Thunder was observed to have deteriorated further, particularly when he discovered that CENTCOM had decided to partner with Shirwan al-Waeli, one of the ringleaders of the airport Sadrist network which ODA 666 had helped to crack.

Things came to a head on July 6 with the killing of three USN SEALs in Sadr City, which drew unusually heavy reprisals from JSOC-controlled air elements. The resulting outcry from the Maliki government resulted in an Iraqi demand for permission from JSOC prior to any future raids in the area.

This did not go down well with ODA 666. Nasiriyah, Dawaniyah, Husseiniya, and a host of other Shi'ite hot spots in the Baghdad belts came under a fierce series of well-coordinated precision airstrikes involving everything from drones to helicopters to bombers. Not surprisingly, casualties (especially among civilians) were high.

Simultaneously, and quite by accident, JSOC's intelligence operations center reported a high volume of ELINT/SIGINT surveillance on a network of cell phones in and around Najaf, with contact points moving several times a day and never staying in one place overnight. The JSOC intelligence officers were shocked to discover that ODA 666 was tracking the cell phone of none other than Moqtada al-Sadr (something no military nor intelligence unit had hitherto accomplished). Worse, an unauthorized AC-130 gunship had been requested to hold on station over the city.

This was the final straw; ODA 666 was ordered to stand down. According to internal JSOC correspondence, a closed-door meeting with Gen. MacChrystal lasting late into the night ended with all members of ODA 666 requesting and filing their separation orders from the U.S. Army. Subject and his men spent the rest of the night at the SAS villa.

All members of ODA 666 were flown out to Aviano AFB in Italy at 0530 Baghdad time on July 21. At noon the following day, a four-car convoy headed east from Najaf was monitored by a UAV operated by newly formed private contractor _____. When the convoy reached Diwaniyah, real-time ELINT confirmed the presence of al-Sadr in the convoy, which continued heading east toward Amara. At 2132 Baghdad time, a flight of two armed Kiowa helicopters operated by contractor _____ moved to engage the convoy inside the city, but both were brought down by RPGs. Oddly, before any coalition CSAR assets could be formally dispatched to rescue the downed crewmen, a transmission routed through the company's drone alerted an SAS QRF in Basra. However, the rescue attempt failed badly, as JAM reinforcements beat the SAS to the crash site. Both QRF Pumas were brought down by ground fire; from a safe altitude, the drone broadcasted live feed of the British crew being dragged from their helicopters and gruesomely executed.

The final footage from the drone before its recall showed

Sadr's convoy headed for Ahvaz. As it crossed the Iranian border at high speed, the phantom transmission to the company drone cut out. Someone had been watching from far away.

The demise of ODA 666 was lost in the ensuing media circus. The September congressional hearings saw the closure of contractor _____ and the relocation of its CEO _____. By Christmas Eve 2007, all members of ODA 666 were officially separated from the U.S. Army with honorable discharges.

Of the remaining information available, official records certify the retention of subject's security clearance (TS/HCI/TK/HCS), for reasons unknown. A brief note records two visits by the subject to government offices: one to CIA HQ at Langley, VA; and one to USCYBERCOM HQ at Fort Meade, MD (both January 2008).

All subsequent records remain classified.

PART III

THROUGH THE FLOOR

SAINT JOHN THE DEMOLISHED

THE RED CLAY made for a bright contrast against the grass, but there were large browned-out clumps. The lines were long gone, and the only reason the bases were still there was that they were screwed into plates buried beneath the ground. Morningside Park's baseball diamonds had seen much better days.

The playground swings were still there, too. Marrone sat on one, absently rocking herself back and forth with one foot. They had talked out the possible variances of the situation and come up with nothing. Santiago had called Marrone first, after looking at the clip from the surveillance video from the day before, when the wet waddling man known as Necator (McKeutchen and DiBiasi had identified him instantly upon seeing the playback) was recorded exiting the subway at Ninety-fourth and Second Avenue, coming out just as a young woman in chef's whites and a bulging military knapsack went in. OCID had uplink to both NYPD Counterterror Ops and the FBI's New York field office less than a minute later. Santiago figured it would be redundant to offer the same to Devius Rune.

Now Santiago stood a few yards from where Marrone swayed, scanning the length and breadth of the park, his jaw set and his hands in his pockets, the badge on his belt clearly visible, silently warning civilian traffic away.

Thanks to creative ratholing by the OCID budget hogs (with more than a little strong-arming from DiBiasi), Santiago's team members all sported Shure UR1M body transmitters with T4AF connectors to lavalier microphones. Santiago and Marrone wore their mikes in their jacket lapels; where the Narc Sharks and More had stashed theirs, Santiago didn't want to know.

So an earpiece and lapel mike kept him connected to Liesl and Turse, parked up on Morningside Drive. More was also out there somewhere, among the jagged cliffs that rose nearly a hundred feet from the park's floor, forming its western border. After Santiago had placed the call to Necator the day before, More had disappeared, returning to OCID three hours later with an insidious piece of luggage containing a .338 Zel Tactilite rifle with a Nightforce NXS scope, "just in case." More covered the high ground from his hidden sniper's blind, while the Narc Sharks took the upper roadway on foot, leaving Santiago and Marrone to watch the lowermost plane of the park, from its southern border at 110th Street to the pond just west of 113th Street and Morningside Avenue.

Santiago had deliberately staged the meeting at the Harlem park to contain the situation away from the crazed morass of midtown and the Convention Week security, and outside the no-man's-land of Central Park, yet close enough to move on the suspect subway station quickly if the meeting yielded enough for a Probable Cause search. To keep things away from the park's fountains and ponds, which drew in tourists and students, Santiago had decided the meeting point should be at the southern border of the park. Necator could approach only from the lower eastern entrances; Santiago's team had the rest of the park sewn up. The other entrance to the eastern edge of the park was at 113th, well within view; the western border north of the Narc Sharks' position had two stationary posts staffed by Columbia University cops. Santiago and Marrone had the southern entrances covered. The meeting ground was as locked down as Santiago could make it under the circumstances.

Still, he had some misgivings about the locale. It was open and spacious, a rarity in Manhattan, with plenty of room for the team to spot Necator from a distance. The western edge of the park, however, butted up against St. Luke's Hospital, Columbia University, the majestic Cathedral of St. John the Divine. Santiago had deliberately placed the Narc Sharks between these and More's general area as a bulwark against unforeseen chaos. There shouldn't be any, as Marrone had reminded him and he had repeatedly reminded himself, but with More around . . . Santiago fervently hoped that if there were to be any gunplay, it would be directed down from the cliffs into the basin of the park, as though from a giant deer blind. Then again, there was a solid line of prewar tenement buildings all along the park's eastern edge to worry about.

Maybe it was the proximity to Manhattan Avenue making him uneasy. From where he stood, Santiago could see where it split off from Morningside. Three years ago, a witness named Renny had lived there, in one of the historic brownstones, in a deluxe apartment More had torn apart, where they'd found Renny's stash and More had dispassionately tortured the kid into literally spilling his guts while Santiago watched in mute, wide-eyed horror. That had been Santiago's *first* case with More. No, despite the park's enduring scenery, Santiago didn't like it here one bit.

"Would it make you feel better if I swore that I have no fucking clue what you guys are into?" Marrone asked from between the chains of her swing.

"Why are you really here?" Santiago asked bluntly, looking down at the dirt.

"I told you, we've been getting a lot of stuff through our database that points to dirty money. This always happens during election cycles, but this year it's off the charts. Both parties have raised record campaign funds, and they're not going through the usual channels."

"What do you mean, usual channels?" Santiago asked, glancing up at her. Santiago was at heart a city street cop, not a federal money cop like Marrone, and he knew it.

"Banks, really big ones like Urbank or Electrum-Horn, and they've reported no large-scale campaign finance activity in their shops—in fact, none at all. I'm talking dozens, maybe hundreds, of billions of dollars, Sixto. You can't make that kind of money just *disappear*."

Santiago sighed and deliberately shifted his eyes away from her. Outside his family, no one ever called Santiago by his first name. Except Marrone. He loved it when she did, and he knew it clouded his judgment. He yanked his thoughts back on track. "So where could the money go?"

"Funds. Big asset-management shops. Like GC Piso.* Or . . ."

"Or," Santiago echoed with a hint of impatience.

"Or something like Redhawk Investments."

That got Santiago's attention. Alex Redhawk had been front-page news for months. A big-shot money manager who was dabbling in politics. More had mentioned him earlier. Which could only mean Devius Rune was interested in Redhawk as well.

"Tell me this," he began carefully, his mouth feeling a little dry, "where

* In *The Big Dogs*.

exactly are you getting your information?"

Marrone perked up; she really did enjoy her work, he thought, and it showed.

"Are you kidding? Our database is the mother lode for all financial transactions. Here and overseas, at least where there's U.S. interests and money. There's rivers of information, it just flows to me, I can get hold of—"

"Liza," Santiago interrupted, savoring her name even as he felt heaviness in his gut, "do all those rivers come from clean sources?"

"What do you mean?"

Santiago felt clumsy, groping for the right words, feeling his way along. "I think—maybe—someone could be feeding you information. To get you to think what they want you to think."

"What the fuck are you talking about?" Marrone sounded dumbfounded and indignant at the same time. "At FINCEN we have all the—"

"FINCEN's a government agency, Liza," Santiago pressed, "just like the CIA. Which, apparently, is interested in Convention Week for some reason. That's why More came back. It's all because of Devius Rune—he called you, didn't he?"

"What are you—"

"He did. He called you or got someone to do it. He's the source of the rivers of information that got you into this. He brought More back, More got me and asked me to get Liesl and Turse. Rune got you. He put our team back together from the GC Piso bust. He set this up, all of it. He's pulling all our strings—don't you see?"

"Bullshit," Marrone almost spat. Now he'd pissed her off. Which, he remembered, was her default reaction when confronted with a truth she didn't like.

"And he'll sell you out, sure as shit," Santiago went on. "If this goes bad, if Washington turns up the heat on him, you're the first one in the fire."

"Really?" Marrone sneered. "Maybe I'll get transferred. Even promoted. Like *some* other people from the Piso case I could name."

This last part stung, as it was meant to. Santiago shook his head, trying not to bite his lip and failing. Marrone was right—at least, by his own logic, she *could* be right. He'd never looked too closely at his OCID transfer, his rise through the ranks; he'd considered it his just reward for suffering through partnership with More. And it *was* a form of payback, just from a place he hadn't wanted to look. The source of the river.

Earlier, DiBiasi had told Devius Rune in no uncertain terms to fuck off, and fuck off he had, to More knew where, but at least it wasn't in Morningside Park. Which had suited Santiago just fine.

Until now. Santiago would have loved to brace Rune and find out just what the fuck was going on.

Goddammit.

The more he thought about it, the more confusing the picture got. Nothing was making sense.

More had said there was something bad in store for Convention Week, which suggested a terror hit, but here he was, riding shotgun for Santiago's meet with a slimy political errand boy who'd had the dumb luck to be caught on-camera. Marrone said she'd been working on some campaign-finance weirdness, but here she was, too. The Narc Sharks—hell, they'd come along on the off chance that they'd get to see Santiago fuck up miserably, but Liesl seemed to think there was some connection between the subway map they'd found at the Mavridez bust and the missing drug money they'd been chasing. Turse wasn't convinced, but he'd never arrested, assaulted, or shot a political figure and was hoping an opportunity would present itself today. DiBiasi had designed the meet with Necator. He had also given strict, loud, and profane orders that all communications would go strictly through him on a closed OCID channel, no exceptions (DiBiasi had saved a special glare of malevolence for More and Marrone at this juncture).

There really wasn't anything tying everything together except whatever was down in the Ninety-sixth Street subway station on the Second Avenue line. Deputy Chief Derricks, the Counterterror Ops chief, was there now, aboveground with a technical team, beefing up electronic surveillance of all the entrances, as well as a few discreetly placed cameras covering the mosque. Santiago's team was under orders not to go down into the subway; Derricks, More, Rune, and even McKeutchen figured it was better to wait for another tempting target like Necator to lead them to the gold mine rather than go shambling around underground without knowing what the hell they were looking for. And possibly scaring off their target in the process.

Still, everyone was itching to get down into the subway except Marrone; she just wanted in on the Necator angle, or so she said. Santiago wasn't buying it for a second. Marrone was a money chaser; if she was here with him now, he guessed her people thought there was dirty campaign cash going underground—something Necator's presence on the surveillance video firmly supported.

Santiago stopped chewing his lip. Marrone had said she was here for dirty political money. The Narc Sharks were here because they'd chased missing drug money. Necator was (supposedly) showing up because he was known to carry money between Albany and New York. More and Devius Rune were back in town chasing a bomb, or something *like* a bomb that the fuckers wouldn't ID. Well, bombs cost money. Moving them cost money. Moving them *quietly* into a city as hysterically phobic as New York would require a great deal of money. All the stray pieces in this fucked-up puzzle were loosely orbiting, bound by the gravitational pull of money. And the pull seemed to be coming from a black hole in the ground around East Ninety-sixth Street in Manhattan. Almost directly beneath the main events of Convention Week. Which Devius Rune, the CIA scumbag, had such a hard-on for.

What the *fuck* . . .

Santiago's earpiece crackled. More: "Ever, Six, worm at your four o'clock."

Liesl joined in. "Got 'im. Can see his sweat from here."

Santiago looked but could not see the pair of OCID detectives, whom he knew to be lurking somewhere around the Carl Schurz monument at 116th, above the massive granite stairway that curved gently down to the park floor. Both Liesl and Turse had blended in seamlessly with the human current. Whatever else the Narc Sharks were (and Santiago could think of many denigrating adjectives), they knew their business.

Santiago could almost hear the squishing steps of the wet flabby mark as he crossed west into the park from the 112th Street entrance; he could definitely hear the grievances Necator was already hurling his way. Santiago figured he'd play it breezily, try to break the ice and calm the guy down.

"What's up?" he began, hands in his pockets, head canted slightly to one side, nonthreatening. Just out for a walk in the park.

"You guys got nothin' on me," Necator panted, closing the distance to about fifteen yards. "You say one fucking thing I don't like, Albany gets your boss on the phone."

"Why don't you tell us something we might like, then," Santiago replied laconically. This was going to be easy. He'd cracked a hundred cases harder than this turd. The guy was sweating right through his suit jacket. This really *was* going to be a walk in the park.

"I work at City Hall and the statehouse. I don't know shit about what else goes on around town. Fuckin' dump anyway," Necator rasped.

Santiago sensed Marrone had come up beside him.

"'Specially 'round Ninety-sixth and Second, right?" Santiago drawled.

"The fuck you talkin' about?" Necator was starting to get his wind back from his grueling thirty-yard march.

"What's down in the subway?" Marrone fired at him.

"Nothin' you fucks got a handle on."

"Aw, now don't say that," Santiago put in, warming to his laid-back guise. "I got a good grip. 'Specially on slimy things that live underground, don't see much sunlight. You feel me?"

"What brought you down there?" Marrone pressed. "The subway's city property, we wouldn't need a warrant for a search."

"I like the decor, the fuck you care? Is ridin' the subway illegal now?" Necator was visibly agitated, his chin and forehead shining, lips trembling, eyes darting.

Santiago was starting to enjoy himself. He began, "Y'know, *we* can call Albany, too—"

A small dark circle appeared just above Necator's sodden right eyebrow, while a bright red cloud sprouted from behind his left ear with a dull *thoop*.

Santiago was already tackling Marrone, the two of them flying backward through a clatter of swing seats and chains, as he registered a muted rifle shot ringing off the tenements along Morningside Avenue.

Turse screamed in his earpiece: "SNIPER—"

Santiago and Marrone were rolling on the rubber matting beneath the swings, Santiago trying to cover Marrone with his body and draw his weapon at the same time, Marrone fighting to get out from beneath his bulk. Jesus, did fucking *More* shoot Necator? A circus played out in his earpiece.

Liesl: "—he's on the rocks by the stairs—"

Turse: "—looks like a fuckin' student, messy hair, red backpack—"

More (in his unhindered radio voice free of its normal pollution): "Ever, Liesl, Turse, fall back, fall *back*, do not engage, repeat, DO NOT ENGAGE—" followed by another shot.

"Get the fuck *offa* me!" Marrone yelled into Santiago's face.

There was another deep shot, and this time Santiago was able to discern a smaller, hollow pop—*silencer,* his mind shouted through the noise in his earpiece. He rolled right, coming up to a kneeling Weaver position, his .45 in a two-handed grip pointed at . . . rocks. The great stone face of Morningside Park's palisade stared back at him in dark gray silence. Until another shot from More brought Santiago's eyes to a pair of erratically moving dots on opposing sides of the long curved stairwell, jinking up and down in the crevasses, thunderbolts at their shoulders. A pair of mountain goats with rifles, running on the rocks, the echo of gunfire filling the seconds as each racked the bolt for another round.

Marrone was kneeling, trying for nonexistent cover behind one of the support poles for the swings, her Walther looking for a target amid the gulches. Santiago could see More approaching the southern wall of the stairs, lining up another shot. Movement yanked his gaze upward—a lone figure, messy hair and backpack indeed, rifle with bulbous suppressor held at port arms, taking stairs four at a time. For a second Santiago thought his eyes had been tricked, that he was looking at More, since from behind the figure moved just like him, *looked* just like him, minus the stupid newsboy cap.

Liesl's voice came through Santiago's earpiece: "I got 'im, I *got* the motherfucker—"

"Yo, wait up, wait UP—" Turse yelled, and Santiago could see his long hair flying just above the wall, moving fast but well short of the stairwell monument. Something else came through the earpiece: a deep, rhythmic thumping.

"Ever, Liesl, fall back, FALL BACK—" More shouted, and Santiago had just enough time to realize that he'd never heard More raise his voice.

Then Liesl came back on the air: "What the fuck is THAT—"

The screams converged in Santiago's earpiece, blurring into one: More yelling for Liesl to get down; Turse hollering, "*Holy SHIT*"; Marrone screaming Liesl's name. But it was Santiago's eyes that jammed and occluded and fed him horrible lies: a massive two-legged armored monster stomping to a stop in front of the stairwell entrance, huge arms extended, one belching flame. This was not and *could not* be.

For the first time in six years, Santiago heard the awful undulation of a machine gun, followed by the crepitation of shattered glass as the armored beast raked the windshields of several parked cars, minivans, and the nave of the cathedral with high-caliber bullets.

Santiago was sprinting, barely conscious of Marrone yelling at him to wait up, trying to get the microphone close to his mouth while looking for a sight picture over the jouncing front blade of his .45 as he made for the stairwell. He caught the briefest glimpse of the sniper—nondescript, slightly disheveled, but Christ, that fucker was *moving*—before he disappeared behind the armored beast's haunches. Then Santiago was at the stairwell, his line of sight with the action above lost.

He knew there was no way he would reach the top. His lungs would explode first. But he could see More off to the side, his rifle slung, moving up the rock face with impossible simian agility. Santiago forced his legs to keep moving even as his quadriceps screamed with acid. He could make out frantic shouts and curses from the Narc Sharks above, but their words were lost in a long fusillade of machine-gun fire. More glass fractured in Santiago's tympanum.

He was stumbling, gasping, his chest on fire, unable to raise his pistol. His vision seemed to cant sideways and brighten, then slide into shades of ocher.

More's voice cut through the thickening red mist in his head: "EVER, LIESL, GET UNDER THE CAR, DO *NOT* GET BEHIND IT GET UNDER, GET *UNDER*, GET UNDERNEATH IT NOW—"

There was a pop, then a flash. An avalanche of shock and noise blew down the stairwell, and Santiago slammed his face into the granite steps. Through the lavalier came an inhuman screech, followed by incomprehensible roaring from Turse.

Santiago managed a spastic push-up that jolted him back to his feet, though none too steadily. He made out strange grayish-white smoke wafting over the park's western wall, about where Liesl had been. He saw the armored beast more clearly, something of this world after all, small riveted windows at the apex of its midsection, both appendages at full extension, spitting fire and bursts of smoke. Another explosion, this time alongside the cathedral, took out an entire stained-glass window. There were other distinct shots, smaller ones—More or Turse or Liesl giving back some, sparks and pings and ricochets festooning the armored beast's frontal plastron. Santiago heard himself yelling hoarsely, calling for Liesl on his mike, finally bringing his .45 up with both trembling arms and putting any and all strength he had left into his hands, clawing and pulling and throttling the trigger in all the ways he'd been taught not to. He did not count his shots, just noticed that his hands froze on the stopped trigger when the slide locked on an empty chamber. He stared at his pistol, dumbfounded, then looked back up the stairs.

And saw the armored beast extending one loglike arm toward him, the wisping barrel of its machine gun protruding from a thick square gauntlet around the hand. He thought he might have heard Marrone in his earpiece; it sounded like she was singing. Santiago had never guessed death would be so confusing.

Then there was a spark off one of the windows at the armored beast's vertex, what would have passed for eyes on a more earthly creature, and the echo of More's rifle. The thing staggered, seemed to shake itself, then swung its gun arm away from Santiago and up toward Morningside Boulevard. There was another long ripping burst from its machine gun, then two pops from its right hand. Santiago heard explosions, screams, breaking glass, and car alarms. Then Marrone really was screaming in his ear and clutching his shoulder, dragging him to one side, trying desperately for any kind of cover on the granite slab, her Walther bucking in her other hand as she fired blindly up toward the Carl Schurz monument.

Time slammed into normal speed again, and Santiago was watching himself clear and reload, his legs shoving him up against the southern banister. Now his arms worked, there was no pain, he drew a solid bead on the armored beast's left flank, and slowly and carefully unloaded, double-tapping the monster's left shoulder and arm. The slide locked again and Santiago reloaded reflexively, no longer thinking, just pointing and shooting, feeling nothing other than alive, until the slide locked again and he reached for a fresh magazine and his fingers scrabbled on an empty pouch. He'd burned through thirty rounds, his entire carry load for the past two years, and now he was dry. Looking up at a thing that was blowing away cars, the cathedral, maybe the rest of his team.

Then tires squealed up above him. The creature seemed to do an odd little hop, half a stagger, and then it was out of sight. The tires squealed again, and Santiago heard rapid-fire shots from a .45. There was More, kneeling behind one of the cornerstones of the monument, some kind of automatic pistol in his hand. Santiago dragged himself to his feet. More ran dry, emptied, and reloaded in milliseconds, spitting out five double-taps and reloading again. Santiago managed a lumbering gait up the last few flights of stairs while More slapped another magazine into his pistol. Just how many did he have? Santiago stumbled onto the monument platform just as another burst of automatic fire tore into the statue. Santiago dropped, bounced off the stone, and rolled behind the northern edge of the platform. He caught a glimpse of More wriggling underneath a bullet-riddled Subaru just as another pop reached his ears, from farther uptown this time. Santiago slammed himself facedown on the stone as shrapnel tore through the trees a few feet above. As the sound of the explosion reached his ears, Santiago saw More bellying along the pavement, underneath a car, then another. By the time Santiago was back on his haunches, daring to peek around the edge of the platform wall, More had disappeared behind a mangled car across the street. A car that was obviously the armored beast's target.

As the shriek of tires receded uptown, Santiago judged it safe to get to his feet, which he did in a series of jerks and jolts. His arms and legs felt like rubber, his shoulders, hands, and eyes burned, and an ongoing tinnitic chime rang incessantly in his ears. The stench of cordite was everywhere; smokes of various hues stained the sunlight, which danced crazily off of dozens, nay, hundreds, of brass shell casings all over Morningside Avenue.

And lo, he beheld the Cathedral of St. John the Demolished.

The northeastern portion of the church had taken the worst of it, though bullet holes stitched a haphazard pattern all along the north wall halfway toward Amsterdam Avenue. Huge smoldering impact sites scarred the apse and nave from street level almost up to the roofline. Guastavino tile from above the dome's crossing above the altar lay in fragments along the pavement a hundred yards away. The northern apsidal shrines had borne the full brunt of the onslaught; both the German chapel and the Scandinavian Chapel of St. Ansgar were almost completely caved in. Fully half of the cathedral had been ravaged, and from the looks of it, Santiago knew in his bones that no matter what the city might do, the church would never be restored. The armored beast had huffed and puffed and blown God's house down.

But it was the sight of More and Turse kneeling on the sidewalk that made Santiago clutch at the wall for support. Liesl, on his back, lidless eyes bulging skyward, flensed face baring tendon and sinew to the sunlight, exposed jaws a denuded rictus of unveiled teeth and gums. Something in the air had reached down and torn Liesl's face off as he crouched behind a car, thinking he was safe.

And then Santiago was on his knees beside Turse, who was yelling and crying and fumbling through CPR, trying for a pulse in his partner's wrists, hands trembling over the ruin of his partner's face, unable to make actual contact. Marrone managed to get a few feet away before vomiting.

There were screams all around them, and the distant rising wail of sirens. An iron grip bit into Santiago's shoulder and shook him with bone-jarring force. More. Saying something like *Ee-ray-dee-dee* . . . Santiago's mind was an overloaded shopping cart sliding along a wet floor through a stand of glass bottles . . .

"—call PAPD, tell them to seal off the George Washington Bridge. It looks like a UPS truck, they headed downhill to 122nd, they'll probably try for the West Side Highway and across the river to New Jersey. It has to come from you. The call has to come from you. *I cannot make this call*. It's got to come from you. Do you understand?"

"GO NORTH, YOUNG MAN"

"**. . . YES, THE PRESIDENT** is planning a special event near where—near the site to memorialize the victims. Yes, it's a terrible tragedy, there's been no word on the perpetrators' identity or whereabouts, the FBI is combing the area. This is just awful, Mel, who would commit such a heinous act right in the middle of Manhattan and blow up a *church*, for God's sake? And what was that *thing* that's all over the news?"

Caduta Massi's aide, Corinne, looked on in stupefaction and mounting malaise at her employer's poise and skilled phone manner as she attempted to coax some truth from the man she privately referred to as "that cocksucker Cordy," Senator Mel Cordryceps.

The office monitors were tuned to various news outlets, all of which showed amateur phone footage of the melee in Manhattan. Corinne's lips parted in mute horror as she watched, for the umpteenth time that afternoon, the explosion that blew a parked car completely into the middle of the street, sending the cop who'd been crouching behind it sprawling onto his back ten feet away, writhing in agony.

". . . haven't been able to reach the mayor, the City Council speaker, not even the chief of police, it's complete chaos up there. Have you heard anything? No? What about your delegation, is everything all right? Yes, all present and accounted for, we're going ahead as scheduled. Yep. Yep. No, I haven't heard from the governor."

Corinne knew this was a lie; she herself had put New York's governor through to the House speaker less than twenty minutes after what some reporters were already calling "The Battle of Morningside Park," live on the air. It had taken Caduta Massi another ten minutes to talk the governor down; the state's senator and representatives had lit up the private line after that. Caduta Massi had had enough of damage control; now she was going on the offensive, trying to figure out what the fuck was happening up there in New York.

Specifically, she was trying to raise Council Speaker Trichinella, whose special "assistant" had not yet reported in from Albany regarding the "plan" to swing the New York legislature vote in favor of the National IRA bonds at week's end. Corinne did not know the specifics but gathered from her employer's demeanor and increasing crassness that the plan was, at best, unsavory. Corinne was finding a lot of that lately, not just in her employer but in all those with whom she did the business of government. There was a kind of pall over the job, a darkness that brought with it anxiety and amorphous revulsion. She was reacting to the toxicity of her environment.

Caduta Massi, on the other hand, was in her element, despite the way she showed it. Slamming down the phone, she snarled: "That fucker Cordy's got to be in on this. We plan Albany, then Necator gets killed. Trichinella's ducking me, which means she doesn't know shit. The cops were after Necator, which means they know about the subway bank, or they *will* know about it. Cordy and those other GOP maggots were trying to blow the whistle on Take It Back, like they haven't got black-money slush funds themselves, the hypocritical fucks. But whatever they were trying to pull, it blew up in their faces. Look at that fucking thing, what would you even call it? Shooting up a *church*, for Christ's sake, on a fucking college campus. Well, now they have truly fucked the duck."

This last graphic visual was meant to be the silver lining of the unfolding storm. The spin-control team supporting the former secretary of state's presidential campaign had gotten right out front when the news broke, sending her concerned face and voice out to the public even before the church stopped smoldering. Preliminary polls from IPSOS and Gallup showed an instant spike in her ratings, with 58 percent of the public approving of her response to the situation (up from a moribund 46 percent on her perceived grasp of the economy at the start of Convention Week). Never one to waste a good crisis, she had seized the moment and was gaining momentum. The GOP candidates hadn't made any speeches about the firefight; they were a complete fucking mess, as usual.

Which left whom, exactly?

That fucker *Redhawk*?

Please. The Democratic candidate for president had scored a TKO without lifting a finger.

But Caduta Massi's job was to lock in the election, and to do that she needed Albany behind the National IRA. And so she'd been diligently working the phones, ringing the bells of everyone along her network from Washington to Manhattan to Albany, trying to take the pulse—or maybe extinguish it—of the crucial vote. If they could swing New York, all other state and municipal governments would fall like dominoes.

Feeling slightly sick, Corinne turned away from her frothing boss to take another call. This one, however, was diffcrent.

"It's the chief of FINCEN at Treasury," the aide whispered, looking at the speaker with wide frightened eyes. "He's asking about Take It Back. How does he—"

The speaker held a finger to her lips. Her face was still, but her eyes had gone from cool gemstones to seething pits of basaltic magma. The aide was seeing a new side of her boss, and it terrified her.

Caduta Massi silently made a fateful decision for which Corinne could have kissed her.

"You're on the next plane to Albany," hissed the speaker. "Now get the fuck out."

• • •

Mel Cordryceps's aide, Drew, was experiencing something he was not used to: fear.

He'd known viscerally, from the moment he'd burst into the senator's office—which earned him an uncharacteristically vicious glare from his boss, who hastily cut the call on his private line—that the mayhem in New York was somehow connected to this very office, his place of employment. He knew it as surely as he knew his own shoe size and blood type. Never in his life would he have fathomed the possibility that the people's government could be so violent to those it purported to serve. The boss had let slip a few hints in the past few weeks, boasting, really, that the "contractor" he'd hired to expose the Dems' financial chicanery during Convention Week had a military background. Iraq. Special Operations, in point of fact. Exactly what was needed. It was about cutting through Washingtonian red tape, about getting things done!

Watching the various monitors in the office, all of which showed the same amateur video of the huge metal monster blowing up cars and machine-gunning the church in New York, Drew thought: *This? This is GETTING THINGS DONE?*

Mel Cordryceps recovered quickly from his momentary loss of composure, bidding his rattled aide to be seated. "It's a terrible tragedy, of course, New York," he began, "but we mustn't let it distract us from our objective."

Drew boggled.

"Convention Week," the senator reminded him.

Unsure how to reply, Drew quickly chose to steer what he thought to be the most prudent and diplomatic course. It saved face, offered him an out, and might be used to defend him in a court of law. And unbeknownst to him at that moment, it would alter his destiny.

"Sir," Drew ventured, "it seems that in light of recent . . . events . . . in New York, it might make sense to focus on more . . . attainable goals." He was doing his best not to stammer. He was used to being confident and unshakable, not the opposite. He didn't like it.

The senator was unfazed. "What do you mean, attainable? You think this mess in New York changes things? It's grievous and tragic, yes, but it doesn't upset the whole applecart. Don't be such a defeatist. I've seen far worse than this in my thirty years in politics, let me tell you."

Mel Cordryceps was playing for time. His aide was proving smarter than he looked, and that was dangerous in this game. The senator was deliberately turning up the wattage of his benign grandfatherly persona, the one he wore for the cameras, while turning over the possibilities in his mind. ODIN had clearly gone off-playbook, off-script, off the goddamn deep end, as far as he was concerned. He had needed that fat little fuck Necator to expose the Dems' black slush fund, and maybe ODIN had his reasons for shooting the courier, but nothing could justify what that *thing* had done in New York.

To add insult to injury, ODIN had the temerity to accuse *him* of withholding vital information, saying that he had deliberately and perniciously withheld information about a certain individual, whose name ODIN declined to give, who had been present in the park. With a rifle. Backing up the cops who'd shown up to grill Necator. Mel Cordryceps had been shocked—no, *enraged* at such effrontery. His trademark composure had cracked as he'd snarled barbed criticisms at ODIN, his impulsiveness, his misreading of a delicate situation, his ham-fisted response to the slightest provocation.

Again he'd been caught off-guard. He didn't think it possible that ODIN would have known about the private SSCI meetings held two years earlier, when Mel Cordryceps was a ranking committee member. When a senior CIA officer named Devius Rune had been hauled over the coals for allegedly running a covert operation in New York, which involved embedding a highly decorated MARSOC operator named Everett More into the NYPD, partnered with the very same police officer who'd called Necator to a meeting in Morningside Park. Where More and ODIN had come face-to-face and all hell had broken loose.

Now, despite his neatly designed plans being blown asunder in a hail of heavy weapons fire, despite the myriad unsettling implications welling up, despite his seething anger at that crazy bastard ODIN and that conniving bitch Caduta Massi, Mel Cordryceps heard the nervous voice of his aide, and the proverbial penny dropped in his mind. There was A Way Out.

As a career politician, the senator was used to being the object of enmity and disgust. He knew how to field anger directed at him. More important, he had learned not only to deflect it but to redirect it. He knew to channel the rage behind angry accusations, and he was well versed in the alchemy by which such negativity could be put to good use, to serve his own needs.

That was how he would handle ODIN, to bring his hired help back on track. After all, to those entrusted with shaping America's future, any crisis should be viewed as an opportunity in disguise. And both ODIN and his own aide had provided him with just such an opportunity.

Mel Cordryceps smoothed himself and began his spiel: "You're right, you're absolutely right, son. This mess in New York proves the wrongness of my direction. We should focus on the election, not its funding. Our business is clean politics, not dirty money. We need to focus on the issue at hand, and that issue is the National IRA. We cannot let this legislative abortion—no, wait, not that word—*abomination* come to pass in what so clearly is a time of crisis." He was mentally editing himself, fine-tuning his speech for his next talk-show appearance on Sunday.

"Here's what I want you to do," the senator went on in his best Calm and Reassuring, "I want you to get up to Albany immediately. The vote's on Friday. I need eyes and ears in the chamber feeding me information right up to the moment the bill hits the floor. I want to know the disposition on both sides, who's a hawk and who plans to abstain. And I need to know the second the votes are tallied. Go north, young man, I'm counting on you. The *nation* is counting on you." Mel Cordryceps actually reached up and put a hand on one of Drew's sizable shoulders.

Drew did his best not to shrug it off. He was experiencing a number of violent emotions, but the overriding one was: LEAVE. NOW. The senator, who apparently had all but forgotten that he'd just helped to instigate the largest terror incident on U.S. soil since the towers fell, was giving, no, *showing* him what he so desperately wanted: A Way Out.

And it pointed toward Albany.

• • •

The Desmond Hotel, Albany: dark wood paneling, labyrinths of dark patterned carpeting, king-size beds four pillows wide flanked by fluted posts and fine details conveniently placed at the level of a recliner's outstretched hand. Such are the simple but sumptuous adornments of its executive suites.

One of these has been occupied, its old-fashioned but functional DO NOT DISTURB card hanging on the outer doorknob for two full days with neither ingress nor egress. There has been a regular stream of room service, trays left and picked up outside the door. Other guests have mentioned it to the concierge. Management is at an impasse: The suite is occupied by a prominent state legislator and a young female guest who arrived several nights ago and has not been seen to leave.

The cleaning staff no longer attempts entry; its members joke about the frenzied sounds of copulation that echo through the adjacent corridor at all hours of the day and night. Such merriment about the sexual escapades of guests is old hat in the hotel business, but this particular instance is proving to be a memorable one. The most remarked observation among the staff regarding the female guest in the locked suite is that she must have an asshole made of Teflon.

• • •

In another bed, in a very different sort of executive suite, in the subway bank 102 feet beneath Second Avenue in Manhattan, LA whispers:

—Time to go. You know the plan. Load the cash, leave the rest. We start packing in five minutes. In one hour we're gone.

LA's mouth and hands are on her paramour and confidante N, moving softly. But her eyes are on the wall-mounted television tuned to a cable news station, which is broadcasting amateur footage of a terrifying armored beast spraying fire and death around a park across town, and they are as hard as the bullets shattering the stained glass of the cathedral on the screen.

EROS, THANATOS, AND A SAINT UNDERGROUND

I ALWAYS KNEW IT WOULD END, BUT NOT LIKE THIS.
Richard is snuffling into his sleeve, on the couch as usual, only this time his soft jolly shell has collapsed in on itself. I did my best, given the circumstances—barely able to walk, let alone speak, I came out of the bathroom only when he threatened to call 911. Given the NYPD's response time these days, I probably could make it to the soup kitchen before the cops showed up here.

Things have been steadily moving in this direction for a long time, I just wasn't ready to face the truth. But my life has been fundamentally altered since . . . when? The lead-up to Convention Week? Since I met Alex? Or Ing Kan? Or when I first started stealing to feed the colony years ago?

Or since the moment I realized that no matter how deeply Richard cared for me, I'd never feel the same way about him?

That's been the main event for the past hour. Richard is as predictable as ever, even during our breakup. His reactions unfold like a menu: shock; anger; denial; and now the raw psychic avalanche that follows denial's inexorable erosion. I cannot drag things out anymore. I can only hold Richard's head in my arms one last time, feeling his tears on my forearms, layering his pain over my own. There are no condiments for the end of the meal, just the cleanup. Whenever you can get around to it.

Richard existed before me; he'll go on without me. He may lose some weight now that he won't have my cooking to live on.

I won't.

I'm done.

The events of the past few weeks knocked me out of my decaying orbit. Now I'm just a rock hurtling toward the sun. It's only a matter of time before Alex finds out about my thieving, whether it's from Ing Kan or Mr. Chiroptera. Or maybe he's figured it out for himself by now.

At least I had the pleasure of cooking for him for a while and knowing he enjoyed it.

At least I got to speak with him as a person, rather than as an employer, if only once.

I got to see him naked once, too. Even if he'll never know it. I only wish I could tell him how beautiful he is.

But that's all finished now. Alex will never know how I've come to feel about him, ever. He'd sooner have me in jail as look at me, and I wouldn't begrudge him.

She saw to that.

Ing Kan won't have me, either, now that playtime's over and she can't torment me anymore. I've lost my job, my health insurance, my boyfriend, my home, and probably my freedom pretty soon. The outbreak triggered by what I saw on the monitors was the worst I've ever faced. But the searing pain has cleared my vision. When I came to on the floor of Richard's bathroom, I knew, for the first time in a very long time, exactly where I stood.

My life with Richard is over.

My life as a cook is over, unless I get a job in the prison kitchen.

But for whatever time remains before the cops close in, I'm free of all my obligations.

Except one.

The colony.

If I'm going down, I'll go doing what I've always believed was the most significant thing you can do with your life: helping those who don't have what you do. When they slap the cuffs on me, I'll be handing out soup and sandwiches to Helm and his friends. Between what's left in my backpack and what Caitlin was able to send down from our last market run, I should have enough food to prepare a final dinner. The Last Supper. Maybe we can even make some menus, Sharpie on brown paper bags.

Which is how, through all the pain, through the rubble of what I'm leaving behind and the imminent collapse that lies ahead, I can find the strength to shoulder my pack one last time.

Richard doesn't know anything I've been through lately. He doesn't need to know about Alex and Ing Kan, and he certainly doesn't need to know about my stealing when the cops take me. This is my parting gift to him: the innocence of ignorance.

There's nothing left to say. I leave him on the couch and close the apartment door quietly behind me.

• • •

"Turse'll be fine," Santiago's sister, Esperanza, was saying. "Audrey's working on him."

Santiago tried to snort derisively, but all that came out was a mucosal glitch. Nothing in his mind or body was working right. He'd thought about going home to his yoga mat but knew that he shouldn't be alone right now.

"I can get Audrey for you, too, if you want," she continued. "She's on call all night."

Audrey Spellman was Esperanza Santiago's answer to the bleak economics of current health care in New York. Before the crash, she'd been a freelance OT, primarily treating children with developmental disabilities. But after the crash, the budget cuts, the hospital workers' strikes, and more budget cuts, with Mount Sinai's entire surgical program teetering on the brink of collapse, the chief nurse of the NTU, Esperanza Santiago, had made an executive decision. She'd brought Audrey on board as a human alternative to anesthesia.

In her years of working with disabled children, Audrey Spellman had developed what Santiago had come to think of as the Voodoo Voice. Whether it was a kid with epilepsy, Down's, palsy, SPD, or any one of the natural wonders inflicted upon children by unknown and merciless device, Audrey's voice could soothe, mollify, placate, or redirect them all. So tranquilizing was her speech that it was a small jump for Esperanza Santiago (who would sit in on the treatments to take catnaps on grueling ninety-six-hour shifts) to apply her vocal talents to pre-op patients when drug rationing began in 2014. It was nothing drastic; abdominal and bone surgery patients still got their happy juice. But little by little, over the past two years—since More had left, in fact—she had learned how to apply

Audrey's somniferous speech to knock patients out cold. To everyone's surprise, it had worked magnificently: Patients actually stayed asleep during minor procedures and recovered well. No drugs meant no side effects, not to mention an immediate and significant conservation of available pain medication, which the hospital bean counters loved. The power of her sleep-inducing speech had earned Audrey an upwardly mobile freelance career at a time when these were largely extinct. She and Esperanza Santiago had both gained mention in several reputable medical journals, as well as becoming unsung folk heroes in city cyberspace.

Santiago was fiercely proud of his sister's achievements with Audrey, but at the moment, he just hoped Audrey was good enough to knock Turse out before he went on an apocalyptic rampage.

Bringing Liesl in was a formality; the techs had pronounced him dead at the scene, too much sudden tissue and blood loss, shock. But no EMT would dare face Turse, who was borderline psychotic over his partner's brutal killing, not to mention the wave of senior cops who flooded the scene while the cathedral yet burned: DiBiasi; McKeutchen; Derricks; and Randazzo. All were apopleptic with rage over the attack; none wanted to hear *can't* or *won't*.

It seemed worse that they couldn't bring Liesl across the street to St. Luke's Roosevelt Hospital, since by CT protocol it was to be fully evacuated following the battle. Inwardly, Santiago was relieved when the brass diverted the ambulance across town to Mount Sinai, where Santiago knew his sister could keep Turse under wraps while the rest of them tried to make sense of the crime scene that Santiago would forever think of as a battlefield.

There was more than enough carnage to justify it. Besides Liesl, they were still counting the casualties among those unfortunate enough to have been nearby when the shooting erupted. A steady stream of ambulances ferried students, teachers, dog-walkers, tourists, and children to Mount Sinai with various injuries. Thus far, Liesl was the only confirmed fatality.

After dutifully calling PAPD to shut down the western bridges and tunnels, then DiBiasi at OCID, then Derricks at CT Ops, then DC Randazzo at One Police Plaza, and finally, McKeutchen at the CAB, Santiago had turned off his phone and stared at the tire tracks left by the UPS truck that had spirited away the enemy sniper and his monstrous cohort. For a moment he thought it would be worth tracing the tread pattern, but he just as soon dismissed it. Whoever had attacked them was good enough to ditch the truck immediately, or at least swap out the tires and tags upon reaching minimum safe distance.

He and More had walked a few blocks north along Morningside Drive, guns drawn and held by their sides; Santiago had borrowed a spare magazine of heavy .45 rounds from More, who seemed to have a limitless supply. Uniformed officers cordoned off the adjacent streets as they passed. Here there were bodies, the Columbia University rent-a-cops in static call boxes, one in a university prowl car. Three had their throats cut; the one in the car had sustained a head shot.

"Small-bore, suppressed, probably a .22 long, subsonic," More muttered, half to himself. "They infiltrated south along Morningside Boulevard, taking out the campus cops quietly, at close range. He went over the wall where the drop wasn't too high before he set up on the rocks. They parked the truck there"— More pointed at the corner, by a nursery school—"to stage as backup. They exfiltrated uptown, straight up the drive, across Seminary Row at 122nd, down to Riverside Boulevard. They would've picked up West Side Highway northbound at 137th, then gone straight for the GWB at 181st. Nobody would look twice at a UPS truck, even on a noncommercial road. Maybe it showed up on PAPD surveillance video before they shut the bridge down." As he talked, More was looking at a digital street map on an outsize iPhone with a rugged outer casing that reminded Santiago of the armored thing that had killed Liesl. And nearly killed them all.

Santiago's mind felt like congealed soup. There were so many questions he wanted to ask. What *was* that thing? Who was the sniper, the one who looked and moved like More did, whom the armored beast seemed to protect? How did they know about the meet with Necator? Who the fuck *were* these guys?

"I need to talk to Devius alone," More said, abruptly wheeling to face Santiago, using his clear command voice, free of its usual clutter. "I don't know *who* hit us, but I know *what* they are, a lot better than you do."

"They're like you," Santiago managed, feeling a momentary lift from hate before his fatigue squelched it.

"Yeah. Someone sent them here. I don't know who or why, but Devius can find out—"

"He got Liesl killed," Santiago croaked.

"No. Liesl got himself killed. I tried to warn him. I've lost men before, more than once. You don't get used to it. You get even. You find those responsible. And I will. And when I do, you'll be with me. So will Turse. I don't care about Marrone. Let me talk to Devius. I'll get back with you at the hospital in an hour."

With that, More was gone.

Santiago went to Mount Sinai Hospital in a numb fog.

Now, as he sat with his sister at a restaurant called One Fish Two Fish, down Madison Avenue from the emergency entrance where hospital staff enjoyed cut-rate Civil Servant Thursdays, he tried to focus his molten mind on the situation. This was proving difficult, as he was sandwiched between a Scandinavian couple with a seriously retarded teenager in a specialized wheelchair to one side of their table, and a group of surgical interns in stained scrubs reliving a recent epic fuckup in the OR on their iPads, the volume turned up high.

"And you have no idea who they were?" Esperanza's voice floated through the mist in Santiago's brain. The Scandinavian couple spoke a singsong tongue, their damaged offspring a gnarled, broken slur of it. One of the interns held up his tablet for his colleagues to see: On-screen, something resembling a swollen, glistening football was slowly herniating from an opened abdomen. There was excitement all around.

Santiago closed his eyes. "No. None. I think More does. I'll bet Devius Rune does, too. I'm used to them keeping their secrets, but they can't play that shit now that Liesl's dead." He wasn't used to saying the words; they seemed to come from someone else's mouth.

"What about the first man they shot? The one you called to the meeting in the first place. Necka—"

"Necator. McKeutchen and DiBiasi recognized him from the surveillance video. They say he's a bagman, carries money and messages back and forth from City Hall to the statehouse in Albany, been around for years. This was all about that fuckin' subway station, Necator, the Mavridez case, whatever it is that More and Rune are lookin' for down there, shit, I don't know—"

"Which subway station?" Esperanza interrupted him. The retarded teenager kept repeating a tortured sentence to his parents, who couldn't understand, and the boy's pitch and gestures were becoming louder and more frenetic. At the other table, one of the surgical interns was saying, "Watch watch watch, right here he cuts the first hepatic lobule—" A wet sucking sound issued from the tablet.

Santiago was getting a feeling he'd had on other cases he'd worked with More, as if he were looking at the world through the wrong end of a telescope. He said very slowly: "Ninety-sixth Street, Second Avenue line."

"You're looking at the subway bank," his sister said flatly, not a question.

"NNnnnnnyyyyyuuuurrrrnnggghhhh!!!" exclaimed the retarded teen, thrashing about wildly, knocking a plastic cup of soda on the floor, where it puddled around Santiago's shoes.

Santiago carefully kept his eyes closed and, with his last shred of equanimity, he asked in a near-whisper: "What do you know about that?"

The intern at the other table held up his tablet for his merry band to see. With a liquid pop, the shiny football, which Santiago guessed to be a massively enlarged liver, squeezed clear out of its owner's thorax and onto a loaded instrument tray, scattering its contents to the interns' delighted cries of "*Opaaaa!*"

Esperanza appeared not to notice. Santiago wondered if her job had cauterized her normal human reactions to such grotesquerie, or if she'd taken to raiding the hospital pharmacy when Audrey wasn't on call.

"Everyone knows," Esperanza said with a simple shrug, "at least everyone who's fed up with the banks, and that's pretty much everyone. The hospital does direct deposit to Urbank, so I keep my account there. But I *was* thinking of getting one of the subway bank's CDs, they're supposed to pay like *forty* percent, I mean, where else can you get that kind of—"

For a moment Santiago heard their mother's voice in his mind, nagging him about how he was too wrapped up in work and school, how he needed to get out more, how he wasn't paying attention to the world around him, and how it wasn't so bad as he thought. He could not remember a single news story, in any format, describing a mass turning away from banks. He couldn't recall a single cop talking about it, nor had anything come up on OCID's radar that would indicate such a groundswell in popular (and illegal) sentiment. Was he really such a hermit, so encapsulated in his OCID cocoon, that he'd failed to notice a tectonic shift in how New Yorkers treated money? He had maintained an account at Banco Popular since his first adolescent jobs. It had never occurred to him, not with the crash or the constantly rising fees or the virtual currencies, that people would simply throw over the banking industry altogether.

For a hole in the ground.

Something shifted in Santiago's mind. His absurd surroundings faded from his consciousness, Liesl's ruined face and the armored beast temporarily turned down in his mental volume. Santiago had caught the scent, the corpuscal musk of dirty money. It galvanized him, filling him with a quiet thrum of energy. "How do you open an account there?" he pressed, his voice and eyes going hard in a way that made Esperanza pull back an inch.

"I dunno, just go down there with cash, I guess. Some of my nurses go there, I can get them to tell you—"

"The route. Just gimme the route down through the station to the bank. Text me. And do NOT go there, not even on the train, until you hear from me. I need—" He needed to move, he needed air, he needed space to think. Shoving brutally past the sniggering interns and shocked Scandinavians, Santiago stomped out of the restaurant, heading angrily uptown without seeing the streets, phone in hand, waiting.

Necator was dead. *Stomp.*

Liesl was dead. *Stomp stomp.*

Everyone in the Mavridez operation was dead. *Stomp stomp stomp.*

Money. *Stomp stomp stomp stomp.*

More had said he was looking for something that could fuck up Convention Week. Marrone had said she'd been getting stuff on dirty campaign money that didn't flow through the regular banks. The Mavridez operation was funneling drug money underground. Ordinary New Yorkers, nurses, his *sister*, for Chrissakes, nobody wanted to put their money into a regular bank. Instead, everybody with a few bucks was ratholing it down into the Ninety-sixth Street subway station.

A fucking hole in the ground, the new face of banking, 2016-style.

Stomp stomp stomp stomp STOMP.

Santiago found himself standing on the corner of 103rd and Madison, looking eastward into his phone. Esperanza had said she'd text him the route down to the bank. More had said he'd get back with Santiago at the hospital; by now he'd have talked to Devius Rune, would've explained there was no fucking way they wouldn't raid the bank after Necator and the armored beast and Liesl. DC Derricks would have real-time video on the bank. Santiago was looking at his phone, willing an avalanche of information from his sister and Derricks, so he could grab More and Turse and get down into the subway and—

He stopped looking at his phone. Something just over its rim had caught his attention. A curved, dark something, a something set in stone and grime. A something called an underpass.

The 103rd Street underpass, leading east beneath the Metro-North railroad tracks, for crosstown traffic to reach the FDR Drive.

And the eastern bridges to Long Island.

Santiago began sweating hard, his pulse rising in his wrists and neck.

The UPS truck with the armored beast hadn't shown up in any sweeps by PAPD, the Jersey cops, the first feds on the scene on the far side of the GW Bridge. They hadn't found anything. Because More suspected the truck had gone west, to New Jersey, and they'd all followed his lead.

What if it hadn't?

What if it had gone *east*, to Queens, Brooklyn, or Long Island?

That would mean the armored beast could still be here.

Why?

Something unbidden and unthinkable arose in his mind: a young woman. In chef's whites. Carrying a bulging military-style knapsack. Who came and went repeatedly from the subway terminal. He could see her image now, blazing like burning propane in his memory, pretty in a haggard sort of way, a hard worker, someone very busy, long hours, high stress . . .

Santiago ran.

His legs still rubbery, he managed to make it back to the NTU ward, where Audrey Spellman would have lulled Turse into a drug-free stupor from which he could be awakened easily. Security desk. Elevator. Corridor. Door. Door.

And More. Standing face-to-face with the son of a bitch spook Devius Rune, both of them on their weird-looking phones.

Still feeling the stress of battle, and newly winded from his sprint back to the hospital, Santiago attempted to articulate the logic of his recent deduction in detail. "East," he gasped intelligibly, "not west. Still here. Them. Bank. Subway. Video girl. Chef. Backpack. Find her."

More turned to Santiago as though none of the previous events had transpired and nonchalantly rasped: "Still have the shotgun I gave you?"

• • •

"You fucking knew about this."

"I fucking did not."

"Bullshit. It's him. You know it's him. You knew all along."

"Stand down, marine."

They were in the corridor around the corner from the stockroom where Turse was being treated—a figure of speech, since they were watching everyone who came and went. What with the flood of casualties from the park, the chief nurse (who happened to be Santiago's sister; Rune wondered what the hell More had done to her on his previous assignments to make her stare at them like she did) had shunted Turse off to a stockroom. There, amid the spare towels, rolls of gauze, and disinfectant, Turse lay sprawled on the floor while an elfin woman with a hypnotic voice murmured to him. More had thoroughly frisked Turse for weapons before "treatment" commenced; they'd watched for a few moments before heading outside for a talk.

An unprecedented one.

Rune's worst fears had been realized: Senator Mel Cordryceps, who'd been on the SSCI panel that had grilled him over More's last New York City op, had decided to launch one of his own. And of all the freelance former SOF talent set adrift after the end of the Iraq and Afghan wars, he'd picked the very worst one.

ODIN.

For someone in Rune's position, especially given his revolving-door standing with CYBERCOM, it hadn't been hard to get wind of who was behind the sudden sabbatical taken by one of the agency's most adept technicians, a civilian employee by the name of Irukanji. Rune had developed an appreciation for the young man's highly specialized skill set; he knew how it could be put to use by another with similar interests.

In the twilight world of Special Operations, one man stood out above all others when it came to battlefield high tech: ODIN. Rune knew him, all right; he'd used him several times in Iraq. His talents and his unit— ODA 666, one of the most decorated and feared A-teams in the history of Special Forces—were legendary. As was his grim outlook and disdain for the military, which had cut him loose when he'd tried to wage his own personal war in Iraq and points beyond.

Which he appeared to be doing again now, only in New York City.

More knew about ODIN, too.

Uncharacteristically for him (and unfortunately for Rune), he was getting emotional about it. Granted, what had happened in the park was a big fucking mess. But More had seen far too much combat over the years to be rattled by one short skirmish.

Except this one had involved ODIN.

And had killed one of the cops More knew.

Rune was close to losing his grip on the situation. It was time for damage control. "Look," he began, "I didn't know that—"

"No," More cut him off with a rasp, "you *did* know. You held out on me. You told me you were looking into this Redhawk guy, who might be an upstart contender for the presidency, and his girlfriend, who you think is a PLA honey trap. You said there was dirty money sloshing around Convention Week. You used Marrone to look into the money, you used me to get Santiago, Liesl, and Turse for local muscle. Now Liesl's dead, Turse is asleep in a closet, and Marrone's set up to be the fall guy for you when the blowback from Washington hits, which it surely will. Santiago almost got killed a couple hours ago doing your dirty work for you—"

Rune thought he might try a different tack. "Since when do you give a shit? You couldn't care less about these cops, you even said—"

"When we operate together, we're a team. A *team*. We deploy together, we go into battle *together*. It doesn't matter if I like them or not. I *depend* on them to help me complete my missions. So far, we've had a high success rate. Until now. Liesl might still be alive if you'd been straight with me from the beginning."

"Will listen to me for just a—"

"No, *you* listen to *me*." More had silently closed the distance between them to just a few inches. Rune held his ground but stood stock-still, as one would when confronted by a cobra. "We never met face-to-face until this afternoon, but I know what he is, what he's capable of, a lot better than you do. You think what happened in the park today was bad? That was nothing; he's just warming up. He'll bring down half the city before he's done—unless I stop him. Which I can't do with the kind of help I get from Santiago's people. This isn't a game for civilians anymore."

More paused. Rune silently hoped More wasn't thinking what he thought More was thinking.

But More was thinking it, all right: "I can have two companies here by tonight, with the rest of my unit coming—"

Now it was Rune's turn to interrupt. "Oh, yeah, that's a *great* idea! Sorry about the church, folks, now for our next trick, we'll drop the Second

MSOB on you. Are you *insane*? Army versus Marine SOF in a grudge match, whoever blows up more of the city wins? Does the term *civil war* mean anything to you? How do you suppose we would contain that?"

"You think you're *containing* things now?" More shot back. "How'd he get the suit?"

Rune's stance deflated a bit, and he sighed through his nose. "I don't know."

"That looked like the Mark III. It's not even supposed to be in field trials yet."

Rune spoke through a clenched jaw. "It's not. Guess he found a way around that."

"That's what he does," More hissed. "It's what he's *always* done. Whoever sent him here had no idea what he was dealing with. Who hired him?"

Rune hesitated. "This isn't exactly a secure—"

"*Who sent him?*" More's voice was very quiet but very clear.

Rune was an accomplished reader of warning signs. It was time to come clean. "Senator Mel Cordryceps," he exhaled.

More waited. Rune knew he was exceedingly good at that.

"He's the Senate Appropriations chair. He's got SOF connections. He was on the panel that grilled me about you two years ago. He presents as a moderate, but underneath he's as radical as they come. He thinks the Dems are out of control, and the GOP's powerless to stop them. His archnemesis is Caduta Massi, the speaker of the House. They *hate* each other. He hates her for backing the former secretary of state for president, among other things. She hates him for standing up to her, especially over the National IRA. That's what the subway bank's for; Caduta's using it to funnel cash off the books to buy votes so that New York can be the pilot program for her new bonds. She figures if she can swing this town, other cash-strapped cities and states will fall in line. Senator Cordryceps means to use the bank to expose her. How *he* found out about it, I don't know. I'm pretty sure GOP's parked cash there, too, or it's the senator's own account, maybe for his pet projects. Like our friend with the Mark III."

More got in another good one: "Who set up the bank?"

"I don't know." Rune was uncomfortable with telling the truth and tired of being on the defensive. "It's someone off our radar. There's foreign money involved—Ing Kan's bringing in Chinese money—but who's in charge, I don't know. Don't look at me like that, I really don't know. I thought maybe you or Marrone could help me out. The point is, this political feud's gotten out of hand, and it's turned Convention Week into a time bomb."

"So you're telling me this is all about *politics*." More fairly spat the last word.

"No," Rune corrected him, feeling the slightest bit more confident, "it's about money. Both political parties are running illegal funds through the subway bank. Judging from what the OCID guys have been working on, and what I've been hearing from my source in the banking industry, I'd say they started a trend. My concern about Redhawk is his potential—his girlfriend's a conduit for black Chinese money out of the country, all the generals and ministers and tycoons who're under the microscope in Beijing trying to save all the profits they stole. Our friend the banker in Hong Kong, the one who first set the honey trap on Redhawk, he's technically not PLA, but his connections to it run deep. They know we've increased regulation of our hedge-fund industry, so they need another way to lower our barriers to foreign capital flows. That means rolling back CFIUS. Redhawk's girlfriend is under orders to push that, and if he gets elected, the Chinese have their hand on the lever. I can't let that happen. Alex Redhawk *cannot* win the White House, no matter how badly we need a change."

"So why go to all the trouble with Treasury and OCID?" More grunted. "Why not just take out Redhawk? Or is that the real reason you brought me back here?"

Rune shook his head, masking his sense of relief. "Deniability. I can't operate in the open any more than you can. I can't look like I'm running a network domestically, and I certainly can't look like I'm conducting overt investigations of politicans, even if they haven't been elected yet. Treasury's a legitimate tool for this. So is Justice. The speaker and the senator are getting subpoenas from both agencies as we speak—"

"Won't do shit," More snarled. Rune's growing sense of solace evaporated. The deep-cover operative More, on loan to Rune at the CIA, was gone; More the MARSOC monster was back at the helm. "If the senator sent *him* here, he's been monitoring all comms, everyone's, waiting for the right time to move on the bank. Santiago tripped his alarm with Necator. He hasn't left." More dug out his phone, thumbing up a speed-dial number without looking. "He still needs to hit the bank, and he can't move the suit too far, too fast, without attracting attention." More checked the screen, then lifted the phone to his ear, his eyes cold and ichthyous. "Ganymede, this is Hydra Two, with an immediate."

Rune knew he'd lost all leverage and fought the urge to panic. "More, what the hell are you doing?"

"Working with what I have," More replied acidly. Into his phone, he rapidly croaked a numerical sequence, then: "I need a Glock 21 fifty-cal conversion package and a .50 Beowulf Overmatch kit for an M4. Eggs for both, eight cartons each. Now." He muttered the address for the hospital, then, to Rune's dismay, began reciting landing instructions for the roof.

Rune tried to intervene: He shook his head, indicating that he wouldn't pick up the tab this time.

More's cold fish eyes slid up to him, and he dropped his phone to waist level. "So now congressmen want to use SOF to fight their proxy wars here at home. Okay. We'll play along. You fast-track that ballistics report?" After the battle, More had given Rune an expended rifle shell fired at him in the park and told him to red-ball it.

Rune frowned. "It's a 6.5-millimeter Grendel." A tactical round, favored by snipers for its retained terminal energy over long distances.

More nodded fractionally. "It's him. No doubt. Make the call. Otherwise look at a map. The subway bank is just a few blocks from the address of the Dems' main fund-raiser, which happens to be tonight. You said the senator wants to hit the Dems in the wallet, right? Only he thinks the guy he hired is, what would you call it, *discreet*." More leaned in a bit and Rune could see a steel spark in those cold, cold eyes. "What do you think ODIN's next target is after the bank?"

Rune shut his eyes, more in frustration than in resignation. More was right. There was no alternative. He pulled out his phone and initiated the transfer sequence. The man on the other end of the line would debit an amount of Wampum, the CIA's virtual currency of choice, equivalent to the cost of the ordnance being ordered by More plus a standard delivery fee, then relay that amount, in code on a secure channel, to a relay banker, who would credit that amount to the account of the private armorer known as Ganymede, who would dispatch the items from a classified secure warehouse on a high-speed tilt-rotor PWUAV, which would deliver the goods within the hour, following a beacon that More would place on the hospital roof shortly. Rune's bankers would then settle accounts between themselves, leaving no trace of the transaction. An ancient method in twenty-first-century guise.

Which was how they were standing, glaring at each other, phones to their heads, when Santiago came flying around the corner, gasping: "East. Not west. Still here. Them. Bank. Subway. Video girl. Chef. Backpack. Find her."

More, implacable as ever, swiveled his head around and said: "Still have the shotgun I gave you?"

• • •

ODIN cut the connection and holstered his secure phone. "Asshole." He was sick and tired of Senator Mel Cordryceps.

"So are we a go?" the Behr asked, strapping on another cold pack. From the bluish hinge of his jaw to his shins, the Behr was a continuous bruise. Bad Boy's armor was able to stop the barrage of high-caliber rounds sustained in the park battle but could not prevent their kinetic energy being transferred at high speed into its operator's body. They hadn't expected the cops to have high-test .45 rounds; they hadn't expected them to have a guardian with a .338 rifle, either. They hadn't expected *More*.

Oh, *that* had pushed ODIN's needle deep into the red. Of course he'd checked out the senator before taking the job, but he'd been more focused on the congressman's legislative track record and connections to the SOF community. He hadn't really paid attention to all the hearings Mel Cordryceps had attended; there had been literally hundreds of them over the years. Not being a politician himself, ODIN had not bothered to open all the envelopes.

But after More's bullets had clipped twigs inches from his head in Morningside Park, after they'd engaged and exfiltrated, after he'd made sure the Behr and the others were okay, and after he'd managed to calm his volcanic rage over the surprise counterattack, he'd gone back to recon.

He'd had Irukanji do a deep-background probe on the senator, all the committee stuff, especially those hearings that had been sealed from public view, even those classified Dark Secret. It took some time, something they'd been short on before the battle, but now they were in turnaround mode, cleaning weapons and replenishing ammo. While they did that, Irukanji used some special software to sort through the tons of files quickly and precisely, searching for the single name ODIN had given him.

And guess what—turned out the good senator had been on the SSCI panel that had grilled that CIA scumfuck Devius Rune two years ago about his last little New York City escapade. Starring Everett "Ever" More, USMC.

Over the years, in Iraq, working for Stan "the Man" MacChrystal at JSOC or Devius Rune at CIA, ODIN had heard the stories. About the mixed-bag unit they called "More's Machine"—MARSOC, SAS, NZSAS, Afghan Special Forces—having fun and games all over AfPak, no strings attached, while ODA 666 was taken bit and bridle over the coals by CENTCOM over every move they made in Iraq. They could've done it all, ODIN's unit could have, broken ISIS, stomped the Mahdi army, taken on the entire Quds Force, and shwacked it—if the brass had the balls.

Now Iraq was the Trifurcate Caliphate, all the lives, all the effort, all the money, all for nothing.

Fucking pathetic.

Rune had tried to keep him in the fold, even tried intervening on behalf of ODA 666 when CENTCOM and JSOC agreed it was time to disband the unit. But there was no way ODIN would stay in their army, not after Sadr City. Not after what had happened at Diwaniyah.

He'd seen to it that his men got out clean, honorable discharges and pensions, all citations and decorations intact, no disciplinary charges brought or pending. With Rune's help, he'd been able to retain most of his security clearances, and with his SOF contacts, he'd set himself up in business after formal separation from the army. His men, loyal, brave, and true, had followed him, and they still did.

All the way to Morningside Park, where he had finally met Rune's other protégé for the very first time.

Fucking More.

Rune was still playing his New York games. Well, now the senator was, too.

"We got the go-ahead, we're shutting down the bank," ODIN declared, hoisting the heavy SAWMAG assembly he'd been cleaning. The dual-drum magazine vastly extended capacity for the M4 carbine but was prone to jamming without scrupulous maintenance. "We've got a secondary target on our way out of the subway, a fund-raiser for the Dems a few blocks away on Lexington. There's a connector from the target terminal on Second all the way to the number 6 line on Lex, big enough for construction cars to pass through. We hit the bank, head west through the tunnel, come out right across the street from the secondary target. Private residence, private security, no problem. After that, you guys exfil. I can do the Albany job myself, we've already got the CMDL programmed, I've got the platform in place, I just need to get the flight plans for delivery, and Irukanji says we'll have those within the hour. So after tonight, you guys get the suit back and get out of sight for a bit. RV at the usual place, first of the month. Got it?"

The other men in the room—the remnants of ODA 666, who'd followed him all the way from Iraq—gave ODIN a silent nod and went back to cleaning their weapons.

The Behr ambled over, water streaming from the sweating cold packs lashed to his massive bruised limbs. He paid scant attention to his injuries; he'd seen much worse. He was ready for Round Two, as were they all. Knowing that Ever More was involved made the assignment more complex, more dangerous, more *fun*.

"So the senator wants to go all the way?" the Behr said. "Cat's outta the bag now. They'll be all over him by nightfall—FBI, Congress, shit, everybody."

"That's why we gotta move fast. By tonight the New York City AO's cleared, By this time tomorrow I'll have the Albany vote fixed." The two men spoke *sotto voce*, looking over each other's shoulders, covering each other's backs—a practice honed by years in hostile territory.

"Is he really serious about shutting Albany down? I thought that was a last resort."

"Like you said, cat's outta the bag." ODIN hoisted the SAWMAG onto a trestle, which already held several boxes of linked M855A1 5.56-millimeter rounds. "He said shut 'em down, we'll shut 'em down. Permanently. We complete the mission *our* way. After today, I figure the senator's in last-resort territory, but we got paid already. Besides," ODIN muttered absently as he began loading the dual-drum container, "he held out on us about *him*."

"You think More's gonna call in the cavalry?"

"No. Rune won't allow it. He couldn't, there's no way he could cover it up. We'd be long gone by the time they could scramble any teams up here, he knows that. And with what More's got up here, NYPD weapons and ammo, he shouldn't be a problem."

"That's what we thought before, that all they'd have would be nines. Instead, they had hot .45s." The Behr gestured toward his own vast chest, a wide yellow and green map of subdermal impacts. "Not to mention that rifle."

"A .338, according to this ballistics report I just pulled," Irukanji called out from across the room. He was bent over his laptop, which had a thick cable connecting it to a high-bandwidth socket in Bad Boy's cockpit, which reeked of the Behr's sweat. "There was a red-ball request out of New York to the FBI lab in Quantico right after you guys left Manhattan. Not local cops, not FBI, not NSA. Signal pattern says Langley, but from off the reservation." Irukanji's fingers rapped against the keys. "It's a SAD signal, for a ballistics fast-track." He looked over his laptop monitor at ODIN. "Looks like your pal Rune's on your trail. They ID'd one of your rifle slugs, and they're suppressing the report on More's."

"So what," ODIN muttered, noting that the Behr was looking directly at him. "All our ammo buys are untraceable." He was just distracted enough not to notice that Irukanji did not look up from his laptop. If he had, he would have seen that the young man had started sweating.

"He knows," the Behr grunted. "More knows it's us."

ODIN pursed his lips but did not stop loading bullets into the SAWMAG. They were enhanced-performance rounds, designed to punch through steel helmets at long range. The SAWMAG held 150 of them, five times more than any tactical magazine the cops would have for More to use.

"Good," ODIN replied, smiling terribly. "We'll do the town together."

(INVESTIGATION)

I SEE THEM ALL THE WAY FROM THE PLATFORM ENTRANCE. Three of them.

There's no mistaking them for anything else. Well, one of them might pass for a colony member, reasonably clean but sort of mangy-looking and disheveled, like a bum or an NYU student, wearing a plaid newsboy cap like my grandfather used to have. One's got long hair and wild eyes; he reminds me of the bikers back home who run meth labs out in the backcountry. The third one's my downfall: a big dark Latino with large warm eyes, outsize hands, and the kind of pebble-link chain around his neck that you just know supports a badge. They're talking with Jonah, but they've come for me. All three of them are wearing long jackets, underground in August, and even from way over here I can spot the ugly bulges beneath. Guns. I'm done for.

In the soup kitchen I created, I won't even get to serve my last meal.

That takes the final bit of wind out of my sails. I slouch down along the platform to the far end, away from the bank, toward the hamburger stand. I need to face the cops standing tall, and at the moment I want to sit down and cry, so I push my way through the throngs of people. I'm really not myself right now, so it doesn't fully register that there's an awful lot of people milling around on the platform. They don't seem to be standing in their usual neat line to get past LA's security goons and enter the bank. Today everyone seems to be at loose ends, some impatient, some angry, most frightened. The majority of them seem to be passing the time by eating hamburgers from the hairballs' stand.

As I reach it, the hairballs aren't there. There's a line, so maybe they went back to their supply area to re-up. Seems strange that they'd leave the stand unattended, though. I push my way through the line and down the corridor, away from the tracks.

I'm not sure what's going on here, but I am sure that I don't care. I just want to sleep, though I know that where the cops are taking me, I might not get any. This is the end of the line, and I just want to rest before I have to get off the ride.

The door at the end of the corridor is locked—naturally. I drop my knapsack, put my back against the door, and slide down to the floor, my head on my hands on my knees.

Let them take me, I don't have the strength anymore, not for them, not for the colony, not for Richard or Alex or Ing Kan. *I tried, Mama, I tried so hard to make things work here.* I just want to sleep now. Maybe, just maybe, the cops won't look back here, the crowds at the bank will go away, and I can sit here and quietly starve to death. At least that way I won't be a burden to anyone.

Then the door behind me is yanked open and I fall flat on my back. Looking up into a pair of feral yellow eyes burning in a pelt so thick, I can't even see the hide beneath.

It's one of the hairballs. God, he's huge, like an ogre. I've never been this close to one before.

He reaches down and grabs the front of my chef's jacket with hands like iron and yanks me inside, turning and hurling me across the room as if I'm a beanbag. I slam into the side of something hard and studded with projections, like a hospital gurney but heavier and more solid.

And wet.

There's a smell in here I know from back home. Once you've been to a slaughterhouse, you never forget it. It's the smell not only of blood but of the various internal bags and hoses that store and carry it around the body. I try to stand but take a vicious kick in the midsection that doubles me over. My old pain rushes up beneath this new one. I'm in agony but afraid to touch anything, I know there's blood all around me and no way of knowing whose it is or what's in it. I curl up into a ball and try to cover my head and groin, my mouth clamped shut. If I try to scream, I'll likely take in a mouthful of blood.

Then I catch sight of something that makes me reconsider this policy:

Helm's head, raggedly severed and lying atop a heap of bloody clothes and shoes. This explains the disappearances.

This is where the hairballs have been getting their hamburger meat.

They've been taking members of the colony and serving them up to the bank customers.

And I'm on the killing floor.

No.

Not like this.

I *cannot* die like . . . this.

I try to scuttle under the object I hit; it looks like a long metal trestle of some kind. There's a scratching sound from the floor beneath me: rats?

No—my knife case.

My Way Out.

I reach down in the darkness and wrap my fingers around the first hilt I feel. It's my Shun eight-inch hollow-ground chef's knife, which I've used alternately for chopping and carving for over a decade. My mother gave it to me for Christmas, had it sent so I wouldn't be caught carrying it on a plane. I know its shape and heft intimately. I can wield it in the dark.

And when one of the hairballs bends down to pull me up on the table, thinking he can slice me up like a side of beef, I put the blade right through his thigh. I can feel it sinking in slowly, then accelerating as the point tears out the far side of his leg.

He howls.

I match his animal bellow of pain with my own screech. This is not pain, not fear. This is the raw, primal instinct to survive, distilled into its purest incoherent blare.

The wounded hairball staggers backward and crashes to the floor in a heap of bloody rags. The other one growls unintelligibly and closes on me, but I'm up in a kneeling position now, the trestle at my back and my knife well out in front. The charging hairball stops when he sees the glint of the blade, bares his teeth, and roars at me. I yowl back at him. We are at an old and fundamental crossroads, the hairball and I, speaking a common language that predates speech.

He'll need to bleed to take me, and he knows it. I will be New York's most expensive burger ever.

But then something happens that's outside of us.

The front of the hairball's shirt seems to mushroom out toward the rear wall above and behind me. The mushroom opens freakishly wide and fast, and for a moment I can see *through* him to the corridor beyond.

Where the mangy-looking guy from the clutch of cops holds a rifle. He's just shot the hairball through the back. But that wasn't a rifle shot, it couldn't be. That was more like a cannon.

The carcass with the bowling ball–sized hole totters in space for a moment, then crashes to the floor across the room from me, yellow eyes going moldy and still as they settle on mine.

Now I can hear the other hairball, the one I stabbed, whimpering and mewling, one hand wrapped around his bleeding leg, the other held high over his head, crying indistinctly for mercy.

The guy in the newsboy cap shifts his rifle slightly and fires again. The kneeling hairball's head disappears. I mean it *disappears*. Gone. What the hell is that guy shooting?

Then the other two are in the room, the big Latino getting between me and the shooter, the long-haired freak bringing up the rear and looking somehow disappointed that there's no one else to shoot. Except me, maybe.

The big Latino's holding a shotgun with a weird pepperbox attachment that makes it look like an oversize baker's tool. I can't help but giggle when I see it; granted, I'm a bit stressed out at the moment. The big Latino's all business, though.

—You're the chef, right? What's your name?

I find that I have to work a bit harder than usual at coordinating my brain, mouth, and salivary glands. My clumsy introductions sure strike a nerve, though.

—You work for Alex Redhawk? the rifleman says in a rusty voice, moving closer, which makes the big Latino hold out an arm to brush him back and bark at him, which he doesn't seem to notice. Once I see him up close, beneath the newsboy cap, there's something familiar about him. He looks like a lot of the guys I grew up with back home, the ones my mother wished I would have stuck around and married. Except for his eyes: They remind me of the fish I had on the table in the penthouse kitchen when Ing Kan first sidled up to me. A lifetime ago.

—Who the fuck is Alex Redhawk? snarls the biker. He's holding an automatic pistol with a dark grip and a gleaming slide. The muzzle bore is bigger than any pistol barrel I've ever seen, even those carried by the security goons in the penthouse. Who *are* these guys?

—Are you cops? I manage. I'm still not great at speaking. I'm on the floor with three corpses around me, two of them headless. It's been a long day.

—I'm Lieutenant Sixto Santiago, NYPD Organized Crime Intelligence Division, says the Latino with the funny-looking shotgun. —We have you on surveillance video coming and going from this location. What do you know about the bank?

Huh? These guys just busted a cannibal franchise, and all they care about is the *bank?*

—You mean LA's bank? Next door? She's been here since before I started the soup kitchen. Can I get up now?

—First drop the knife. You gotta come with us, Santiago is saying as I try to get to my feet.

—Who's LA? the rifleman wants to know.

—Who gives a fuck? rasps the biker. —Whadda you know about those assholes in the park?

—What park? I'm lost. Things have overtaken me. Santiago's arms are strong and warm. They feel good around me, the shotgun aside. Now I know how my dishrags feel at the end of dinner service: wrung frayed. I could go to sleep on Lieutenant Santiago, I really could, but he's bundling me up and hustling me down the corridor toward the platform. I catch snippets as the cops yell at each other along the way:

—*Turse, call Central, tell 'em we're gonna need crowd control down here fast. These people are all probably bank customers lookin' for their money.*

—*Is this the place that was on that fuckin' map me and Liesl found at the Mavridez bust? There really IS a fuckin' bank in the fuckin' subway?*

—*Waste of time, whoever was running this place is long gone, we should find out who LA is and*—

That's as far as the rifleman's contribution gets.

That's when the conversation stops.

That's when all hell breaks loose.

We've just made the platform. The one called Santiago is half-walking, half-dragging me to the stairs leading up to the southern exit at Ninety-fourth Street, on the downtown track. The crowd in front of the bank has grown unruly; if the customers haven't put it together from the cops' guns that something's not right with the bank, they will soon enough.

At the far end of the platform, near the big access conduit that leads west toward the Lexington Avenue line, is a monster, a huge armored thing with arms like tree trunks, clomping toward us, one tree trunk extended, spitting machine-gun fire. A dozen people, both bank customers and colony members, are mowed down in seconds.

That's it. I'm done. My brain shuts down. I grab Santiago's arms and freeze. *I'm sorry. I've stepped away from my desk. If you'd like to leave a message, wait for the explosion.*

The explosion comes a few moments after the monster extends another tree trunk and something bounces off the ceiling of the terminal toward us. A few moments after the rifleman spreads his arms wide and shoves the three of us, with astonishing force, back through the entrance to the soup kitchen. The explosion, when it comes, isn't nearly as loud as the screams that erupt from the crowd on the platform.

Now I can see other men with weapons pouring through the corridor between the soup kitchen and the bank. They're aiming for us, but the colony members and bank customers are in the way. One of the men raises to his shoulder something that looks like a big bicycle pump, and there's a long, loud zippered sound tearing the air. Santiago throws himself on top of me—God, he weighs a ton—and the other cops hit the ground as well. The rifleman takes charge:

—*They're trying to flank us. The suit's coming around the front entrance, the rest are coming through the back. They're trying to box us in. Turse, get that table down.*

I'm looking at the world sideways through a kaleidoscope. The biker tips over one of the long common tables from the soup kitchen, spilling plates of my would-be last supper everywhere, forming a makeshift barrier between us and those trying to kill us. It doesn't seem to stop bullets tearing through, though. I can't really tell. Maybe I'm already dead. It doesn't seem so bad right now.

Apparently, I'm alive enough to catch the rifleman telling Santiago in a surprisingly calm and low voice, to *set up on the other door, they don't know what you've got yet, we'll hold off the others,* and then he turns and makes some gesture to the biker that I can't see, and the two of them go flat on their bellies and wriggle around to opposite ends of the capsized table.

I'm in the middle. Since I don't want to see what's in front of us, I look to the back.

Straight into the terrified eyes of the colony members, who are trapped back here, with hit men and an armored beast bearing down on us all.

These people have nothing left, they've lost everything in their lives, from their jobs to their homes to their minds, and now they're up against the wall of a subway soup kitchen, about to be slaughtered like Helm. No, not like Helm. They'll see their death coming, on two legs, with tree trunks that spit fire.

And they'll die looking at me, the one who tried to save them.

Which will be my final act, if I can manage it.

I stand up. I've never felt so heavy, so lead-limbed, so filled with mortar and crusted with dried mud. I turn. The one called Santiago, on the far wall just to the left of the platform entrance, is yelling something at me, waving furiously with one arm, the other holding his weird shotgun aloft. There's obviously plenty of noise, but I can't make out distinct sounds. Except one. A deep, rhythmic thumping . . .

And then I'm looking at it.

And it's looking at me, tree trunks protracted.

And all I can do is draw another knife, since the cops didn't take my case. Another Shun. This one's a Sora paring knife, my standard for vegetable prep. Also excellent for cleaning shrimp.

Goodbye, all. It's been a pleasure serving you.

A tree trunk pops and puffs smoke. Something pings off the ceiling, then banks off the far wall and into the colony. I can't tell what happens next because Santiago takes me down as if we're playing football in the park and covers my body with his own and my face is pressed to the floor and I can see the rifleman doing the same thing to the biker and then there's an explosion and screams I can hear and both the rifleman and Santiago come up onto their asses and let loose with their weapons and my hearing is replaced by a high-pitched constant tone and the monster seems to stagger in the doorway, pieces of it flying out onto the platform behind, and it starts to stumble back out onto the platform, but as it does it raises its other trunk and sprays a long ribbon of fire out over my head into the colony and I still can't hear anything save the bell tone in my head though I can tell that the floor's getting wet. Then the monster's out of sight and Santiago's throwing me back down against the side of the table next to the rifleman, who's firing single, careful shots toward the other entrance, where the monster's allies lurk.

Then I know I'm not dead because my hearing returns and I can discern that there are fewer screams and I see the colony, or what's left of it, behind me, a scattered heap of heads and limbs and corpses, the sum of our parts. And I can hear the rifleman evenly saying:

—. . . *drive them back through the west conduit. He's got a SAWMAG*—

—*The fuck is that?* Santiago yells back.

—*Hundred and fifty rounds, you'll run dry before he does. But we've got more firepower than he expected, we've got to press our attack, otherwise everyone down here dies. You hit the suit. I'll get behind and drive it toward the conduit, you and Turse take the rest of his team. Pick your shots, use fire discipline, but remember, you can shoot through most of what's around you. Now cover me.* The rifleman crouches, then zip, he's gone, covering the distance to the doorway in the blink of an eye.

Santiago and the biker are shooting regularly from behind the table back toward the second entrance, and they must be having some effect, because the other team is pulling back across the room, though in a ritualized, crisscross manner, almost like some sort of dance. The music stops when one of them, ducking into a supply closet I use for storing bulk dry goods, jerks spasmodically like a puppet as four big holes are punched right through the room's thick metal door.

—*THAT'S FOR MY* PARTNER, *YOU* FUCK*!* the biker screams.

Two men, including the one with the bicycle pump, run back down the corridor toward the west conduit. I hear more thumping from behind the wall separating us from the platform, the monster's on the move, and it's moving fast for something that size. There's shooting from where the rifleman went, he must be keeping busy. Santiago and the biker are up around the table, running in fits and starts down the corridor. The biker checks the supply closet where he shot one of the monster's men, turns and smiles horribly at Santiago, and gives him a thumbs-down.

And then they're gone.

It's time for the reckoning.

I try to walk, decide it may take a while, and begin the slow crawl toward the remnants of the colony.

• • •

"Mr. Alex Redhawk?"

The band, a chamber quartet, was doing Bach. The crowd was richly dressed, expensively coiffed, and hungrily scrounging for money, as usual.

"Yes?"

"I'm Captain Anthony DiBiasi, OCID. This is Agent Liza Marrone,

FINCEN. Come with us. Don't say no."

The press gang hadn't registered the newcomers' arrival until DiBiasi flashed his badge. Then it moved en masse, a great wall of life, striving to eat or be eaten in the mad rush to break the story first. A barrier reef of bright TV anchor fish, reporter bottom-feeders and slow, undulating camera polyps.

"How could I resist such a warm invitation," said Redhawk drily, baring his electrifying smile at Marrone, who managed to refrain from throwing herself at him. "May I ask what this is about?"

"A young woman by the name of Beth Hutiak," Marrone replied just as aridly, "who was involved in a huge gun battle down in the Second Avenue subway tunnels tonight. She says she works for you. Is that correct?"

That did it. Redhawk's leading-man visage vanished, replaced for a moment by the kind worn by someone who knows they've just blown the audition, then in turn by a look of genuine concern. "Jesus! Beth? Yes, she works for me, she's my private chef. A *gun* battle? Is she okay?"

The media reef surged with sound and motion, and DiBiasi dialed up his signature scowl and jerked his head toward the arched doorway. Redhawk looked a question at DiBiasi, then seemed to think better of it, put his head down, and followed him out of the gallery. Marrone walked behind him, trying not to swallow her ears with a shit-eating grin and failing. The crowd muttered, the reef swirled and clicked, and the band played on. The crowd took momentary notice, then returned to its milling and murmuring.

After all, Alex Redhawk, the maverick of Convention Week 2016, had just announced that he *wouldn't* be running for president; that meant one less mouth feeding at the trough, nothing more. The common attention would turn to those remaining, and the competition would intensify. Time for more *hors d'oeuvres*.

From his vantage point at the magnificent chessboard on the far side of the room, hands on his special cane, Julius Exmoor watched the exeunt with a frown. This wasn't part of the plan. Then again, Exmoor reminded himself, Devius Rune had a way of rewriting the script on the fly.

• • •

Over the years, Santiago had seen his share of accidents. Be it motorcycle, car, truck, bus, or (as a rookie, in the smoldering rubble of the towers nearly a decade earlier) airplane, he'd had occasion to witness up close and personally the violent unintended embrace of man and machine. But nothing in his past could have prepared him for the sight that confronted him now.

He and Turse were gingerly making their way along the side of the train over the wreckage, keeping away from the third rail, watching for any remaining enemy fire, and scanning for survivors. More was at the front of the wreckage; the only survivors he cared about, Santiago knew, were those he was about to terminate.

The armored beast was dead, though, Santiago was fairly certain of that.

More had seen to it.

He'd led the charge, the three of them chasing the enemy sniper's group back through the west conduit, dodging cover fire from the armored beast, which had clumsily walked backward, protecting the leader, the one who moved like More. Who had the SAWMAG. Santiago had emptied his whole load, twenty rounds of explosive, illegal FRAG-12 rounds, at the creature, scoring a few hits, but more important, keeping it moving backward while More and Turse traded fire with the men in the enemy group. More finally nailed one of them, putting two .50-caliber rounds from the modified police M4 right through a steel support column behind which the man had sought cover. Santiago had seen the other man's rifle, along with the arm that still held it, fly halfway across the chasm of the tunnel toward the downtown track. Only then did he register that they had driven the enemy group all the way down the conduit, like prehistoric brush-beaters on a mammoth hunt, right onto the Lexington Avenue line.

Where the armored beast, crippled by multiple hits from the modified weapons and struggling to cross the tracks, was hit head-on by an arriving number 6 train.

The Kawasaki R160.

Eight cars.

Forty-seven tons of steel traveling at fifty miles an hour.

The armored beast's undoing.

Santiago didn't bother looking beneath the train, which had remained on the track throughout the collision. He concerned himself with the living, knowing that More would see to the dead and soon-to-be.

He found himself able to go through the motions more or less on autopilot, the nuts-and-bolts management of terrified humans in crisis, because that was how he'd come up in the job. The falling towers. The crash. The riots. A single sniping in Chinatown; a massive firefight in the Bronx. Now an armored beast that had wreaked havoc aboveground and below, granulated into an unguessable recipe beneath the wheels of a subway train. As always in such moments, there was More, both instigator and resolution, architect of chaos, prince of disequilibrium, whom Santiago hated, feared, and ultimately depended upon. He would admit this to no man.

But even that observation, to which Santiago had by now grown accustomed, quickly faded into the white-noise soundtrack of the First Responder. There was a greater contingency.

Because they hadn't found *him*.

The man with the SAWMAG. The enemy sniper. The armored beast's master. The one who moved like More.

Santiago had seen him silhouetted in fast-moving frames as the 6 train sped between them, an indescribable shriek of metal on metal tearing out from beneath the train. He even looked like More, in that disheveled white-guy way. But where More's eyes were cold and flat, this man's eyes burned like a white-hot plasma torch. This was more than anger, Santiago knew. It was the incandescence of hatred, and it would not burn out on its own; it would have to be extinguished by force.

Santiago saw, with a quick glance down the length of the slowing train, that More was looking at the man, too. They were staring across the chasm at each other, through the windows of the train.

But by the time the train had stopped, by the time they'd brought their weapons to bear on the far platform, by the time Santiago had radioed for backup and a three-block perimeter aboveground and a shutdown of the entire subway system and a systematic subterranean sweep of all East Side subway tunnels by heavily armed and armored ESU squads, the man was gone.

"We'll find him," Turse had panted. He'd just clambered up a service ladder to make sure they'd checked every last inch of the platform, brandishing Santiago's Glock 21, modified by More into a .50-caliber handheld bazooka.

"No," More had grunted, his voice reverting to its usual glottal mess, "I will."

To which, in his mind, Santiago silently added:
Just not here.
You've done enough.
All of you.

• • •

Alex Redhawk was, in TNU Chief Nurse Esperanza Santiago's professional opinion, a real pain in the ass.

Throwing his weight around, talkin' 'bout how he was tight with the chairman of the board, how much money he gave to the hospital every year, didn't they see the plaques? She just *knew* that was what would get the chief of medicine to sign off on the release of the girl, Beth Hutiak. Who, in Nurse Santiago's opinion, was lucky to be alive and had no business going home with that asshole Redhawk. Even if he did belong to the Asclepius Group, one of the members-only outfits formed by doctors who'd escaped the constraints of the disastrous decade-old health care law by forming private medical clubs catering to the ultra-wealthy. Leaving those like Esperanza to improvise care strategies for the teeming masses bearing subprime federal coverage, if any at all.

But Esperanza had been stymied in venting her frustration to her brother, who still carried that goddamn shotgun, the one More had given him on his first destructive visit to the city. No, Sixto wouldn't talk to her, just waved her off and shook his head, right after that creepy older guy, Devius Rune, had shown up at the hospital and kicked everyone but Redhawk and More out of Beth Hutiak's room (which *she* had arranged as a personal favor!) and shut the door.

Her brother, reeking of cordite and not saying a word, had slouched off down the hall with a similar-smelling Turse and their glowering boss, DiBiasi.

No one had told her a thing, just shown up with another wave of human tragedy and expected her to clean up the mess.

• • •

Devius Rune was having a Bad Day.
He hated it when More was right.
And he had been dead right about ODIN.
The mess at the church across town would take ages to resolve. There

would be a real media Mardi Gras, on-camera smoke and sobbing for the foreseeable future. Followed by endless finger-pointing, hand-wringing, and pontificating. Rune figured he had at least a month of internal inquiries and Senate committee hearings on his calendar already.

But the massacre underground, that was a whole new level of trouble. The cops were still counting the bodies, the injured were being brought up to the street for transport to Mount Sinai (because of the goddamn NYPD terror regs that mandated evac of the nearest hospital, Metropolitan, right above the fucking soup kitchen), where Santiago's sister was throwing a shit fit over the number of casualties and the severity of the injuries. The city's OME would be brought in, no way around that, not with the kind of ordnance the surgeons would be pulling out of the survivors in the coming days.

There was no way to cover up the Mark III, even if it was in pieces. That meant DARPA would get involved, the Pentagon, too, and Congress again. ODIN's teammates, the ones More and his buddies had taken out, would be identified as former ODA 666 members, and even though they'd been discharged for years, the army would get dragged into it, the Joint Chiefs would see to that. Devius Rune would have his hands full trying to explain ODIN's past and present links to USSOCOM and CYBERCOM; they'd press him on how and why ODIN retained his security clearance even after his stormy separation from the military. That would put the dogs on the trail of Irukanji, which Devius Rune couldn't allow, since he was one of Rune's assets, and hackers of that virtuosity were hard to come by.

Nor did Rune want to spend any more time in front of a bunch of self-righteous morons in some congressional committee trying to obliquely deflect questions about the likes of ODIN—and More—and why such men were permitted to exist, let alone be turned loose on U.S. soil.

Because the answer was so painfully obvious.

Because those in power would always need men dispatched with hidden motive, silent machination, and parting subterfuge. Men beyond law, beyond morality, beyond the illusions that those in "civil" societies draped over their eyes like veils to shroud them from the less comfortable truths about the world and the ungentle creatures inhabiting it.

Those on Capitol Hill didn't have a clue how the real world worked. And they were the lucky ones. For those who thought they did know—such as Caduta Massi and Mel Cordryceps—were delusional to the point of psychosis.

As they had just proved in New York.

When mired in adverse circumstances, Rune looked for so-called bright spots. These were circumstances (or people) that he could exploit to strategic or tactical ends to turn even the worst situations around.

Right now he had exactly two: Beth Hutiak and Alex Redhawk.

This was due to the fact that he no longer had Ing Kan, who was beyond anyone's reach.

There was little left of her for anyone *to* reach.

It had been McKeutchen, the CAB captain, who'd broken the bad news. He'd come waddling into the room, grinning from ear to ear behind a saturnine DiBiasi, who'd ignored Rune's protest for privacy by pointing a finger at his face, then jerking it back over his shoulder without a word. Grudgingly, with a familiar feeling of disappointment, Rune followed him into the hallway, More on his heels, leaving Nurse Santiago and her team to finish cleaning up Beth Hutiak, who was holding up well considering her ordeal. Redhawk's presence seemed to help; he'd refused to leave Beth's side from the moment the cops brought him to the hospital to the moment Nurse Santiago threw him out of the room. Redhawk had remained on station, occasionally checking his phone but more often waiting and asking any medical staff who went in or out of the room about Beth. Rune wondered if Redhawk was putting up a screen to throw the cops and decided he wasn't; the man seemed genuinely concerned about his chef in a way that seemed to transcend a business relationship.

Beth Hutiak, for her part, had been solid and unflinching in her recall of events, from Ing Kan's bizarre behavior to the mystery cameras and the blackmail scheme (surprisingly, Redhawk had met her gaze when she described it in detail) to the slaughter in the subway. She'd left nothing out, not even her own thievery. And she didn't freak out when they administered the ELISA test, checking her for God knew what pathogens she'd been exposed to from rolling around in the carnage. The preliminary results were, amazingly, negative. Beth Hutiak had dodged more than one bullet this evening. The others wouldn't have noticed, but Rune had detected a flicker of interest even from More. A lucky woman, to be sure, but also a strong one.

Rune had been pondering ways to use this observation to his advantage when DiBiasi and McKeutchen had burst in and dragged him away from a crucial debriefing. Until now the city cops had been remarkably cooperative, an abnormality Rune was trying to exploit.

But now that fat slob McKeutchen had blown everything to hell. DiBiasi served as relay: Approximately one hour earlier, when Redhawk and Beth Hutiak were at the hospital with Rune, More, and Santiago's team, a Chinese diplomatic attaché named Ing Kan had done a swan dive off the terrace of Redhawk's penthouse, decorating the corner of West Fortieth Street and Sixth Avenue with her innards.

Rune had already mobilized the local FBI office; the head fed there, SAC Totentantz (who *loved* dealing with Santiago, More, and Rune) was just getting into his car with his DSS counterpart to detain Ing Kan, revoke her diplomatic immunity, and speed her deportation proceedings. There was no police activity at the scene prior to the incident. There was no staff at the penthouse, either: The security detail was all outside with Redhawk (which was escalating tensions with the cops and hospital staff). Also present was Redhawk's house manager, an odd little man Redhawk referred to as "Mr. Chiroptera", who informed the cops that Ing Kan's behavior had been increasingly erratic of late, the most recent instance of which was her abrupt dismissal of her two Filipino maids. Mr. Chiroptera looked straight at Devius Rune when he said he hoped the now-questionable immigration status of the young ladies might be overlooked and they would be "provided for," which was readily echoed by that asshole Redhawk, who kept bitching about wanting to see Beth Hutiak.

Rune couldn't understand what had happened. He'd set and sprung the perfect trap, and Ing Kan had escaped in the most unimagined way possible. PLA agents weren't supposed to be captured, but she couldn't have known the CIA had been on her so closely in New York—hell, since Hong Kong, when she'd been introduced to Redhawk. Rune knew Ing Kan was deep into moving black money for PLA generals, Chinese tycoons, Triad kingpins operating between the mainland and Macau, even Shan warlords running heroin from the Golden Triangle. All dangerous foes, to be sure, especially with the most recent purges from Beijing's latest anti-corruption drive making headlines worldwide.

But to *kill* her?

In a way that made it look impossible to be anything other than suicide? Why?

Had they somehow gotten their money back?

And there was the crucial question: Where WAS all the fucking money?

Ing Kan was moving millions. But she hadn't washed any of it through the consulate—Rune's undercover agents there would have picked up on it. Local businesses? No, that's why he'd brought in Marrone—to sift through the massive FINCEN database to track unauthorized dollars connecting Ing Kan to any business in the U.S. and its allies. It had saved him plenty of time and effort, allowing him to focus on other priorities. But so far, Marrone had come up dry.

The banks? Well, Rune hadn't maintained his working relationship with Julius Exmoor over the years for nothing.

And now he couldn't even address this latest conundrum. Instead, he was on a landing overlooking the Guggenheim Pavilion's atrium, which was filled with milling hospital staff, worried relatives of patients, and free-floating coffee kiosks. Rune and More faced a gang of scowling cops, from that headcase Turse (still covered with grime and GSR from both battles) right up to Deputy Chiefs Randazzo and Derricks. Santiago stood silently behind them, hands in his pockets, staring and saying nothing. Not one of them looked anywhere close to friendly.

Then there was More, smelling as foul as Turse, who'd been curiously standoffish, even for More. Rune hadn't forgotten their earlier spat; he knew More never would. Rune himself hadn't been thrilled with the way his latest New York op had played out. The objectives had been met, yes: Ing Kan was neutralized; Redhawk was out of the White House rat race; ODIN was on the run, his operation all but destroyed; Senator Mel Cordryceps and House Speaker Caduta Massi were being subpoenaed, probably at that very moment. In theory, Rune's op was a success.

The reality was quite different.

Feeling the anger from the cops swelling toward the ceiling, Rune, in typical Runian fashion, thought it best to be proactive. He got as far as "Look—" before every cop in the room snarled, "Shut the fuck up." Even More stood at a distance from him.

This would not end well.

A long table stood between Rune and More and the clutch of cops. DC Randazzo cantilevered his huge grizzly frame onto his massive paws and grunted: "Let's get vestibular."

Each of the cops assumed the same position, hands on the table, heads down. Rune sighed and played along. Working with local law enforcement was always a nuisance, but the NYPD was a different breed of bother.

"You should've told me you were in town," Randazzo opened. "I backed you in the past when you were playing your games here."

Rune attempted, "I couldn't—"

"Fuck you, Secret Agent Man," Randazzo snapped. "You shoulda called me the second you knew you'd have to go operational here. I don't care what rules or regulations you invoked, that was a formality after the fact so you could say you'd followed the rules. You withheld vital information about an imminent threat, and now I've got bodies aboveground and below all over my town.

"They're stoking up the fire for you in Washington, and they're sharpening the spit. I'm gonna watch you roast, and I'm gonna enjoy it, because after they're done with you, it's *my* turn. For the moment, I'm going back to my office, and I'm gonna put my feet up and think about all the different ways New York can fuck you the way you've fucked us. That's the only good part about this whole sorry shitstorm: You're gonna be the last one left out in it." Randazzo pushed his ursine bulk up from the table and headed for the stairwell, by which stood a uniformed NYPD sergeant with a shotgun.

It was DC Derricks's turn. He leaned farther over his hands and whispered: "You held out on me, motherfucker."

"Hey, don't give me that," Rune started. "I contacted you first—"

"Fuck you, Secret Agent Man," Derricks spat, his voice rising. "You knew *he* was part of this, you shoulda warned me first thing. I could've mobilized ESU, gotten SIGINT surveillance up sooner, scrambled riverine units to cut off their exfil route, even brought in the Air National Guard to blast that fuckin' suit from the sky. We coulda stopped him before all this shit went down. But *you* had to do it *your* way.

"I'll send you a final body count when we have one," Derricks rasped. "They're gonna pull a train on you on the Hill that'll make you forget what it was like to walk normally. Have a nice ride back to D.C., asshole." With that, Derricks strode to the stairs.

Next in line was DiBiasi, who looked like he might fly over the table and go for Rune's throat with his teeth. He skipped the preamble, and this time Rune kept his mouth shut.

"You've got quite a chess game going here," the OCID captain hissed. "Politicians, spooks, Special Forces fucks. Dirty money for dirty tricks. A shooting gallery in a park, a slaughterhouse in the subway. Derricks is getting ahead of himself: We don't even know where all the bodies are, let alone started counting 'em.

"What gets me isn't your twisted fucking subterfuge. It isn't the warped way you got to checkmate. It isn't that the church I got married in—the second time—is now a miniature version of the Twin Towers. It isn't that the Ninety-sixth Street subway terminal looks like the set of some fuckin' zombie movie. It's this: *You got one of* MY *men killed.* Liesl might be alive if you'd been straight with us from the beginning, and maybe your pet viper there"—he gestured savagely with his chin at More so that the vertebrae in his neck popped audibly— "could've stopped that sick fucker before he got started. But you didn't. And now OCID's one man short."

DiBiasi stood up, jaw set and eyes bright, stuck his hands in his pockets, and turned for the door, followed by McKeutchen and Santiago. Halfway to the stairwell, DiBiasi stopped and turned back to Rune. "If I see you at Liesl's funeral, I'll kill you," he said slowly and evenly. "Fuck you, Secret Agent Man."

DiBiasi's shoulders brushed the sides of the doorway on his way out; McKeutchen had to practically squeeze his girth through. Rune overheard McKeutchen say something like: "I got married there, too. My first time. By the second time, I couldn't afford it."

Santiago glanced back over his shoulder at More and was gone.

Rune sighed as he pushed himself up from the table, rotating his head on his neck, letting the blood drain from his head. It was good to let them vent; the cops' threats meant nothing to him. But they were right about one thing: Washington would be sharpening the knives for him. He might have better luck facing the ire of the NYPD.

He turned toward More, who'd been silent and motionless the entire time. "Well?"

"Did you do Ing Kan?"

"No. That's what I can't figure out," Rune replied curtly. "We were up on her comms, her finances, everything at the embassy, and the blackmail, but termination wasn't an option."

"The penthouse peepshow cameras? I thought those came from embassy PLA plants."

"As far as Ing Kan knew, they did."

"So the blackmail crew was really *your* people, working for her?"

Rune allowed himself a small, wry smile. "They don't call us the Special Activities Division for nothing."

The problem with talking to More, Rune reflected, was that he didn't care how long he kept you waiting for him to speak. That and his damn fish eyes, which didn't seem to blink as much as human eyes.

"The cops are right," More finally slurred.

"Which ones?"

"All of them."

"So keeping compartmented information from being compromised by a notoriously leaky and corruption-prone local law-enforcement agency was bad judgment?" Rune was getting a mite testy.

"The bad judgment was in your strategy, not your tactics," More sibilated. "Your execution went well up until the end. But this wasn't a counterintel assignment—you came up with it on your own. You weren't just carrying out policy, you were *making* it. Satisfied with the results?"

Rune bruxed his molars, looking into More's depthless eyes. "Perfectly. And I wasn't making policy, I was carrying out a mission, as were you. Speaking of which, I've got your next one."

More turned soundlessly; no joints popped, no clothing or harness creaked. As he floated past Rune on silent feet toward the stairwell, he wheezed: "Fuck you, Secret Agent Man. I've already got my next mission. Once I find him."

• • •

The private doctor from the Asclepius Group, Larry, looks like a vole. But he's by far the cheeriest person I've met today.

—I wouldn't worry, he's saying as he stows away some of his arcane gear. This guy has better equipment in his bag than they had at the hospital. —The Western blot test showed no pathogens. You're quite a lucky young lady.

He just gave me a test the hospital would have had to send out for, wait at least a week for the results, and charge God knows what. Dr. L. did it for me for free in under five minutes. That was after putting me through Alex's at-home body scanner.

I'm in yet another penthouse room that I never knew existed. It's like a private hospital in here. There's a huge machine with the words SIEMENS SOMATOM SENSATION CARDIAC 100 stenciled on the side, which I read as he slides me in. After he asks if I'm pregnant. Even low-level rads aren't fetus-friendly, I guess.

—Ah, there we are, says the doc from behind a monitor showing him my inner topography. —Genital neural inflammation. No malign fungals or bacterials, no neoplasms. Textbook vulvodynia, generalized. That explains the chronic pain you told me about. Don't worry, this is an easy fix.

Maybe easy for *you*, Doc, I mutter to myself.

—Let's get to it, he says, rummaging around and coming up with another odd-looking little kit, which he unzips to reveal a Mag-Lite and a series of swabs of different lengths.

Oh no. I've been on a pretty even keel the last few hours, all things considered, but the sight of the examination kit brings back a surge of fear and pain that hasn't switched on since the attack of the hairballs.

—It's okay, it's all right, I won't hurt you, Larry the Vole promises. —Whatever you may have been given in the past, great strides have been made with treatment. Here, feel how fast this works.

And he swabs me.

Just like that. So fast I hardly see his hands move.

The first man to touch me between my legs besides Richard in four years.

With a cotton-tipped stick.

That's coated with some sort of—

Oh.

Oh.

Oh my God.

There's such a mix of sensations rippling through my core that I can hardly distinguish among them. But none of them is painful, not one.

—Feeling better, I take it? Larry smiles.

—I don't . . . I can't *believe* it. I feel . . . What did you use on me?

—A modified gabapentin derivative, Larry replies rodently. —There's been real progress made in the last few years with engineering new tricyclic antidepressants for analgesia. You'll take another swab tonight. The rest of the regimen I'll leave with Alex. We'll keep you at this dosage for the next few weeks, then gradually bring it down as your outbreaks diminish. A few months from now, you'll forget you ever had it.

I have no idea what he's just said to me except the last part.

I'm going to be cured.

I can be whole again.

I feel . . . new.

Dr. Larry is packed and at the door in under a minute. He must have a lot of house calls to make tonight.

When he holds the door open for me, Alex is sitting right outside. Something in me stirs, expands, and moves toward him. But the two men go off to Alex's office. Alex looks back over his shoulder at me before they go inside and close the door.

I cannot imagine what the annual membership fee for this medical club costs.

I cannot believe what's happened to me today.

I need to talk to Alex.

Dr. Vole-Face emerges from the office, heading for the front door. He tips an imaginary hat to me, smiles, and winks, and he's gone.

Replaced by the unsmiling visage of Mr. Chiroptera.

My heart does a momentary little flutter—what does he have in store for me? Jail? A lawsuit? Working off what I've stolen?

But after so many extraordinary events today, he gives me one last one.

He smiles at me.

For the very first time.

And says:

—Go on in, my dear, he's waiting for you.

He holds out his arm toward the office door and even gives a tiny little bow.

I don't know what's going on here.

But I am propelled into the office by a force I don't want to fight.

The last time I stood in this doorway was just before the wine tasting. Now I'm completely inside Alex's inner sanctum. There are no guards here. Ing Kan is dead. The monitors are all dark.

Alex Redhawk, maverick money manager, the Man Who Would Not Be President, my boss, is hunched forward in his leather swivel chair with his hands clasped uselessly over his knees. He's looking up at me, his eyes almost apologetic. This man holds my whole life in his hands. What's he going to do with me?

I'm steeling myself for recriminations, but what I hear from him is:

—I didn't know. About any of it. I'm sorry.

Apparently, the extraordinary stuff-making machine isn't finished with me for the day.

—She never told me anything, not about the thieving, the way she was treating you, none of it. She'd definitely been getting, well, more unusual the last couple weeks, but I put that down to pressure from the embassy about her friends in China. Before that, I thought she was genuinely pleased to have you here. But now I know it wasn't just for your cooking . . . His voice trails off.

Alex looks down at the floor. In a way, his awkward modesty is amusing. Considering what I saw him doing on-camera not so long ago. To a certain extent, it's entirely understandable. I've forgotten that this is a man whose girlfriend just committed suicide for no apparent reason.

But his girlfriend was Ing Kan. I haven't forgotten that.

For the first time tonight, I feel no sympathy.

I have literally wallowed and crawled through pain and blood and death this evening.

Now I want to live.

And I don't want to be alone.

I feel . . . new.

—Beth, I don't know what to say. Alex is talking to the floor. —This has been such a completely fucked-up day—

—It's not over yet, I whisper.

He looks up from the floor and stares. He's not used to seeing me like this, I know; he's only ever seen me wearing chef's whites. Now I'm not wearing anything at all. The clothes I had on in the subway were a biohazard. The hospital johnny I've been in for the last few hours is pooled around my feet. Alex blinks, puts his hands on the arms of his chair, starts to stand, then abruptly sits down.

I want to laugh.

Instead I say:

—Dr. Larry said he left my regimen with you.

Alex opens his mouth, his lovely mouth, and nothing comes out. He manages to nod, his jaw hanging open.

—Take out a swab, I whisper.

He's just sitting there. I hope I haven't overloaded his circuits. I also hope he won't keep me standing here all night.

He doesn't. The swab is in his hand, while everything else that was on his desk a moment ago is now on the floor.

His hand is far from steady.

But that'll be just fine.

—Roll your fingers over the swab, I tell him softly. —Get the medicine on them.

He barely manages to comply, his hands trembling visibly. Oh, Alex, you little boy in your big man's costume, I can see you now. But don't worry, it'll be all right.

—Come here, I say to him.

I've wanted to say those words for I can't remember how long.

He's none too steady on his feet, and his eyes are confused and wild. But I can see the bulge in his pants from across the room. Good. At least I haven't terminally freaked him out.

He's standing in front of me, quavering, his medicated fingers curled and shining, like his lips. I can feel the heat coming off him in waves; I can hear his pulse throbbing. It's time.

—Put the medicine on me, I barely manage to susurrate.

At our first contact, the tremors in his fingers vanish, the heat coming off his skin suffuses into mine, and we flow slowly into each other, his hand melding perfectly into my creases, already finding delicious caressal form and rhythm, arcs of electricity banding up and down my body and heat building within my core like a broiler coil and absolutely no pain, no pain at all, and Alex gradually ups the tempo and I can feel a whirlpool I'd thought long extinct starting to gyrate within me, and his mouth, his lovely lovely mouth, is on mine and I can taste all that I have forgotten and thought was never mine to savor again and Alex's fingers are moving faster and farther and my legs are beginning to feel like gravity no longer applies to them and my hands are inside his shirt and his nipples are hard and sharp beneath my fingertips and the heat is rising through my chest and neck and now I'm floating on his digits and drinking sustenance and delicacy and flavorfume from his mouth and my hands are between his legs and there is fierce calidity here, too, and churning force and insistent life and the friction on my manumitted vulva passes the point of no return as the heat from my core razes up through the base of my skull to my scalp and the horror-pain of the day obliterates itself in whiteout and my mind is made of marigolds.

PART IV

WELCOME TO THE SUBDUCTION ZONE

(NEUTRALIZATION)

SENATOR CORDRYCEPS'S AIDE DREW could no longer stay inside. Not after witnessing all the hobnobbing and backslapping, the glad-handing and sustained glances from knowing and half-concealed eyes. Not after hearing the legislators (both chambers, both sides of the aisle) passing detailed instructions to one another on when to withdraw *en masse* from the main assembly chamber to each camp's conference lounges, thus triggering automatic affirmative votes by their absence. Not after seeing the Budget Committee chairman, Terry "Tee" Saginata, swaggering into the chamber with a sated leer, hand in pocket visibly massaging his crotch, already starting into his tale of novel conquest and debauchery that the aide knew was coming even without hearing it. Once, before taking the job in Washington, Drew had seen a nature special about baboons. At the time of viewing, when he'd been a little drunk, a little horny, and plenty bored, he'd thought the animals' peculiar form of aggressive/sexual/excretory display rather amusing.

Now, watching almost the entire New York state legislative body engaging in starkly similar behavior, it was too much for him. He slammed through the outer doors, thinking he'd head up to the Corning Tower observation deck, as far from the imminent vote on the National IRA bond as he could get without leaving Albany. He needed time to think. He did not relish the thought of returning to Washington. Or, for that matter, to Cordy.

Trotting down the stairs outside the colonnaded entrance, he nearly tripped over her. He couldn't believe it. Although he'd been thinking about her constantly since the start of Convention Week, he'd never even remotely considered the possibility that Caduta Massi's aide would be *here, now,* at the same time he was!

But she *was* here, and she was pulling on a cigarette like she wanted to choke, and boy, did she look worn out.

When she noticed the pair of long legs standing too close to her and not moving, she looked up at him.

And smiled, in a weak, almost sickly way, like she felt as bad about being there as he did.

And he sat.

Sat right down next to her, just like that.

He wanted to hug her. Well, no, that wasn't entirely accurate, he wanted to do much more than that, let's be honest. But the overriding protocol, the one that he found himself following without question or doubt, was to sit next to her without touching her and offer the hint of a smile in return. He'd never been this close to her. She was so different from the others he'd known, with her pale, pale skin, her hard and nervous eyes hidden by dark artifice, lines of metal and ink threaded through her skin. She looked exotic, and she looked wounded. He did want to touch her, badly, but at the same time, he sensed that she needed someone to talk to.

And he did not want to ape the boorishness of the baboons he'd seen inside the state grand assembly chamber.

• • •

There was excellent signal clarity on the radio exploit Irukanji had engineered for ODIN to put through the CMDL unit in the back of the pickup. He could hear the tower controller at Shaw Air Force Base in Sumter, South Carolina, as clearly as if he were parked there. Instead of on a hill by a landfill in Troy, New York, just a few miles north up I-787 from Albany. He'd driven all night from Manhattan, stopping only for gas.

ODIN was a master of military systems—their use, their strengths, and their weaknesses. He could not only procure them, he could undermine them. It was a skill he'd honed to deadly effect on foreign fighters. Now it would be brought to bear on a lone American one.

Irukanji's intel (which he'd delivered to ODIN right before they deployed to the subway bank, a day and a half earlier) was as good as promised. The "flight" was actually a one-man "squadron," the kind of exercise that the air force, bloodied by years of slashed budgets, had turned to in order to maintain bare-minimum levels of competence. This amounted to breaking the wingman model that had been in service since the dawn of powered flight. No longer would pilots train in pairs or groups on a regular basis; now fuel and ordnance were parceled out in single servings for live-fire exercises. This was officially known as "maintaining operational readiness."

And so it was that young Captain Bobby "Ramf" Rhamphorhynchus was making the qualifying bomb run necessary for any pilot prior to active-duty deployment—solo. As per Irukanji's intel, he would refuel in the air flying to and from the target, a cluster of abandoned barges and refinery scrap that had been towed into restricted U.S. waters just off the coast of Lubeck, Maine, right at the Canadian border. He would take his navigational cues and fuel from drones on station at pre-positioned spots in the sky, like buoys in the sea. His only human contact would be the voice of the Eastern Air Defense Sector controller, fifteen hundred miles away.

ODIN made a few final adjustments to the intrusion program on his laptop and sent it through to the receiver, a high-bandwidth data link in an olive-drab casing no bigger than a beer cooler, with an effective tactical range of five hundred miles. Which was about where Captain Ramf was now, topping off his tanks from the KC-135T drone orbiting a patch of ocean off the Delaware coast. He was scheduled to hit the same nozzle on the return to Shaw. Since the aerial refueling sequence was entirely automated, there wasn't much for ODIN to listen in on other than some desultory back-and-forth, the pilot advising the controller when he was lining up the probe to the robotic teat, and when he'd detached and resumed course. ODIN checked his watch, a matte-black MTM Cobra. At this airspeed, he had another three and a half minutes. He double-checked the CMDL and transmitter array, splayed out in the pickup's bed like a massive aluminum sunflower, then hopped back into the cab. To find the white noise, he needed to keep his mind on the mission and off the previous day's losses. He chiseled into a subscriber-only paleo-rock program from a satellite in high geosynchronous orbit somewhere overhead. He got some ancient eighties caterwaul, the signal rough and low compared with the equipment in use in the pickup:

Moving forward using all my breath
Making love to you was never second best

I saw the world thrashing all around your face
Never really knowing it was always mesh and lace . . .

• • •

They averted their eyes while the deputy state comptroller and the city public advocate went bounding up the stairs, the Three Pauls in tow, obviously impatient for the outcome of the vote and the spoils to be divided thereafter. She hung her head, grinding out her cigarette beneath her heel. "Hail, hail, the gang's all here," she proffered. This wasn't what she'd planned for, any of it. At least she had some company, even if it was that big dumb jock who worked for Cordryceps, whose nearness and size were reassuring in this strange and uncomfortable place. His not so surreptitious glances at her back in D.C. had been the only silver lining of Convention Week. She couldn't believe he'd been sent up here, too. Mel Cordryceps and Caduta Massi must not have wanted any of their staff to see what could only be an epic shitstorm blowing up between them. No, she was glad to be far from there, even if it meant being here.

Next to Cordy's aide. Big Boy. Who, she grudgingly admitted to herself, was actually really cute up close.

And who was saying: "Not quite. The governor and the senator are down in Manhattan right now. Some kind of powwow with the City Council speaker there. I hear your boss had something to do with it."

Caduta Massi was the last thing the aide wanted to hear, discuss, or think about. Instead, she parried with: "What's your name?"

"Drew," Big Boy replied right away, but calmly, without desperation, looking at her fully for the first time since sitting down. Maybe not so dumb after all. Promising.

"I'm Corinne," she found herself saying quite easily. "Call me Cory."

• • •

EADS CONTROLLER: HARBINGER ONE, THIS IS SHAW CONTROL, WE HAVE YOU APPROACHING LAUNCH COORDINATES. MAINTAIN COURSE, SPEED, AND ALTITUDE, OVER.

PILOT: HARBINGER ONE, COPY.

C: ROGER. INITIATE PRE-LAUNCH CHECK.

P: INITIATING NOW.

The array in the pickup bed whirred and clicked, locking in on the signal being transmitted from the cockpit to the weapon nestled comfortably within the internal weapons bay, safe from weather and slipstream.

But not safe from ODIN.

The platform was the original version of the F-15 Silent Eagle, the existence of which was still officially denied by DoD, despite years of sales to Arab League nations that had bolstered the bottom lines of numerous defense contractors with heavy lobbying presences in Washington, and sustained scores of first- and second-tier contractors to the Pentagon through seven lean years. While the plane was now in its third manned variant (there had been numerous drone prototypes, all of which had crashed; they were still working the bugs out), the alpha model had been relegated to training young aviators like Captain Ramf to take over the skies.

The weapon was a GBU-100 SDB. It was a five-thousand-pound monster with an onboard AI self-navigation module and a glide range of a hundred miles, which could be doubled if launched from forty thousand feet or higher.

C: HARBINGER ONE, CLIMB TO FIFTY THOUSAND AND ASSUME LAUNCH ATTITUDE. STATE WEAPON STATUS.

P: TOWER, WEAPON SAFE, INS ENGAGED. REQUEST TARGET DATA.

C: COMMENCING TARGET DATA TRANSFER. TARGET ELEVATION THIRTY-TWO METERS. AIR AND WATERS CLEAR, ZERO FRIENDLIES IN TARGET ZONE, OVER.

P: ROGER THAT. CLIMBING TO FIFTY THOUSAND.

There was a messy rush of noise as the sound of the afterburners flooded the radio. He checked his gear one last time to make sure it was locked on the Eagle. All readouts told him the time was right.

ODIN thought of the Behr and clicked on the command marked EXECUTE.

An invisible, silent hand, moving at eight hundred megabits per second, reached upward, through space and storm cloud and a thousand bands of wireless sky-road, moving effortlessly through the Eagle's carbon-composite skin, its silicone vessels, its titanium bones, to wrap wraithlike around the miles-long filigree of its Ethernet nervous system.

(You should know better) Dream of better lives, the kind which never hate
(You should see why) Dropped in a state of imaginary grace

(You should know better) I made a pilgrimage to save this humans' race
(You should see why) While comprehending a race that's long gone by . . .

• • •

"I'm as surprised as you are," Drew was saying. "My boss just sent me here out of the blue."

"Same here," said Corinne, snapping shut the lid of her Zippo with a clack, blowing smoke away from Drew, giving her hair a quick carefree tousle. She was feeling much better. The best she'd felt in weeks, in fact. She was determined not to lose it.

"Did she tell you why?"

"To watch the National IRA vote, I guess."

"Which we're not doing."

"Nope."

"Because we're out here talking."

"Yep."

They were both smiling now.

• • •

ODIN was using a penetration program called a Separator, designed to break up the coded connections between complex operating systems at the capillary level. As it was a memory hog, it took time to load and transmit, which was why ODIN had selected this particular CMDL, a compact surface module from L-3, for the Albany job. The Separator was already inside the Eagle's systems and poised to strike while Captain Ramf was going through the safety procedures prior to arming the bomb.

Once he did, however, the Separator didn't take long.

C: HARBINGER ONE, I'M SHOWING UNSCHEDULED ACTIVITY IN YOUR WEAPON'S INS MODULE. YOUR WEAPON APPEARS TO BE TRACKING. YOU ARE NOT CLEARED TO LAUNCH. REPEAT—YOU ARE NOT CLEARED TO LAUNCH. CONFIRM WEAPONS STATUS AND STAND BY TO RUN TARGETING SYSTEMS DIAGNOSTIC, OVER.

P: UH, YEAH, CONTROL, WILL DO. WEAPONS STATUS IS—

C: HARBINGER ONE, YOUR WEAPON IS TRACKING, REPEAT, YOUR WEAPON IS TRACKING. WE HAVE NOT YET COMPLETED TARGET DATA TRANSMISSION. YOU DO NOT HAVE A TARGET. REPEAT: YOU DO NOT HAVE A TARGET. OVER.

P: WHAT THE—

C: I SHOW FIN STABILIZER ACTIVITY ON THE WEAPON—

P: WAIT—IT'S NOT ME, IT'S—

C: PRE-ARM SEQUENCE INITIATED, REPEAT, WEAPON IS IN PRE-ARM MODE—RAMF, WHAT THE HELL IS GOING ON?

P: IT'S NOT ME! I'M NOT DOING IT!

C: HARBINGER ONE, ENGAGE MANUAL SHUTDOWN *IMMEDIATELY.* REPEAT—

P: I'M TRYING— WHAT THE— CONTROL, MY WEAPON JUST WENT ACTIVE, IT'S NOT ME, I DID *NOT* DO THIS, CONTROL, I'M—I'M—

C: HARBINGER ONE, I SHOW YOUR WEAPONS BAY DOORS OPEN, CONFIRM YOUR STATUS, REPEAT, CONFIRM STATUS—

P: CONTROL, I'VE LOST CONTROL OF— HOLY SHIT, BREAKAWAY, *BREAKAWAY,* WEAPON IS FREE, WEAPON IS FREE, SAY AGAIN THE WEAPON HAS DETACHED, CONTROL, *I DID NOT DO THIS—*

C: RAMF, WHAT THE FUCK?

P: CONTROL, IT WASN'T ME, REPEAT, IT WASN'T ME, *I DID NOT DO THIS—*

• • •

"Do you like your boss?"

"What—is this some trick question so you can get me to give up dirt on my boss that you can give your boss and score some brownie points?" Cory was in the game, enjoying herself, testing, prodding. Mapping the terrain of Drew Island.

It was the most fun he'd had since before Convention Week began. But at the mention of their employers back in the Capitol, the fun deflated, like air leaving a balloon.

She saw it in his countenance. *Oh, shit, girl,* she lashed herself inwardly, *you went and fucked it up before it even got started. Nice one.* She tried to recover, a little too earnest, a little clumsy, annoyed with herself. "Look, I didn't mean—"

"It's all right." He sighed, leaning back on his big arms.

He really was built, she thought, none of her boyfriends had been near Drew's size. She wondered if—

"Right now I feel like not going back there, ever," he said, looking away from her, throwing her thoughts into disarray. She heard the thud of utterly deflated sincerity as he gave voice to what she'd felt since watching the footage of the melee in Morningside Park.

He meant it.

And his thoughts echoed her own.

Slowly, tentatively, trying not to say or think too much, she flicked her cigarette away and reached out to him.

• • •

The real beauty of it, mused ODIN as he watched the weapon redirect itself to the new target coordinates he'd uploaded through the Separator program, was that it all came down to the weather.

Not that the bomb would have any trouble finding its target in any kind of conditions. Short of maybe a tornado or a Cat 5 hurricane, there really wasn't anything to stop it.

Not the Shaw tower controller, whom he could hear shouting frantically at Captain Ramf over the radio. *Waste of time, pal.* The Separator had severed all links between the aircraft, the tower, and the weapon, which was on the course he'd given it, gliding at a speed of roughly six hundred miles an hour, closing the distance fast.

And certainly not Captain Ramf, the dumb shit, because he was USAF, and the USAF, in its wisdom, had decreed that not only would there be no more wingmen in training flights, there would be no ordnance carried other than what was specific to the exercise. This was officially known as materiel conservation, and it meant that the Eagle carried no missiles, bullets, or even flares with which to try to bring down the bomb. All Captain Ramf carried with him besides the weapon were external fuel tanks for the long trip.

No, the bomb would continue serenely on course, taking its navigational cues from a benign solar-powered weather drone, a twin-rotor cigar tube of a UAV making lazy circles six miles above Schenectady.

Just like the Millennium game, he thought, all those years ago. It was really so easy to turn a big military machine against itself once you knew how it worked.

• • •

C: DO YOU HAVE A VISUAL ON THE WEAPON?

P: NEGATIVE! NEGATIVE! I SAW IT BANK LEFT—UH, WEST, I DON'T KNOW—

C: I'M SHOWING ACTIVE RESPONSES FROM THE INS, IT'S TAKING NAVIGATIONAL CUES FROM SOMEWHERE. RAMF, ARE YOU TRANSMITTING?

P: NO NO NO—

C: ARE YOU BEING JAMMED? CHECK YOUR ECM POD STATUS—

P: THE POD'S FINE! MY FLIGHT SYSTEMS ARE FINE! BUT I CAN'T GET A READ ON WEAPONS SYSTEMS, IT'S LIKE THEY'RE—

C: WAIT, WAIT, THERE IT GOES, BANKING AGAIN, NOW IT'S HEADING— OH MY GOD.

P: WHAT? WHAT?

C: ALBANY. IT'S HEADING FOR ALBANY. WEAPON HAS REDIRECTED TOWARD ALBANY, REPEAT, WEAPON IS ON COURSE FOR ALBANY— SOMEBODY CALL FORT DRUM, SCRAMBLE SOME INTERCEPTORS, QUICK QUICK *QUICK*—

P: ALBANY?

I'll stop the world and melt with you . . .

• • •

"All in favor . . ."

You could hear a pin drop in the assembly chamber two floors beneath the Capitol's grand dome. This was largely due to the fact that, as instructed, nearly every legislator with a vote had withdrawn to their respective camps' halls, away from the floor, thus locking in an affirmative vote with their absence.

The Budget Committee chair kept checking his phone. Clearly, there was someplace else he would rather have been.

The deputy comptroller and public advocate were privately ensconced in the governor's office, throttling their phones, awaiting the outcome with bated breath, watching the vote on a monitor in a conference room one floor below the grand assembly chamber.

The Three Pauls were illegally smoking up a fire stairwell, jabbering excitedly on their phones to their delegates and reps in Manhattan and points beyond about the spoils soon to come.

(I'll stop the world) You've seen the difference and it's getting better all the time . . .

• • •

P: FORT DRUM CONTROL SAYS ALL THEIR INTERCEPTORS ARE GROUNDED FOR MAINTENANCE! THEY SAY IT'S BEEN ON THE SCHEDULE FOR WEEKS! THEY'RE SCRAMBLING SOME CHOPPERS, BUT THEY'VE GOT NO MISSILES! THEY'VE GOT NO SAMS, NO TRIPLE-A, THEY GOT NOTHING! JESUS, ARE THERE ANY ANG UNITS UP THERE?

C: I'M TRYING TO RAISE THE GOVERNOR'S OFFICE, BUT NOBODY'S ANSWERING THE DAMN PHONES, THEY MUST ALL BE AT A FUCKING CONFERENCE OR SOMETHING—

P: I JUST GOT THE SAME RESPONSE FROM ATC AT ALBANY INTERNATIONAL, THEY SAY THE WHOLE LEGISLATURE'S SEQUESTER-ED FOR SOME BIG VOTE ON—

C: OH SHIT—

P: WHAT THE HELL'S GOING— CONTROL? CONTROL! COME IN, CONTROL! MY WHOLE SYSTEM'S GONE INTO TACTICAL MODE, I DIDN'T—

C: AFFIRMATIVE, WEAPON HAS GONE HOT, REPEAT, WEAPON IS ARMED, I SHOW FLOOR SENSOR ACTIVATED—

P: JESUS—IT'S TARGETING A STRUCTURE?

C: AFFIRMATIVE. FIN STABILIZERS BARRED AND RETRACTED, WEAPON IS LOCKED ON TARGET, REPEAT, WEAPON IS LOCKED ON TARGET. TARGET IS— OH MY GOD WEAPON IS LOCKED ON THE CAPITOL, WEAPON IS LOCKED ON THE CAPITOL—

P: WHAT THE *FUCK*—

C: WEAPON IS TARGETING THE CAPITOL BUILDING, REPEAT, WEAPON IS TARGETING THE STATEHOUSE, RAMF, CAN YOU RAM IT?

P: *WHAT?*

C: I HAVE VISUAL ON THE TARGET FROM THE WEAPON FEED, HOLY SHIT, GET ME SOMEONE, ANYONE, *I NEED COMMS TO THE CAPITOL NOW*—

P: HARBINGER ONE TO FORT DRUM CONTROL, EMERGENCY, EMERGENCY, WE HAVE A ROGUE WEAPON TARGETING THE CAPITOL BUILDING IN ALBANY, WE NEED TO WARN THEM, REPEAT—

C: I NEED COMMS TO THE CAPITOL RIGHT FUCKING NOW, SOMEBODY—

(Let's stop the world) There's nothing you and I won't do . . .

• • •

She had to reach up to kiss him, and he held her, lifted her to him, effortlessly, it seemed, and drank so delicately from her lips, she could not help but kiss him deeper, harder, feeling the rush of heat between their mouths, their tongues twining together like curious young animals exploring their newfound world, and she felt herself falling into him, dissolving into his embrace, his mouth a lifeline through the rising wind, and she clutched him, digging in, cleaving unto him against the heat consuming her and she felt his clothes scorch and his skin simmer and pop and his hands were sinking through down to her bones and her hair was on fire and their faces ran together in a liquid drapery of flesh and metal and the last thing she felt as her breath left her was the rush of her lungs flowing into his mouth . . .

(Let's stop the world) I'll stop the world and melt with you . . .

THE NEW ORDER

THE WALL STREET JOURNAL ONLINE

(UNSUBSCRIBED READERS WILL BE INTIMIDATED,
IMPOVERISHED, AND INCARCERATED)

MONDAY, AUGUST 27, 2016

Shocking Attack Leaves New York in Federal Custody

* * *

Routine Military Exercise Gone Awry?
Horrific Malware Leap from Cyberspace to Reality?
Many Questions, Few Bodies, No Answers

By Ronney Radiant

ALBANY—They sat entwined on the blackened steps of the statehouse, joined forever by a blast of such extreme temperature and pressure that it fused flesh, metal, and extruded organs.

A grisly forensic investigation usually reserved for the scene of mass graves exhumed for leveling war-crimes charges has identified Drew Tether, 22, and Corinne Bocce, 21, as the young couple whose charred remains have made the front page of nearly every news outlet in the world since the shocking air strike on the Capitol Building in Albany, New York, last week.

Mr. Tether was an aide to **Senator Melvin Cordryceps** (R—Virginia), chairman of the Appropriations Committee; Ms. Bocce was an aide to **Representative Caduta Massi** (D—California), the speaker of the House.

Both legislators are the subject of new federal probes by differing agencies. The Justice Department has recently opened one for Senator Cordryceps, while Treasury is investigating Speaker Massi. The nature and scope of the inquiries is unknown. Calls to both federal agencies, as well as both legislators' offices, were not returned as of this writing.

It remains unclear whether the federal investigations are connected to the unprecedented attack on the statehouse, from which 217 are confirmed dead, most of them state lawmakers, and which has left New York (city and state) a ward of the federal government. It is the first time in U.S. history that a federal takeover of this magnitude has occurred.

Under current law, a federal manager, appointed by the president, will take over custodial duties of the stricken state. While the identity of the executive appointee has not yet been announced, highly placed (surviving) sources in New York's government, as well as several in Washington who have asked to remain anonymous, have strongly intimated that **New York City Council Speaker Isabella Trichinella** will play a leading role in the transitional government.

General elections for city and state offices to replace those legislators killed in the Albany attack have yet to be scheduled. So many lawmakers died in the strike that it will take weeks, if not months, to fill each vacant slot. The repercussions on both New York City and State are as unimaginable as they are unprecedented. Until now, terror attacks on the city have been endured. Now the entire political machinery of one of the richest, most populous states of the nation's densely settled Northeast, with a major global hub city at its heart, has been literally blown apart.

The heat from the blast melted the building's iron girders and turned human flesh to charcoal. The explosion (which preliminary forensics indicate took place in the main assembly chamber, suggesting a "smart" weapon that detonated only after penetrating the Capitol's dome and tunneling down several stories) leveled the entire nineteenth-century edifice. The pressure wave in the wake of the blast caused a vacuum strong enough to yank out internal organs, as evidenced by the star-crossed lovers on the burned and broken steps of the Capitol, mute witnesses to the extent of the carnage. So extreme was the destruction that the current body count rests mainly upon the roll call conducted that morning, records for which were stored in the state's cloud data net (whose servers are located elsewhere and so survived the attack).

Almost the entire legislative body for New York State was present at the time of the bombing, having convened for the long-anticipated vote on the new urban-assistance bond issuance known generally as the National IRA, a program originated by Speaker Massi with the strong backing of the president and Democratic-majority Congress. With New York under de facto federal control, the program is all but assured for implementation in New York City. The House speaker has publicly stated that New York will be a pilot for enacting the bond issue in other declining cities across the country.

As for the investigation into the attack, there are almost no answers to the landslide of questions. All that is known at this time is that the pilot of the plane allegedly carrying the weapon is in federal custody. The pilot's identity was not released. The U.S. Air Force has barred all media access to its personnel, in blatant violation of the Freedom of Information Act . . .

• • •

City Council Speaker Isabella Trichinella's back was arched, one hand encircling her left breast, the nipple sharp between her left forefinger and thumb, her right hand deeply twined in the thick brown tresses of the head between her legs. The speaker had not waited an hour since receiving the call from Washington to celebrate her latest conquest. Giardia, her new aide, was currently ministering to her. Trichinella had met her only twice, once at a fund-raiser with that pig Terry Saginata (good riddance!) and once at a certain West Village bar with a select clientele.

When the word had come down from on high about the new order, indicating that the press conference wouldn't be until the following day, the speaker made a personal call on a cell phone she thought secure, knocked off early, and locked up her office. Tsetse Fly had been missing in action for days, and the speaker couldn't be without a special aide for long.

There had been no word from her former assistant since she'd gone up to Albany. But while the smoke still billowed from the crater that had been the Capitol Building (playback on a million phone screens surrounding her as she slipped anonymously from City Hall into a cab on Chambers Street), Isabella Trichinella stopped thinking about her. *Quel dommage.*

The speaker had no illusions about the Albany attack. It was easy enough to connect the dots between the shoot-out in Morningside Park, the massacre in the Ninety-sixth Street subway station, and now the obliteration of the entire state legislature. Which took care of the solidly Democratic downstate core but also wiped out the upstate Republican majority.

Somebody hadn't done his or her homework.

Once again, the former secretary of state's A team was on the ball, getting her Shocked and Awed mug in front of the cameras on her bus tour even as fire crews raced to the bomb site in Albany. It *was* a bomb, no question of it, human error or computer malfunction, it didn't matter, the air force already had the pilot locked up. The Joint Chiefs were convening, the Pentagon press pit was screaming, but for once, the speaker's private line wasn't glowing.

Because in New York, the survivors were running for cover.

Senator Theodore Usanius Rickover Davidson III had caught a private flight out of JFK for points unknown.

Governor Mario Mansoni had taken his official helicopter to his family estate in Rhinebeck.

Everyone else was dead.

Except City Council Speaker Isabella Trichinella. Or, as the anonymous caller from Washington had put it, *Emergency Executor* Trichinella.

The new order was coming.

For the first time in its history, New York—city and state—would come under direct federal management. The manager would be a direct appointee of the president, since Peter Fasciola, who by law was to take control in the event of a crisis, was a puddle of protoplasm in the rubble of the statehouse. Word had gone through back channels, from the executive branch (the president's chief of staff) to the legislative (Caduta Massi, who, strangely enough, was the subject of a Treasury probe), and thence to Trichinella (since the entire DNC now considered New York's mayor to be *persona non grata*). The manager would be at the top of the food chain, Trichinella would be next, and every local representative, councilman, alderman, ward heeler, and community board leader under the party's banner in New York City would answer to her.

Everyone else was dead.

The new order was coming.

As was newly appointed Emergency Executor Trichinella.

Who had been told in no uncertain terms by the voice in Washington that as long as she toed the line and didn't fuck things up any further, she could expect to be mayor herself within the year.

Trichinella arched her back into a perfect capital *C*, balancing herself on the balls of her feet and the crown of her head, aligning herself precisely with her new paramour's tongue and fingers, both hands white-knuckling around clumps of her linen Frette sheets, and as she felt the delicious inexorable surge of sensation start at her core, she discerned the percussive sound of a door opening, followed by an asymmetric clomping, and she opened her clenched eyes and beheld her former aide, her hair a wild shrubbery, her eyes pinwheeling fireflies, walking lopsided on one manta ray slingback (just like her own! Where did the bitch get *those?*), a smoldering hot mess if ever there was one. She limped to the foot of the bed, pointed her other shoe at Trichinella like a pistol, and screeched: "Where the FUCK is my MONEY?"

• • •

OCID Detective Sergeant Peter Konrad Liesl had been the black sheep of an old Lutheran family that emigrated to New York from central Europe around the time Otto von Bismarck was pulling together a bunch of tattered ancient kingdoms to form the nation of Germany. Shunned for his career choice and wild ways, Liesl had a few somber relatives who'd sighed in resignation when they got the call from Santiago, and managed to direct their lost kinsman's remains to the corner of Border and Sassafras avenues, wherein lay the family plot (#206) in Greenwood Cemetery in Brooklyn.

They'd stood silently, the three who'd deigned to show up in a warm rain that was just enough to slow everything down. Santiago stood at the end of a row that began with the commissioner and the mayor, ran through DCs Derricks and Randazzo, then down to Captains DiBiasi and McKeutchen.

The promotion had been a purely stealth maneuver, coming right after Devius Rune, calling from an undisclosed location, had broken the news that New York would be brought under direct federal control.

After the initial outburst of profane oaths and vehement threats against fate, the government, Democrats in general, and that rabidly anti-NYPD dyke who would be the "emergency executor" in particular, the heads who occupied the top of the food chain in Santiago's world got vestibular again. Santiago got the results in the OCID men's room just as he stepped away from the urinal. After making him wash his hands, McKeutchen and DiBiasi treated him to a back-and-forth surge of information that made him feel like a tennis ball at the U.S. Open.

DiBiasi served: "Randazzo's out—that cunt Trichinella's had a hard-on for him for years—which means my head's next on the block."

McKeutchen returned with a smooth forehand: "They're coming after all of us, everybody that ever tangled with 'em, insulted 'em, or ignored 'em, and that's pretty much the whole officer corps between captain and commissioner."

Santiago got in a lob. "Who is?"

"The new order, kid, the whole fucking DNC machine. They may have lost a few upstate just now—I'd still like to ask your fucking friend Mr. Fish Face about that—but there's plenty more to take their places. They've got the whole thing sewn up now, from D.C. to DeKalb Avenue. They're gonna move up all the local suck-ups and ward bosses, put the mayor in a box, and squeeze him right out of City Hall. That cunt Trichinella's already the princess of the city. She shoulda blown up the statehouse a long time ago."

McKeutchen: "Think she did?"

DiBiasi: "Who else would pull something this fucking stupid?"

Santiago was losing control of his neck muscles with so much whipsawing between the two men. "But why do you think they'll come after NYPD brass?"

"It's insurance, kid," McKeutchen put in. "They wanna make sure they've got as many of their own in the top public jobs. They already owned the unions, but they only had a piece of the main city agencies. Until now."

"Once they've got the public sector locked down, they can work on the private one," DiBiasi backhanded acidly. "You think they squeezed the banks before, just you wait. A year from now it'll be shelters and shanties all they way down Wall Street. The banks and brokerage houses will shut down and move away. They'll throw half a million out of work overnight. Then all the other industries that depend on the money trade will dry up and die, and another half million will be out on the streets. It'll be like the riots again, but this time there won't be enough of a department left to stop 'em."

Santiago asked, "So where do I fit in?"

"You're our ace in the hole, kid." McKeutchen beamed like a proud drunken grandfather at a new birth. "You're our finger in the dike. The department's gonna need guys like you. You're seasoned, you know how to clear cases even when the bullshit's piled up to your hairline—"

"You're not a yes-man," DiBiasi aced through the center of the OCID men's room. "You don't bend over for the bosses, and you're not afraid to fight. The city's gonna need you. There's a major shitstorm coming, and it's gonna last a lot longer than forty days and nights. All of us, captains or above, we're marked men. You're not; you were just below the radar. If the Dems are gonna seed the department with their own people, we want to make sure there's a couple of ours left behind. To balance the scales. That's where you come in."

They'd bestowed the rank on him right then and there, Santiago filling out the paperwork and a "captain's exam" while leaning against the side of the toilet stall in the OCID men's room.

Now, as the Emerald Society played taps at Liesl's graveside in the rain, Santiago could see what they'd meant. There were new faces in the senior officers' ranks, some of whom he recognized, none of which he liked. It had already begun. Both McKeutchen and DiBiasi had summonses from One Police Plaza, the City Council, and City Hall. The knives were out. Randazzo was already gone, as were a number of standing deputy chiefs. Only Derricks had survived the purge; in a target like New York, it would be political suicide for the heads of the new order to sack a capable CT Ops chief. The "seeding" was under way.

And Santiago was part of it. He was no longer a deskbound lieutenant. He was Captain Sixto Fortunato Santiago, head of the NYPD's vaunted OCID unit, with fifty people under his command, two gold bars on his uniform to go with the new blue and gold badge, a .50-caliber pistol, and a twenty-round shotgun full of three-inch anti-vehicular shells, all illegal, which DiBiasi and McKeutchen had told him to keep as a parting gift, with the following well-intentioned caveat: "Keep yer fuckin' mouth shut, kid."

As the Emerald Society blew taps, Santiago found himself gazing at Marrone. She stood tall but ashen-faced, holding on to Turse's arm, the one not saluting. She had shown a strange caring for the lone Narc Shark in the wake of the maelstrom that had claimed his partner, at odds with her otherwise jagged persona. When they'd arrived at the cemetery, she'd even referred to Turse as Nick. In all their years of working together, Santiago had never used Turse's first name, nor had he heard anyone else do so. Turse was Turse. And now, with Liesl gone, Santiago knew Turse would need someone to hold on to. Santiago just wished it weren't Marrone. He knew in his bones that Rune's use of her would have serious consequences down the line. Plus, he still had mixed feelings about her. He would admit this to no man.

The Honor Guard loosed its rounds skyward. Santiago hardly noticed; he was now immune to gunfire. With the casket going into the ground, he felt no desire to attend the inevitable boozefest that followed the burial of a cop KIA. He noticed Marrone and Turse heading off together, still arm in arm; he could not bring himself to join them. She could keep an eye on Turse for now. Santiago had to keep an eye on him as long as he was in OCID, making sure he did not wreak bloody vengeance upon those who, even if they were scumbags, were not the scruffy sniper who moved like More.

Excusing himself as diplomatically as possible while the funeral gathering broke up, Santiago walked alone up a slight rise toward a tree beneath which he'd parked his old Anticrime taxicab, back from its overhaul at Odilàn's pirate garage. Driving the cab to the cemetery had brought the first smile to Santiago's face in nearly a month. The old Crown Vic still looked like a city hack on the outside, but under its skin it was now pure street dragon. McKeutchen said he'd slip-slide the paperwork to shift the car from CAB to OCID, one last gift. It was understood that with these, Santiago was assuming more than the mantle of command: He was now a protector, a rabbi to watch over others as others had done for him, one of the few remaining bulwarks against the chaos engulfing the city. Santiago understood his new position but took it with a grain of salt.

He had not told anyone of his new Plan: He would stay on to protect New York City, but he himself was moving *out* of it. The events of the past few weeks had sounded a primordial alarm deep within him, which, over a period of sleepless nights, took shape as a decision to relocate outside the city limits. When the time came, he would leave his hometown quietly, without making a ripple.

As he passed the tree near the cab, a shadow detached itself and glided into silent step beside him.

"DiBiasi wasn't bluffing," Santiago muttered without turning his head. "He sees you, he'll kill you."

"He can try," More gurgled.

"Whatchu still doin' here? I figured Devius woulda had you on a plane outta town before we secured Ninety-sixth Street."

"I'm taking a break from Devius," More gluttered. "I wanted to make sure you got your promotion."

Santiago sighed to cover his surprise at More's twin revelations. "I shoulda known that was you."

"They let you keep your weapons, too?"

"Yeah. Thanks. But the next time I use 'em, the ME'll be all over my ass."

"I doubt it," More furged. "They need you now more than ever."

Santiago considered telling More about his new Plan, then bit his tongue. "Why you here, then?"

"Tell Turse I'll get him. I don't know where he is or how long it'll take me to find him. But I will."

"I know." Santiago closed his mind to the devastation sure to ensue from More's hunt. He was still digesting the current cataclysm. He paused for a moment. "So you buy the chef chick's story?"

More shrugged. "Doesn't matter."

"Well, whaddya think?"

More pursed his fish lips, then came as close to a smile as he ever did, off by a few decades. "She'll be all right. She's a survivor."

Santiago saw no point to continuing this line of conversation. Beth Hutiak had Alex Redhawk taking care of her now. More apparently couldn't care less about her. Though it had seemed to Santiago, for a moment, that he might have.

Another thought struck Santiago. "Would do Turse good to see your ass again 'fore you left."

More shook his head soundlessly. "No time. Can you get me to JFK?"

Santiago chuckled. "In the trunk?"

Then More said something which, despite all the shocks he'd endured since before Convention Week began, jolted Santiago to his core.

Nodding at the cab, More hissed: "Can I drive?"

• • •

The new aide was a bit older, a bit wiser, and knew when to speak and when to keep her mouth shut. "Who's the target?"

House Speaker Caduta Massi, resplendent in a muted green-sequined suit that strongly suggested scales, rummaged through piles of memos, files, official and personal correspondence, and message slips. Her office had gone to hell since Corinne had been killed.

And her with the National IRA set to roll out over New York.

And her with a whole state to run.

So much to do.

But now, with a glut of congressional aides left unemployed by the Albany attack, she could pick and choose. And she'd snagged a veteran hatchet woman.

Ah, there it was. "A nuisance," she replied, holding up the message slip, the last one written in Corinne's own hand. "With the potential to become a problem. She needs to go. Now."

The new (older) aide raised her eyebrows, hands poised over her tablet like talons.

"A FINCEN investigator at Treasury," the speaker read, "named Marrone. Liza Marrone."

No more was said after that.

• • •

A nuisance. Such a damned nuisance. One more atop a mountain of others. Senator Mel Cordryceps sat at his desk in his expansive northern Virginia mansion, a bottle of Defiant whiskey next to the phone, which held the latest bother. He hit the replay button.

"*Senator, this is Special Agent Cody Sarabande, FBI. I've been trying to reach your office, but no one seems to be there. I need to speak with you as soon as possible. It concerns the recent . . . events in New York. I'll be at your office within the hour, and if I don't see you there, I'll*—" The senator shut the machine off.

Such a nuisance. Really, with so many bigger problems to address, this had to happen. He sighed. Too bad about Drew; the senator could've used his bonhomie and broad shoulders to deal with this new pest.

Mel Cordryceps sighed again and opened the top center drawer of his desk, pulling out a compact .45 with a walnut grip, a Terry Tussey Junior custom job he'd picked up years ago. So much to do, and now he'd have to leave it all unfinished. The senator felt no remorse whatsoever for the outcome he'd brought about. It had all been going as planned, but then that wack job ODIN had botched everything.

Now he had other considerations. If he went through the temple, the bullet would hit the library and damage the custom carpentry, a lengthy and expensive fix. If he went through the mouth, Hitler-style, he'd either break the Swarovski crystal chandelier or, worse, the bullet would go through to the bathroom above and take out the irreplaceable French claw-foot tub. Either method would have a considerable effect on the resale value of the house, a difficulty he'd hoped to spare his wife, who'd have her hands full in the days ahead.

So much to consider.

Such a damned nuisance.

• • •

As usual, Exmoor was seated at his stupendous chess table, this time working through a Morphy-Anderssen defense he'd laid out on the board. As usual, Lanark was seated across from him. But this time he was as subdued and gloomy as Exmoor always was. The effusiveness and elevation standard to the fund-raising scene was gone. The party was ending, and everyone knew it.

The federal takeover had occurred with such shocking rapidity that it seemed to have been planned long before, its architects awaiting the suitable moment to erect their monstrous new bureaucratic edifice. The catastrophic loss of so many seasoned legislators turned out to be no significant hurdle. The new overseers simply filled vacancies from the ranks of local groundling politicos—aldermen, ward heelers, party bosses—with little administrative experience and few apparent qualifications beyond loyalty.

A siege mentality was settling in across the city, and its lengthening shadow was felt most acutely in opulent bunkers like those of Julius Exmoor. And his ilk.

All was not gloom, however. One pocket of life throbbed ebulliently in the far corner of the gallery, where Lanark, fairly drooling into his fourth Scotch and water, cast his gaze. "Who . . . *is* . . . that?" he managed.

A fair question. One that Exmoor had been asking himself ever since the woman, a fortyish, extremely well-preserved and self-assured specimen, came through the arched entrance and immediately took up with the City Council speaker and the lieutenants of the new federal manager, whose identity had yet to be made public.

Exmoor knew nothing about this woman (whose bare arms belied a great deal of physical training) or her accompaniment, a substantially younger Latina of singular magnificence in both physiognomy and physiology. Exmoor figured it was even odds whether Lanark's misproportioned head, craned in the direction of the striking couple, would lead his ass right out of the chair to the floor.

What little Exmoor knew of the woman with the chiseled physique was that she'd arrived at the mansion as part of the "extended" retinue of the new municipal governing body; she had been described in passing as an entrepreneur with an eye toward the redevelopment zone along the Lower West Side waterfront in Manhattan, which, it was rumored, was to be designated as a "free-enterprise zone"—a euphemism for the new designated areas in Manhattan where gambling was to be permitted. The new arrival, it was said, came with very deep pockets, though the origins of her wealth remained unclear.

Watching the muscular woman confidently making time with the city's new overlords, Exmoor made a mental note to place a call to Devius Rune as soon as covertly possible.

"Dieter," Exmoor grunted.

"Yeah?"

"Shut the fuck up."

• • •

I've forgotten so many things.

What it was like to get charged up about planning menus instead of dreading them. Or what I can do in a really great kitchen, with great ingredients, for a uniquely appreciative audience. Or the little things: a luxurious bath in a magnificent bathtub; sleeping in; rising to face a new day without fatigue or apprehension, the weight of another slog ahead.

The energy derived from being able to work out again, every day, even twice a day, made easy now that I'm living with a man who has a full gym in his apartment.

Or savoring the anticipation, not just the act but the delicious *anticipation,* of sex without pain.

This last thought makes me smile around Alex's still-trembling cock, which I just drained again so I can revel in his unique flavor: vanilla bean, yes, and allspice, with notes of saffron and cardamom. This may be due to his newly expanded diet. Good thing I'm here to exercise him regularly.

Which I can do without fear now.

The cops, especially that nice one, Santiago, seemed much more interested in the subway bank and Ing Kan than me. It almost looked like they were looking for some kind of connection, though what it was, I have no idea. The other one, More, the one who sort of reminded me of back home, told me the Chinese consulate was making a big fuss over Ing Kan's remains; they wouldn't allow an autopsy. It was almost like he *knew* . . . But he couldn't have.

No one could have known how I'd been lacing Ing Kan's food with all those antidepressant drugs Caitlin takes all the time. With all the exotic spices and sauces, Ing Kan never tasted what I was giving her. I had no clue about dosages or cross-effects; I just ground up as many of the pills in her food as I could. Funny, I finally found out where Caitlin gets all these: She goes to open houses pretending to be interested in the apartment and raids the medicine cabinets, can you believe it? She keeps the mood drugs for herself and gives the others to her pillhead friends.

Sometimes I get the feeling that Mr. Chiroptera knows, but he's not saying. He's warmed to me quite a bit since that night in the subway. Seems like a million years ago now. And I know he doesn't miss Ing Kan, not one bit.

I make sure Alex doesn't, either.

No one will ever know.

Which suits me fine.

The colony . . .well, there's not nearly as much of it as there used to be. But the slaughter in the subway had the effect of shining bright lights underground. The survivors—I'm happy to report that Jonah was among them—are now front-page news. After the battle, when the cops sifted the living from the dead, the city got involved, mostly staff working directly for the City Council speaker and the new federal management office. They're now the poster children for the National IRA program, which went online right after the bombing in Albany. I won't have to worry about feeding them anymore; the new bonds are doing that. Or maybe your tax dollars are. They're big stars, all over the news every day. I don't know when—or if—I'll see any of them again.

But we won't be around much longer. Convention Week soured Alex on more than politics. He's been thinking about retiring for a while, it turns out, and the past few weeks have cured him of staying in New York—or this country, for that matter. He's got lots of friends in Asia (not like Ing Kan!), and he wants to travel around there, the southern seas, Australia, and New Zealand, really look around before settling on any one place. He says he's through with America and Americans for the time being. "The future's in the East," he says, "let's go meet it."

Alex Redhawk, Maverick Big Cheese billionaire. The Man Who Would Not Be President.

Who'd leave this gloomy fortress in a heartbeat to take me to greet the rising sun.

Mine, all mine.

This is crazy.

But I'll take it.

Wherever it takes us.

GLOSSARY

AAA: anti-aircraft artillery

AFB: air force base

ANG: Air National Guard (U.S.)

AO: area of operations

ATC: air traffic control

AWACS: airborne warning and control system Black budget annual funding for U.S. non-military intelligence services

CAB: Citywide Anticrime Bureau

CCTV: closed-circuit television

CENTCOM: Central Command (U.S.)

CFIUS: Committee on Foreign Investment in the United States

CMDL: compact multi-band data link

CSAR: combat search and rescue

CT: counterterrorism

CYBERCOM: Cyber Command (U.S.)

DARPA: Defense Advanced Research Projects Agency (U.S.)

DC: deputy chief

DoD: Department of Defense (U.S.)

DSS: Diplomatic Security Service (U.S.)

EADS: Eastern Air Defense Sector (U.S.)

ECM: electronic countermeasures

EFP: explosive formed penetrator

ELINT: electronic intelligence

ELISA: enzyme-linked immunosorbent assay

ESU: Emergency Services Unit

FDR: Franklin Delano Roosevelt

FINCEN: Financial Crimes Enforcement Network, Department of the Treasury (U.S.)

GCT: Grand Central Terminal

GDP: gross domestic product

GSR: gunshot residue

GWB: George Washington Bridge

HUMINT: human intelligence

HVAC: heating, ventilation, and air-conditioning

IED: improvised explosive device

IRA: independent retirement account

ISIS: Islamic state of Iraq and al-Sham

IWB: inside the waistband

JFK: John F. Kennedy International Airport (NYC)

JSOC: Joint Special Operations Command (U.S.)

MARSOC: Marine Special Operations Command (U.S.)

MSOB: Marine Special Operations Battalion (U.S.)

NTU: nurse triage unit

NYC: New York City

NYFD: New York Fire Department

NYPD: New York Police Department

NZSAS: New Zealand Special Air Service

OCID: Organized Crime Intelligence Division

ODA: Operational Detachment Alpha (U.S. Special Forces)

ODIN: Observation, Detection, Investigation, Neutralization (U.S. Army)

OMB: Office of Management and Budget

OME: Office of the Medical Examiner

OT: occupational therapist

PAPD: Port Authority Police Department (NY and NJ)

PLA: People's Liberation Army (China)

POS: point of service

PWUAV: propulsive wing unmanned aerial vehicle

QOS: quality of service

QRF: quick reaction force

RG: Republican Guard (Iran)

RPG: rocket-propelled grenade

RV: rendezvous

SAC: special agent in charge (FBI)

SAM: surface-to-air missile

SAS: Special Air Service (UK)

SAWMAG: squad automatic weapon magazine

SBD: small-diameter bomb

SIGINT: signals intelligence

SLAP: saboted light-armor-piercing

SFQC: Special Forces Qualification Course

SFAUCC: Special Forces Advanced Urban Combat Course

SOF: Special Operations Forces

SPD: Sensory Processing Disorder

SR: special reconnaissance

SRO: single room occupancy

SSCI: Senate Select Committee on Intelligence (U.S.)

STOCK: Stop Trading on Congressional Knowledge

ST/SO: small team/single operator

TF: task force

TIF: tagged image file

TS/SCI/TK/HCS: top secret/sensitive compartmented information/ talent keyhole/HUMINT control system

UAV: unmanned aerial vehicle

USAF: United States Air Force

USN—United States Navy

USSOCOM: U.S. Special Operations Command

WAV: waveform audio file

ACKNOWLEDGMENTS

Saint Underground is a work of fiction. May the world it describes never exist.
I should begin by thanking political scientist Gerald Benjamin and former New York Assemblyman Daniel L. Feldman, co-authors of *Tales from the Sausage Factory: Making Laws in New York State* (SUNY Press, Albany, 2010), who graciously schooled me in the Byzantine workings of the political machinery between New York City and New York State.

I am equally grateful to Dr. Charles M. Brecher, of the Wagner Graduate School of Public Service at New York University, for setting me straight on voting procedures and contingency plans for city and state government in times of crisis. He is also the co-editor of *The Two New Yorks: State-City Relations in the Changing Federal System* (Russell Sage Foundation, 1988) and a co-author of *Power Failure: New York City Politics and Policy Since 1960* (Oxford University Press, 1993), all of which I used in my research.

Aboveground: For city affairs and planning with regard to mentally ill homeless patients, thanks to Sonia García of the Community Advisory Board at Metropolitan Hospital Center (Behavioral Health Pavilion). Below: Deep thanks to Alan Saly and Mario Galvet of the Executive Board of the Transport Workers Union (Local 100); and to Behrouz Fathi, former president of the Civil Service Technical Guild (Local 375). These men shone a bright light underground, into the nebulous world of new subway design and construction in NYC, as well as the commercial interaction between this crucial transit system and the spaces between and above its subterranean terminals.

For the nitty-gritty of urban planning, I referred to *The Heights: Anatomy of a Skyscraper* (Penguin Press, 2011) by the ever informative Kate Ascher, as well as the mesmerizing photography of Stanley Greenberg's *Invisible New York: The Hidden Infrastructure of the City* (Johns Hopkins University Press, 1998).

Beth Hutiak is the sum of many parts. Her name derives from a groggy transposition of waiters' names from a staff list back when my wife ran catering for Fred's at Barneys. Beth's occupation of private chef, a vocation unknown to me before I started working on this book, was described to me in detail by those who walk the walk—Beth "Grill Bitch" Aretsky, Michael Ferro, and Marc Valois. The inspirations for her recipes are duly credited below, so please don't sue me. As for Beth's affliction: Vulvodynia is a serious and chronic condition affecting one in twenty women in the U.S. alone, according to the *Journal of Women's Health* (and that was back in October 2008, the last comprehensive study for which I could find statistics—I suck at statistics). As to its symptoms and treatment (both medical and homeopathic), I am indebted to Dr. Stephen Gallousis, OB/GYN, Fairfield County Medical Group, New Canaan, CT. Thanks also to Dr. Lily Wong, West Care Medical OB/GYN, NYC. Lanark's osteoabrasion procedure does not actually exist. I know this because Dr. Christine Hamilton-Hall, of Darien Aesthetic and Maxillofacial Surgery, told me so, and since she's a plastic surgeon, I figured she'd know.

I am greatly indebted to those at the following public agencies who kept me on the righteous path when it came to procedural details: Candice Basso (FINCEN); Lieutenant Rick Khalaf (NYPD); and Special Agent Cody Monk (FBI).

ODIN is the result of so many people and events that I know I will fail to do justice to them all. But first and foremost, I owe a debt of incalculable gratitude to those on the ground who worked the air: Alphabetically, they are Bill Burgum, Mike Haytack, Conan Higgins, John Knipe, and Chris Spann. Gents, take a bow.

There is no book focusing solely on the use of ODIN units in Afghanistan and Iraq that I could find. There were some people who might write one someday. These are: Christine Roe, speaker for the Houston World Affairs Council (who herself served in an ODIN unit); Peter Singer, formerly of the Brookings Institution and author of *Wired for War* (Penguin Press, 2009) and co-author of *Cybersecurity and Cyberwar* (Oxford University Press, 2014), who introduced me to her; and Thom

Shanker, *New York Times* senior Pentagon correspondent, for his toothsome 6/22/08 article "At Odds with Air Force, Army Adds its Own Aviation Unit" (http://www.nytimes.com/2008/06/22/washington/22military.html?_r=1&partner=rssnyt&emc=rss). The full list of periodical sources consulted regarding ODIN units will be available to all on my website, www.dunnbooks.com.

There are a few other peripheral works consulted for ODIN's genesis. The biggest and baddest is *The Endgame: The Inside Story of the Struggle for Iraq, from George W. Bush to Barack Obama* by Michael R. Gordon and General Bernard E. Trainor (I used the paperback edition—Vintage, 2012). Also: *Beyond Hell and Back* by Dwight John Zimmerman and John D. Gresham (St. Martin's Press, 2007); *Masters of Chaos* by Linda Robinson (Public Affairs, 2004); *The Night Stalkers* by Michael J. Durant and Steven Harton with Lieutenant Colonel Robert L. Johnson (ret.), G. P. Putnam's Sons, 2006; and *The Mission, the Men, and Me* by Pete Blaber (Berkeley Caliber, 2008).

A few words on tech. First, tactical. Both the Beowulf M4 and GI Glock.50-caliber conversion kits have been on the market for years. ODIN's rifle is a fictitious future variant of the current .308 MacMillan CS5, while More's Zel Tactilite rifle and optics are on the market as is. The 6.5-millimeter Grendel round is still around, as is Armatec's SAWMAG dual-drum magazine for the M4 and AR-15. Santiago's shotgun mods can be found online at RCI or Brownells (but don't try looking for FRAG-12 shells!).

The armored beast is, necessarily, a product of my own feverish imagination. The Defense Advanced Research Projects Agency (DARPA) hung up on me when I called to ask them about prototype battle exoskeletons. So did Ceradyne Systems when I tried to get some background in new trends in ballistic armor composition. I did score a helpful copy of John Edwards *Geeks of War* (Amacom, 2005) for a dollar at a library sale. John Knipe helped me out with Bad Boy's armament, all of which is currently in use with the U.S. military. Oh, the grenade launcher is officially known as the counter-defilade target engagement (CDTE) system; unofficially, it's called "The Punisher." It was jointly developed by Alliant Techsystems and Heckler & Koch, while L-3 developed the targeting system by which the operator can manually adjust the detonating distance, thereby making a plain old 25mm grenade "smart." It will ruin your day.

Ganymede's delivery drone for More's goodies was inspired by a blend of the Horten Ho-229, the B-2 Spirit, and AVOLT's Hammerhead UAV. The bomb used in ODIN's air-strike hack is fictional, though based on the current GBU-39 small-diameter bomb. Wet thanks to Conan Higgins and Chris Spann for describing the more gruesome effects of thermobaric weapons; the morbidly curious can also visit www.globalsecurity.org to read up on the BLU-118/B.

Additional how-to for ODIN's air-strike hack was graciously provided by Bill Burgum, Dr. Steve Call, Jason Montgomery, and Jon Rahoi. The F-15 "Silent Eagle," which allegedly does not exist, is already on sale to Saudi Arabia, (at least according to Wiki, maybe Ed Snowden had first dibs, if Julian Assange didn't).

As for more utilitarian equipment: Redhawk's home CAT scanner is based on the current SOMATOM CARDIAC 64 model from Siemens. The 427IR crate engine can be readily found at Roush Performance's website. Centurion II HVAC monitors, HI-SCAN X-ray systems, Shure body transmitters, and T4AF lavalier connectors are all market standbys. ODIN's "easel" is a fictionalized big brother to the current IBM Thinknote. I got my Shun knives at Williams-Sonoma.

Now to locales. Exmoor's mansion really is the Frick Collection, through which I've spent countless happy hours wandering. Morningside Park and the Cathedral of St. John the Divine in Manhattan, and Greenwood Cemetery in Brooklyn, are likewise fond old haunts; each has an excellent website that distant readers may visit for further information. Also: I have never visited Albany and relied on the Internet to map the Capitol Building and the Desmond Hotel. They may have changed the carpeting in the latter since this writing.

Exmoor's chessboard is my own invention, but the moves he lays out are taken directly from Emanuel Lasker's *Manual of Chess* (Russell Enterprises, 2010, though the original copyright dates to sometime in the 1940s, I believe). All other references inside the Frick's gallery are real.

As is Audrey Spellman of Family First, kind souls who permitted me to use their actual names in this novel. Not to mention Nick Turse, author of *The Complex: How the Military Invades Our Everyday Lives* (Holt, 2008).

When faced with the difficult prospect of naming political characters, every writer should have at least one professional parasitologist whom he can call friend. Mine is Dr. Rosemary Drisdelle, author of *Parasites: Tales of Humanity's Most Unwelcome Guests* (University of California Press, 2010).

Everything involving famine and cannibalism in this book is directly inspired by the 1941–44 Nazi siege of Leningrad. The authoritative work on this is Harrison Sinclair's *The 900 Days* (Harper & Row, 1969) from whence my fictional hamburger hairballs spring. However, I would argue that a worthy successor is Anna Reid's *Leningrad* (Walker, 2010), which benefits from its position well after the end of the Cold War (and perhaps before its rekindling in 2014).

On the subject of shadow banking, there are simply too many citations to list. I eagerly follow reportage on the subject in *The Wall Street Journal*, *Financial Times*, *Barron's*, *The Economist*, Bloomberg.com, the U.S. State Department (www.state.gov), and the European Commission (ec.europa .eu). However, I wish to spotlight two individuals who have given selflessly of their time to educate a mindless clod like me on the finer points of the subject. They are: Richard Bove of Rafferty Capital Markets; and once again, Dr. Eric Anderson of National Intelligence University—author, teacher, biker, shooter, sounding board, and friend.

Regarding Beth's recipes, I adapted most from the cookbooks of several high-flying chefs, with alterations made so as not to plagiarize. Do NOT treat the recipes as gospel—*buy the cookbooks*. Take it from the pros, your dinner guests will thank you for it. My works consulted are *Two Meatballs in the Italian Kitchen* by Pino Luongo and Mark Strausman, Artisan (New York), 2007, p. 25; *Testsuya* by Tetsuya Wakuda, HarperCollins (Australia), 2000, pp. 24–25, 42–43; and *Bold Italian* by Scott Conant, Broadway Books (New York), 2007, pp.123–25).

Beth's wine-tasting menu was entirely the product of Kerry Dolan, *chef de cuisine*, and Steven Semaya, proprietor, of Boulevard 18 in New Canaan, CT; and John Kapon, head of Acker Merrall & Condit Fine and Rare Wines, NYC. Savory thanks to all.

Once more I will provide a disclaimer for my characters the Narc Sharks. The name sounds so natural that people think I must have seen it before. Once again, for the record: I have not. The closest I ever came to this was the "Nark Ark" described in Joseph Wambaugh's seminal 1982 police novel *The Glitter Dome*, which does not refer to his fictional undercover narcotics detectives but, rather, to the car they drive (a beat-up Toyota).

Deep and humble thanks to the Dunn Books team: Thomas Eldon Anderson; Colleen Brown; Michael Coppola; Chuck Dorris; Dean Eaker; Max Fanwick; Archie Ferguson; Steve Gaynes; Matt Gillick; Marc Halpert;

Amanda Harkness; Susan Heller; Joel Higgins; Katie Hires; Jae Hong; Madeline Hopkins; Ed Katz: Alissa Letkowski; McKenzie Morrell; Meryl Moss; Alan Neigher; Gerri Silver; James Sullivan; Beth Thomas; and Michael Kevin Walsh.

One final point. The Mavridez Operation is based on actual events. Interested readers can Google 492 Amsterdam Avenue, New York City, 12/19/09, or they can just read http://cityroom.blogs.nytimes.com/2009/12/17/three-men-fatally-shot-on-upper-west-side-police-say/. I took my then-infant son to see the chalk outline of the fallen shooter's body on the sidewalk beneath the fire escape after the shooting. I fear it will not be his last.

CPSIA information can be obtained
at www.ICGtesting.com
Printed in the USA
BVHW071402141121
621551BV00001B/44